Books by Anina Collins

The Eleventh Hour (Poppy McGuire Mysteries #1)
After Hours (Poppy McGuire Mysteries #2)
Top of the Hour (Poppy McGuire Mysteries #3)
The Darkest Hour (Poppy McGuire Mysteries #4)

THE DARKEST HOUR

ANINA COLLINS

The Darkest Hour

Poppy and Alex come up against their toughest case yet, and they may never be the same again.

When someone close to both Poppy and Alex is found brutally murdered, all the clues point to Alex as the killer. But Poppy knows in her heart that her partner could never commit such a heinous crime. As the evidence begins to mount against him, Poppy must race against the clock to prove that the man she trusts with her very life isn't the murderer, even as everyone around her is convinced of his guilt.

But if Alex isn't the killer, who is? As the mystery unravels, the past and present finally meet in Sunset Ridge.

Chapter One

THE SOUND OF my Jingle Bells ringtone woke me from a sound sleep, startling me from a recurring dream of me running and stopping only to be buried alive in sand. I'd begun having the dream right after my mother died, and whenever my subconscious felt helpless, the dream crept back into my nighttime mind. This was the first time I'd had the dream in months, though.

As I opened my eyes and looked across the room to see the frost framing my bedroom windows, I had no idea why the dark recesses of my mind thought I should feel helpless or lost. The holidays had been a flurry of good times with my father, and things between Alex and me had never been better. We hadn't gotten as serious as I'd hoped to yet and still hadn't slept together, but I chalked that up to his inability to let the past go. I'd known he was haunted by the ghost of his wife when I kissed him that night in October, so I worked to quietly temper my desire for more.

All of this ran through my mind at lightning speed as my phone continued to jingle on the nightstand next to me. Forcing my eyes to remain open, I rolled over and grabbed it without looking at the caller ID. There really was no reason to look anyway. Only two people in the world called me in the middle of the night, so it was either my father or Alex whose voice would hit my ear momentarily.

"Hello?" I groggily mumbled, silently asking why they'd interrupted my sleep.

"Poppy, it's Derek. I'm sorry to wake you, but something's happened."

Hearing his deep voice instead of my father's or Alex's surprised me. Pulling the phone from my ear, I looked at the time. 4:17. Why was Derek calling me at four o'clock in the morning?

"What do you mean something's happened?" I asked as my brain tried to recover from sleep mode.

"I need you to get down to the apartment building across the street from *The Eagle*. Hurry, okay?"

"What? What are you talking about?" I asked, slowly coming out of my fog, but it was no use. He was gone already.

I hopped out of bed and quickly dressed as my mind kicked into full panic mode and questions exploded one after another. Why was the police chief of Sunset Ridge calling me about something happening in the early hours of the morning? He had officers who handled the overnight shifts and hadn't worked one since becoming chief nearly a year ago. What awful event had roused him from bed before his usual nine AM arrival at the station?

Then a horrible thought tore through my brain and made tears fill my eyes. Derek would only call me if something had happened to my father. Nothing else would make him involve me in one of his cases.

As I raced down the stairs to head out to my car, I

called my father but it went directly to voicemail. That wasn't normal. My father's phone was always left on. He was one of those people who never let his phone run out of a charge. Over and over, I called and every time my heart sank a little lower when his comforting voice intoned that same voicemail message he'd had for as long as I could remember.

I backed out of my driveway like a bat out of hell and tore down the road toward the apartment building on Main Street where Derek waited to break the news that I'd lost my father. I wiped the tears rolling down my cheeks, warming the ice cold steering wheel with them. What had happened to him? Why would he have been at that building instead of at his place over the bar? My father hadn't told me about anyone new in his life recently. Had he met someone at McGuire's and gone back to her house?

A million ideas flashed through my mind. He'd been told by his doctor right before the holidays that he needed to lower his blood pressure, but his love of salt had continued unabated through Thanksgiving and Christmas. Had he had a heart attack and been found dead?

The last words I said to him echoed in my head as I parked my car a block away because of the police barrier. He'd called right before nine to remind me to turn on my humidifier since the heat had been running in my house and it tended to make it almost unbearably dry. I'd brushed him off because I was thinking of something Alex had mentioned about going to Baltimore for dinner one night this week and told him I'd be sure to get the humidifier running, the idea leaving me as soon as the words left my mouth. I'd then said goodbye and that I loved him, but it had been more rote than anything real and full of feeling.

How could I have been so thoughtless? My last words to him and they'd been nothing more than a daughter's dismissiveness to the only real family she had left.

I wiped the tears from my cheeks and steeled myself for what Derek had to tell me. Craig stood in the middle of the street redirecting curious onlookers away from the apartment building about a block away and smiled at me when I approached him, but it wasn't his usual happy smile. His face told me this wasn't just some crime scene like usual.

And then he spoke and I knew it was bad.

"Poppy, I'm sorry. I know you two were close."

Tears welled in my eyes again. Close wasn't the word for what my father and I were. I had no grandparents left alive, and after my mother died, he was all I had in this world.

I thanked Craig with a gentle pat on his shoulder and made my way to where Derek stood on the sidewalk in front of the apartment building. As I walked toward him, my legs moving as if on their own since my brain was occupied with thoughts of how I'd go on without the man who'd been there every day of my life, I tried to decipher Derek's expression to figure out what had happened. His frown made him look much older than his thirty odd years, and in his eyes I saw real sadness like when he lost his brother.

Reaching out, he put his arm around my shoulders and quietly said, "A neighbor found her sitting in her car. I want to warn you, though. It's bad."

I leaned against him, thankful for the support, and

then stopped dead in my tracks as his words finally made it through all the other thoughts in my brain. "Her? This isn't about my father, Derek?"

He shook his head. "No. Why would you say that?"

Relief washed over me as tears of joy now filled my eyes and began to roll down my cheeks. I wiped them away and smiled. "You didn't tell me what had happened, so I naturally thought my father had been hurt or worse."

"No, it's not your father. As far as I know, he's home safe and sound in bed, like I wish I was."

My eyes dry now, I stood there confused by Derek's still sad look. "Then why am I here at some crime scene and speaking of that, where's Alex? You know I do my amateur sleuth thing with him."

Derek didn't cheer up at all from my attempt at being cute. "Not on this one, Poppy. Come with me."

I followed him to a car surrounded by nearly all of Sunset Ridge's police officers and Donny, the county coroner, and his assistants. All four doors were open, and as I stepped closer, I saw a woman sitting in the driver's seat.

"Who is that, Derek? What happened to her?"

"That's Bethany, Poppy. Someone slit her throat sometime tonight."

I looked at the woman behind the wheel again and saw he was telling the truth. It was Bethany. Covered in blood, her beautiful face was frozen in a look of shock. The sense of relief I'd felt when I learned my father hadn't been hurt disappeared, replaced by a feeling similar to the one I'd had on my way there. Bethany was the closest thing I had to a best friend, and there I stood looking at her as she sat in her car murdered sometime that night. I'd cried so much already since waking up just a short time earlier, but now as I thought of Bethany attacked like she must have been, I couldn't stop the tears from coming again.

Turning away from the sight of her, I asked Derek through my sobs, "Why would someone do this to her? Everyone loved Bethany."

He avoided my gaze and looked past me to where a woman stood with another of his officers. "Yeah, I hope it's not worse than that. Come with me."

Worse than that? Had her killer sexually assaulted Bethany before slitting her throat? My stomach roiled at the mere thought of that happening in addition to the son of a bitch killing her.

I followed Derek as the bile rose in my throat. Why would anyone do this to her? I hadn't exaggerated when I said everyone loved Bethany. They did. Men and women alike took to her naturally. She had a way of lighting up a room by just walking into it, and her smile never failed to make everyone around her feel better.

It's one of the many things that made her a great member of *The Eagle*'s advertising group. Nobody sold more for the paper than she did, and even as she beat her team members every time in their quarterly sales competitions, none of the other people in the sales department resented her for it. I always had the feeling they understood she'd been blessed with good looks, an infectious personality others couldn't help but love, and a way about her that made sales the perfect career for her.

That she wouldn't be there to pop into my office and chat each day made my chest tighten. That same bright soul who sold better than anyone else at the newspaper had been the one person I called my friend there. Even when she and Alex began dating and I secretly hated it, I never truly felt anything but friendship from her.

We'd drifted apart slightly in the past weeks after he'd told her he couldn't see her anymore. I sensed she knew he and I had gotten closer, but she never once mentioned it or gave me any sense she resented me.

Alex had been a blip on her very busy social radar, for sure, so I always assumed she easily walked away from whatever they'd been and continued on with her life. She never wanted for dates in all the time I'd known her, so what was one guy in a world of men who clamored for her attention?

As Derek and I drew nearer to the officer, I heard the woman next to him say something about a boyfriend of Bethany's. That couldn't be right. We may have drifted apart a little recently, but she would have told me about a new man in her life, especially someone she was calling a boyfriend. Bethany Lewis wasn't exactly the type to award that title to just any man.

"They were fighting bad," the woman said, shaking her head and sighing. "It's such a shame."

Derek tapped Stephen on the shoulder to get his attention. The newest officer to join the force, he came on a month after Alex. I had only met him once or twice as he always seemed to get stuck with the overnight shifts, but he was unforgettable with his pale blond hair and dark brown eyes, a combination that seemed misplaced like one or the other trait should be changed. Combined, they gave him a startling look I didn't much like.

"Chief, this is Mallory Michaels, one of the victim's neighbors. I think you should hear what she has to say," he said as he flashed me a snide look.

I'd heard Bethany mention her neighbor Mallory once or twice at work when she was having problems with her landlord not fixing things. A tall, thin woman in yoga pants and a t-shirt, she had fried looking hair as a result of too many bad bleach jobs and reminded me of a stripper past her prime. Her makeup looked old and faded, like she hadn't washed her face before she went to bed that night.

Derek gave her a forced smile. "Just tell us what you know, Miss Michaels."

She twisted her expression from frustration and huffed, "I already told this officer my story. I don't want to stand out here in the cold with her over there in that car any longer than I have to."

"I understand," he said in a tone that made it clear to anyone who was paying attention that he was struggling to keep his cool. "If you could just repeat it for us, I'd appreciate it."

Mallory's mouth contorted into a shape similar to what a snake might look like as it slithered away after killing something. "Fine, but then I'm going inside. This has been awful, and I think you people have a duty to one of Sunset Ridge's citizens to do better by her than leaving her in that car for hours in a pool of her own blood."

Derek tensed up next to me, and for a moment I thought he might yank her right out of her sneakers and drag her to the police station for being so difficult. He looked like he wanted to, but he knew even better than I did that he couldn't arrest someone for being a horrible person. Even if Mallory was more than deserving for being so damn difficult.

"Thank you, Miss Michaels. If you could just tell us what you know."

"I called 911 when I heard a strange noise outside in the parking lot and was afraid someone was getting attacked. I didn't see anyone, but I heard someone scream, so I hurried to my phone and called you guys. When I looked out my window after, I didn't see anything but a car leaving the parking lot."

"Did you see anyone at all?"

"No. Just the car. It looked like a sports car or something and it was dark."

Stephen interrupted and directed her back to the idea of a boyfriend I'd heard her mention as we walked up. "I think you should tell them what you told me about what happened earlier last night."

Again, the officer shot me a look, and this time I had to believe it was intentional. What was his problem? I didn't even know him.

Mallory folded her arms and turned to face Derek. "I heard her and a guy fighting outside last night around nine o'clock. It was pretty heated too. She was angry with that guy she's been seeing lately."

I couldn't stop from saying what I knew was the truth. "Bethany wasn't seeing anyone. I'd know if she was. She didn't have a boyfriend. Whatever you saw, it wasn't her fighting with anyone she was serious with."

Derek looked down at me still frowning. "Are you sure, Poppy? I know you two were close, but she might have decided to keep some guy a secret from even you. She might have had good reason to."

I stared up at him and couldn't believe what he'd just said. "Do you remember who we're talking about here, Derek? Bethany didn't keep any men in her life a secret. I'd bet my last dollar on it that even you knew practically every guy she dated in the last year. She wasn't exactly a shrinking violet about those kinds of things. Bethany liked to have a good time, and she didn't care who knew who she was having those good times with. At the very least, I would have known."

Mallory didn't seem swayed by my argument any more than Derek did, though, and insisted it was a boyfriend Bethany was fighting with. He pressed her for a description of the man, and when she began to speak, I felt my stomach drop.

"It was the guy I've seen her with before. She's been seeing him for months. Dark hair, dark eyes, about six foot, in good shape. I don't remember his name, but she knew him. He wasn't a stranger to her."

She'd described Alex to a T. He wouldn't have been a stranger to Bethany and it was likely Mallory would have seen him in the time the two were dating. But he'd told me he broke it off with Bethany and hadn't seen her except for in passing at The Grounds or the Madison Diner since fall.

Had he lied to me?

"Are you sure?" I asked, not wanting to believe what I was hearing.

Mallory nodded, sure that she had seen the man there a number of times before. "He didn't come around for a long time. I know that, but he started coming back around in the past few weeks since the holidays. I've seen him at least two or three times since Christmas. I just figured they got back together."

My heart sank a little more with each word that came out of her mouth. She was saying Alex had begun to see Bethany in the past few weeks, but how could that be when he spent every night with me? Even when he worked the overnight shift, we saw each other at the Madison for at least a few minutes.

I stared at her as she spoke and knew she had to be wrong. She had to be mistaking Alex for someone else. "Are you sure it was the same man she'd been seeing before? He couldn't just look like the same guy?"

She shook her head. "Nope. It was the same guy. I'd remember someone like him. I thought they made a good looking couple, but from what I saw last night, they weren't a good couple at all."

"What did you see?" I asked, my heart in my throat as I waited for her answer.

"They were fighting and she was furious at him. I'd never seen them fight like that before. He grabbed her shoulders to stop her from lashing out and hitting him after he said something I couldn't hear. I just know it was bad."

Derek interrupted her story and asked, "Did he hurt her as they fought?"

I wanted to scream that Alex would never hurt anyone like he was insinuating. I didn't know what was going on, but I knew Alex. He couldn't have hurt Bethany like that.

"No," Mallory said with a shrug. "It wasn't like that. He wasn't trying to beat her up or anything. She was the one who was getting physical. Whatever he said to her made her angry as a hornet, and she let him know it. She got one shot in before he grabbed her shoulders to keep her from getting another one in."

"How did you see this?" I asked, my mind scrambling for anything that would discredit her claims. "Where were you when this was all going on?"

Turning to look at her apartment on the first floor next to where I knew Bethany lived, she pointed and said, "Right there in my front window. They weren't more than five feet away from me since it all happened in front of her door."

Disappointed, I looked at where her window was in relation to Bethany's front door. Each apartment was set up the same—a large front window that took up the left half of each one's façade and a front door at the right edge of it. I'd teased Bethany once when I found out she'd moved in there that the place had always reminded me of a motel on the side of the road with the way it looked.

"Is that all? Can I go back inside and try to forget this whole night now?" Mallory asked in a pleading tone.

Derek gave her another forced smile. "Don't forget anything you saw, but feel free to go home for the time being. If we have any more questions, we'll let you know."

She hurried off to her apartment as everything I'd heard whirled around in my brain. None of what she said was possible. It couldn't have been Alex.

As my world began to crumble down around me, I heard Derek ask me something and turned to see his sad eyes looking at me. "What? I didn't hear you."

He struggled with his words before finally saying, "I know you've gotten closer to Alex lately, and I don't want to think what Mallory said is true any more than you do. The fact is, though, that the person she described is Alex. I know this isn't what you want to hear right now, but is it possible he started seeing Bethany again?"

Without thinking, I answered, "No! I don't care

what she said. Alex wasn't back to seeing Bethany. He wouldn't do that. He'd tell me."

"Would he?" Derek asked, obviously skeptical that a man would tell his current girlfriend that he'd decided to go back to seeing his previous one. I didn't blame Derek. I would have been skeptical too if it wasn't my personal life at the center of this case.

Then something Bethany had told me right before Christmas popped into my head. "Her sister was in town. I remember Bethany had told me that her sister was coming to stay at the beginning of January for a couple weeks. Where is she? She should still be staying with her."

"There's no one in the apartment, Poppy."

"Then someone needs to find her sister. She's her only relative since her mother died three years ago and I know for a fact that she said she was coming to stay with her. We need to find her. Her name is Mariah Lewis."

Derek whistled for Craig to come over. "Bethany's sister was staying with her. We didn't find any evidence of her in the apartment, so I want an APB put out for her. And ask that neighbor if she saw anyone staying with Bethany recently."

Craig hurried off to start the search, and I saw an even more worried expression settle into Derek's usually appealing features.

"What are you thinking?" I asked, afraid to hear his answer.

He shook his head and then finally said, "I don't know. I'm worried whoever killed Bethany did something to her sister and I can't ignore the fact that the person Mallory Michaels described is the ex-boyfriend of the victim and one of my officers."

"Alex couldn't do this. I know him better than anyone else and I'm telling you he wouldn't do this."

Derek gave me one of his forced, official smiles. "I hope you're right, but I don't have a choice in the matter. I have to look at him as a suspect, Poppy. I hope you understand."

I didn't. I couldn't figure out what had happened to Bethany and if Alex was involved at all. My heart said he wasn't, and my gut agreed, but my head wasn't so sure.

Chapter Two

DEREK STOPPED HIS squad car and shifted into park before turning to face me. His expression troubled, he opened his mouth to speak but nothing came out. I'd known Derek Hampton since I was a little girl, and never once had I seen him not be able to say what was on his mind. He had become more diplomatic since becoming police chief, but that wasn't what was going on as he stared at me saying nothing.

"I just need to know you're going to remember he's innocent before being proven guilty, Derek. I know in my heart Alex would never do this, but if you have to go on facts alone and won't allow yourself to admit you know him too, then at least give him the chance you'd give any other suspect. Don't rush to judgment."

Hanging his head, he said, "I'm not a bad guy, Poppy, but I have to go where the evidence takes me. You know that. I just want you to accept the fact that the person Mallory Michaels saw fighting with Bethany last night was Alex."

Before Derek could go any further, I cut him off. "That doesn't make him a murderer. I won't believe Alex did that to her. He couldn't. I know him better than anyone else and I know he couldn't do that, so just remember that."

He nodded, but I knew he could believe Alex could do this horrible thing. What I didn't understand was how he so easily allowed that thought to settle into his mind as a possibility. He knew the type of person Alex was. He'd seen him work with me for nearly a year. How could he believe in any way that he would ever hurt anyone, much less murder someone he once cared about?

I didn't ask because I didn't want to know, to be honest. Whatever Derek had conjured up in his mind to justify even considering Alex as a suspect wouldn't make sense to me. All I knew was he was wrong.

Derek got out of the car and I followed him to the front door of Alex's house, my heart pounding like a sledgehammer in my chest. Never in my worst nightmares had I ever thought I'd be standing there on his porch with one of his fellow officers to question him on a murder he was suspected of committing.

"Let me do the talking, Poppy. I shouldn't even have you here since he's your partner, so I need you to promise me you'll stay quiet."

I looked up at him and shook my head. I couldn't promise that and mean it, no matter how much he wished it was so. Alex was my work partner, but he was so much more than that. How could I just sit idly by if I saw Derek do something to hurt him?

"I won't get in the way of your questions, but I won't promise to stay quiet either, Derek. You knew who I was when you got into that car with me. My guess is you're hoping I won't keep my mouth shut and Alex may say something that will help you."

He banged on the door and sighed. "What I'm

hoping is this is all a huge mistake and one of my best officers didn't slit a woman's throat."

As I stood there in the January cold waiting for Alex to come to the door, all I could hope was he had an airtight alibi for the hours after nine o'clock last night when he left my house. He'd said he needed to go home because he wasn't feeling well. Had that been a lie to allow him time to go see Bethany? I didn't want to consider that possibility because even letting that tiny question into my brain meant a legion of other questions would follow that would make me doubt everything Alex and I had become in the months since that first kiss on my couch.

I couldn't handle finding out it had all been a lie. No, not Alex. Not the man I knew.

The front door opened slowly and we saw him standing in black sweatpants and a grey t-shirt, his expression one of confusion as he looked out at us. Nobody said a word for what seemed like an eternity, and then when he finally did speak, he sounded like he'd just rolled out of bed seconds earlier.

"What's wrong?" he groggily croaked out, his eyes squinting from the brightness of the porch light.

"We need to speak to you, Alex. Can we come in?"

I hated the sound of Derek's official tone. He didn't have to be like that with one of his officers.

"Derek, what's going on?" Alex asked as he scrubbed the sleep from his face.

"Can we come in, Alex? There's been a murder and we need to speak to you about it."

That time Derek dropped the veil of his position and let the real man come through his words. The real man who sounded scared to find out the truth.

I stood there staring at Alex, looking for something to tell me he couldn't have done this crime so I could show Derek he was wrong. I saw nothing to prove his innocence or guilt. He looked like a man who had been asleep all night, but I couldn't use that to defend him. I knew all too well how easy it was to playact just having woken up. I'd done it many times to avoid going out with friends when all I wanted to do was stay home and curl up with a good book.

He stepped back out of the way and opened the door to let us in. I saw the confusion in his eyes as I passed and wished I could pull him aside to say I needed him to know I didn't believe he could ever commit such a heinous crime. I knew I couldn't and risk being thrown off the investigation, though, so I hoped my gentle squeeze of his hand as I walked by would let him know I was in his corner and wouldn't be leaving, no matter what happened.

He closed the door and followed us to the living room, offering us a seat like we were friends come to visit. If only that was true. I took my place on the couch next to Derek and Alex sat down in the chair across from us, but my position felt wrong. I shouldn't have been seated next to the person who was there to question him about committing a crime. I felt like a traitor to everything I felt for him sitting there next to Derek.

"What's so urgent about a murder that you need to come see me at five in the morning?" Alex asked with a smile. "This couldn't wait until I got to the station in a couple hours? Did someone important get murdered?"

I looked to my left to see Derek studying him just as Alex always did when he and I went to speak to murder suspects. I knew just what he was looking for. Did Alex sound guilty? Did it sound like he was forcing the calmness in his voice? Was that smile real? Had he truly been sleeping or was that all an act?

And then Alex looked over at me, and I saw the concern in his dark eyes. "Poppy, what's going on? Who was murdered?"

Before I could answer him and somehow let him know that I didn't think he could ever do this horrible crime, Derek spoke up and began his questioning. "Bethany Lewis was found murdered in the front seat of her car a few hours ago. Her throat had been slit from behind."

His words hung like a thousand pound weight that threatened to crush whatever friendship and love had grown between the three of us, and I watched Alex's expression change from that playful joking look to one full of utter sadness. I couldn't help but think that even though he could never had killed her, maybe he and Bethany had rekindled their relationship and I had been wrong about that. I didn't want to think that, though, because if I had been wrong about him seeing her again, had I been wrong about anything else?

Alex lowered his head and mumbled, "Jesus. Poor Bethany."

When he looked up again, I saw tears in his eyes. I wanted to take him in my arms and be the one who comforted him like he had been for me when I needed a shoulder to cry on. I didn't, though, instead remaining next to Derek even as my body ached to hold him.

He sat back in the chair and shook his head in disbelief. "How did this happen? Who would do that to her?"

Wincing like he was in pain, Derek took a deep

breath and said, "Well, that's what we wanted to talk to you about."

Unlike when he announced Bethany had been murdered, this news settled in between us like some uncomfortable ugliness almost too much to acknowledge. Alex's eyes opened wide in surprise and his mouth dropped open.

"You think I had something to do with this?" he asked in a tone of disbelief mixed with shock and hurt as he stared at Derek, thankfully. If he had been facing me when he asked that, I wasn't sure I would be able to handle it.

"One of her neighbors said she saw you and Bethany fighting outside her apartment hours earlier. I'm just doing my job here."

"My wife was murdered, Derek. I remember the investigators coming to me first since they always look to the husband first. I also remember the pain of knowing she was never coming back again. I'd never see her smile, hear her laugh, feel her arms around me. Your job may be to ask me these questions, but I just found out someone I once cared about was murdered. I hope you'll understand that I have no answers for you just like I had no answers for the cops in Baltimore when Helena died."

I'd never heard Alex so angry before. His brown eyes so caring and mysterious flashed his rage. Derek saw it too and leaned back away, surprised by his reaction.

"I'm not saying we think you did this, Alex. I'm just saying I have to ask you some questions. I want to clear this all up as much as you do."

Alex stood from his chair and looked down at us as

he shook his head. "You have no idea what it's like to be questioned as a suspect in a murder, Derek. I see it in your eyes even as you sit here in my living room. You think there's a possibility I did it. You think I could have taken a knife and slit someone's throat."

Then he turned to look at me for the first time, and the agony in his expression nearly took my breath away. Searching my eyes for the truth, he asked, "Do you believe I could do this, Poppy?"

My emotions jumbled, I just shook my head as the words got caught in my throat. No, I didn't think he could kill Bethany! I didn't think he could kill anyone like that. He was honorable and good. Alex wasn't a murderer. No matter what happened, I wouldn't be able to believe that.

He turned back to face Derek. "My chief and my partner come here to find out if I murdered a woman I used to sleep with. Is that how it is? Well, I didn't. I was here all night asleep."

"Are you saying you didn't go to Bethany's last night and have an argument with her outside her front door?" Derek asked sharply.

Now it was me who looked at Alex for anything to cling to. He glanced over at me and then quickly looked away. "I did go to Bethany's last night. I was home before ten, though."

His admission hit me like a punch to my chest, taking my breath away. He had gone to see Bethany last night? Why? From what he'd told me the last time I asked a few weeks ago, he and Bethany didn't even talk much anymore since he and I had decided we wanted to see what was happening between the two of us. We were taking it slow, but we'd professed our feelings to each other and I'd believed him when he told me I was the only woman in his life.

Had I been a fool to trust him when he said that?

Derek continued with his questions as I sat next to him reeling from Alex's first answer. "Why did you go to her apartment?"

Taking his seat again, Alex blew the air out of his lungs and answered, "She called me and asked me to come over."

"I had been under the impression that you and Bethany had stopped seeing one another a while back sometime in the fall. Why would she want to see you now?"

"Sunset Ridge really is a gossipy little town, isn't it?" Alex snapped. Avoiding my gaze now firmly settled on him as I awaited the rest of his answer, he continued, "Your impression was correct. She and I stopped seeing each other early in the fall. As for why she wanted to see me, we'd remained friends so it isn't so surprising she'd call me."

They'd stayed close enough friends that Bethany felt comfortable to call him and he responded by going to her house after claiming he was sick and leaving mine? I didn't want to admit it, but I was beginning to doubt him. Nothing he'd ever said to me since we began seeing each other in October had given me any indication he was still speaking to her in any way, friendly or otherwise, and now I had to find out they were still close enough that if she called him he immediately went running to her?

"And did you have an argument?" Derek asked.

Alex shook his head and pressed his lips together before he said, "I don't think it's any of your business if we had an argument or not. I just told you I left her place by ten and I was home all night asleep, so I'm not your killer."

Turning to look at me, Derek frowned. He'd asked a simple, straightforward question and Alex had intentionally hedged answering it. The question was why, and I knew Derek wasn't going to let it go with his evasive answer. I wanted to know what they'd fought about too, but for different reasons.

"So are you saying you did or didn't have an argument?" Derek pressed. "I just want to be sure I'm understanding things here."

Alex leveled an angry stare at him. "I didn't say one way or the other."

I knew he was feeling defensive answering Derek's questions, and I understood that. I also knew it wasn't exactly Alex's nature to be loose with details about much of anything, but this was a murder investigation and his chief was the one asking him the questions. I couldn't believe he wouldn't answer him.

Frustrated, Derek asked his question once more. "Did you and Bethany argue when you visited her last night? It might help you to know that there was a witness to your argument."

Wincing like answering caused him pain, Alex nodded. "Fine. We had an argument, but when I left her apartment before ten last night, she was alive."

"And what was the argument about?"

I'd waited for nearly five minutes for this answer, but all Alex did was shake his head as he refused to even give the tiniest detail about what Mallory Michaels had seen them fight about on the sidewalk in front of her apartment.

"That's none of your business."

"You know full well it's my business, Alex. I'm trying to solve a vicious murder, and right now, you're the last person to see our victim and that's when you and Bethany were fighting loud enough for her neighbor to witness the two of you. Now what did the two of you fight about?"

"I won't tell you, so don't bother asking again, Derek."

I didn't know why Alex was being so difficult about what he and Bethany had fought about. How bad could it have been? Was he refusing to answer because I was there and he didn't want me to know how close they still were? It was a little late for that.

Even though I wanted to speak up and plead with him to just answer Derek's question, I didn't. Not because Derek had told me to keep quiet but because I honestly wasn't sure I wanted to hear the answer anymore.

Derek took a pen and a piece of paper out of his coat pocket and asked, "What's the make, model, and color of the car you drive?"

As Alex freely answered this question by telling him he drove a black 1969 Ford Mustang, I looked around for any evidence that could point to him having been the one who slit poor Bethany's throat and left her to bleed to death. Alex had taught me well in the months I'd been his partner, so I scanned the rooms around me for signs of blood or a knife and had to admit to myself I didn't know if I was doing it to prove he hadn't done it or to help Derek prove he had.

I saw nothing, though.

I wanted to believe he couldn't be our killer, but

after watching him refuse to answer Derek's questions, I wondered if my faith in him had been misplaced. Maybe he'd been seeing Bethany the whole time he and I were together and taking things slow. The thought occurred to me that I was the woman he spent time with laughing and talking and she was the woman he slept with.

Turning away so he couldn't see my face, I wiped away a tear that escaped as that truth settled into my brain. Maybe everything I thought we were wasn't the truth at all.

Derek's phone rang, breaking the tension and the silence that had settled in among us, and he excused himself to take the call as I wished for the first time to be anywhere but near Alex at that moment. Out of the corner of my eye, I saw him get up from his seat and was surprised when I felt the couch dip next to me as he sat down close enough that his leg touched mine.

"Poppy, I need you to believe me. I would never hurt anyone like this. Please, you know me. You know me better than anyone else in the world. You can't think I did this."

His words sounded like they were being pulled from the depths of his soul, and I turned to see him looking at me with desperation in his eyes. I'd never seen him look like that. It stirred something in me that made me want to burst into tears at how betrayed hearing he had gone to see Bethany made me feel.

"You never told me you and she were still talking. What was she in your life, Alex? You told me you wanted to take things slowly with me, but were you sleeping with her on the side all along?"

He took my hands in his and did exactly what any accused man would. "No! It wasn't like that. I hadn't seen Bethany in months, at least not alone. She and I were finished. I love you, Poppy. I wouldn't do that to you."

In all the months we'd been together more than mere partners solving crimes, he'd never told me he loved me. I'd wanted to believe he did and was just afraid to take that next step, and now as he begged me to believe he wasn't a killer, he finally said those words that should have made me happier than any woman in the world.

But they didn't. Defensive and hurt, I couldn't help but wonder if he said those three precious words to convince me he wasn't guilty.

"You love me? You've never told me that before right now. So why did you go to Bethany's last night after you left my house early because you said you were sick?"

He got an uneasy look on his face. "Don't do this, Poppy. Whatever she and I talked about doesn't have anything to do with us."

I ripped my hands from his hold and shook my head in disbelief. "Doesn't have anything to do with us? You're the prime suspect in her murder, Alex. Right now Derek is probably on the phone with Donny or Craig and hearing that they found some evidence that he's going to want answers about, so if you want me to believe anything coming out of your mouth, you need to answer my question right now."

Alex let out a heavy sigh and nodded. "Okay. She called me a little after nine last night as I was driving home and she was all depressed about something she wouldn't talk about over the phone. She didn't even sound like herself. When I got there at around nine-thirty, she acted like I was just playing games with her feelings by saying I didn't want to see her anymore but then coming by for what looked like sex. She was crying and a mess. I tried to calm her down, but she ended up screaming for me to just go and never come back. That was the last I saw of her."

"Why would she call you and then act like that?" I asked as his explanation filtered through my skepticism.

He took my hands in his again and looked into my eyes with a look of pure sadness. "I don't know, Poppy, but I swear to you there was nothing going on with her."

"Her neighbor said she's seen you at Bethany's a few times since Christmas, Alex."

"Well, she's wrong. I'm with you every night, Poppy, and even when I have to work an overnight shift, you and I still see each other. I wouldn't do that to you. You have to believe me."

Derek returned from his phone call before I could tell Alex I believed him. It hurt like hell to know he'd seen her the night before and I had to find out about it in the course of her murder investigation, but I believed he was telling me the truth.

"Alex, do you own a hunting knife?"

I felt Alex's hands squeeze mine for a second and then release their hold on me. "Why would you ask me that?"

Frowning, Derek said, "Because the coroner has determined that Bethany's throat was slit with a hunting knife. So I'll ask again. Do you own a hunting knife?"

I waited for Alex to answer his question so we could get back to our conversation, but he stood up from the couch and walked toward the door. Holding it open, he said flatly, "I want you to leave now. I have nothing else to say."

Derek simply nodded his head and did as his officer asked, obviously resigned to the fact that he wasn't going to get anything else from Alex, but I wasn't ready to let it go so easily. When Derek had walked out, I ran to Alex still holding the door open for me to leave and pleaded for him to tell me what was going on.

"Alex, why won't you answer his question? Just tell him the truth so he can eliminate you as a suspect and we can go back to our lives again. What harm can come from just admitting you have a hunting knife if you're innocent?"

He grimaced and shook his head over and over. "Something's very wrong, Poppy. I would never hurt anyone like this, but I can't say anything more. Just don't forget what you know about me. Don't forget."

Tears rolled down over my cheeks at his answer to me. I didn't know what he was talking about, but I knew this man. He didn't want to believe he could kill Bethany for any reason.

"Please tell the truth, Alex. I care about you. That won't change no matter what evidence Derek thinks he has, but I don't understand why you won't just tell the truth."

He pressed his lips to mine in a desperate kiss, and when he pulled away, I looked up into his eyes and saw real terror in them. His voice shaky, he pleaded, "Please prove that I didn't do this. I'm innocent. If anyone can prove it, it's you, Poppy."

I stumbled out into the cold winter night unsure of practically everything in my world except one. Alex wasn't a killer. Now I just had to prove it.

Chapter Three

DEREK DROVE BACK to town saying nothing, his deep frown telling me everything I needed to know. Not that I didn't understand his unhappiness. Alex had been less than helpful and didn't exactly do a lot to make his chief think he was innocent.

I sat in the passenger seat listening to the sound of the rubber tires rolling over the hard ground as the events of the night replayed over and over in my mind. Bethany dead. Alex the prime suspect, at least according to Derek. And me caught in the middle. I wanted to catch the killer and see him pay as much as anyone else, but I couldn't deny my allegiance to Alex. He was my partner in crime at work and the man I loved.

The car turned onto Barn Street and my house came into view. Just a few hours before, I'd been happily tucked into bed having that strange recurring dream and now everything in my life felt like it had been turned upside down.

Derek parked the car in my driveway and sighed as he stared out the front window. "I just remembered you drove to the crime scene. Do you want me to take you to get your car?"

Surprised at his comment after expecting him to say

something about what had happened out at Alex's, I patted Derek's arm through his coat. He turned to look at me, and I saw the sadness that had been in his eyes since telling me about Bethany was gone now, replaced by something else.

Concern? Anger? I wasn't sure.

"I can get it later. Thanks, though."

"It doesn't look good, Poppy," he said in a somber voice I rarely heard from him.

"You're always a glass half-empty kind of guy, aren't you, Derek? It's going to be okay."

I didn't know if that was the truth or just my hopeful optimism taking over because I'd experienced an overload of bad already that day. What I did know was I trusted Alex Montero with my life every time I left my house to work on a case with him. I couldn't change that because things looked bad, even if I wanted to.

Derek looked away from me and said, "With his past history, I have to wonder if things are like people whispered when his wife died."

"What do you mean?" I asked, stunned he would mention Alex's wife at all.

"I don't know. It just seems odd that this guy has had two women he's associated with die violent deaths. Most guys can't say that."

Barely able to get my thoughts together, I finally found the words and said, "That makes him a killer? Two people die around a cop and that makes him a killer?"

Whipping his head around to face me, Derek grimaced. "You're blinded by how you feel about him, Poppy. I don't know if it's that you idolize him or love him, but ever since you two began working together, you've had that puppy dog look in your eyes when it comes to Alex. How much do you really know about him?"

"I guess not as much as you think I should," I snapped, hurt that someone who'd known me nearly all my life would think of me like some schoolgirl with a crush. "If you suspected he had a part in his wife's death, which I think is ridiculous, by the way, why did you have him work as a cop in our town if you thought he was a killer?"

"Nothing was ever proven to show he was his wife's killer. She was murdered while he was on duty, and there was no real evidence to show he did it. But rumors flew all over the place saying he was the killer."

My voice trembling, I asked, "And yet you not only hired him to work in Sunset Ridge but partnered him with someone you've known since she was knee-high to a grasshopper? If you truly thought there was a chance he killed his wife, you wouldn't have let me work with him for nearly a year."

I felt the tears well in my eyes, but I willed them away. I didn't want Derek to see how upset his words made me. Whatever he thought, I knew Alex. He couldn't have hurt his wife any more than he could have hurt Bethany.

"Poppy, I would never put you in harm's way. I didn't have any proof Alex had done anything, but now another woman in his life has been murdered. I don't want to see you get hurt next."

"So with no proof and just rumors, you're willing to convict him, Derek?"

He wore that look on his face he always got when we knocked heads about something, like I only knew part of the story and he didn't want to be the one who had to tell me the missing piece of it. "Alex's wife was killed the same way, Poppy. Her throat was slit. They found out it was cut with a hunting knife. I don't know if it's all a coincidence, but I've got a bad feeling about this."

I felt like someone had just slapped me across the face. The same way? No, this wasn't happening.

"Are you sure, Derek? They were both killed like that?" I asked, all at once understanding why Alex had been so unwilling to cooperate.

Nodding, he blew the air out of his lungs until there was none left inside him. "Yep. Two women murdered in one person's life is one thing, but two women murdered the same way? That sounds like a pattern. He always seems so calm and rational, but maybe when it comes to his personal life, he's the exact opposite."

Although I didn't want to discuss my personal life with Derek, I knew I had to so he would forget this craziness he had in his mind about Alex. "You know he and I have been seeing each other, don't you? Do you think I wouldn't have seen some hint of him being completely different in his personal life?"

Shrugging, he sighed again. "You haven't been together all that long, Poppy. Maybe there was something different about those women from you."

I shook my head in disbelief. "No, I would have seen something that told me at some point he'd turn into a murderous monster. For God's sake, I'm not a fool! I can be infuriating on my best days, Derek. You can attest to that. Why would I still be alive and Bethany, who was more than accommodating to anyone she dated in many ways, lies dead? It doesn't make any sense."

"You can be maddening. That's true," he said with a

tiny smile.

"So I think I would have gotten some indication from him by now that he's not the calm man he appears to be. Derek, I know him. He's not a murderer. If you want to convince me he is, you're going to need a whole lot more than some rumors from the past."

Derek's smile faded away, and he said in a low voice, "It's not you anyone has to convince, Poppy. It's twelve people."

I couldn't believe my ears. He already had this case in front of a jury! "So you've tried and convicted him not even four hours into the case? What happened to innocent before being proven guilty?"

He held his hands up in surrender. "I'm not doing anything here, Poppy. I'm just worried this isn't going to turn out the way you hope it will."

"Well, I intend on finding out the truth, no matter what it is, so don't try to stop me from working on this case."

I knew Derek could stop me with just a word, but I hoped he wouldn't. No one knew Alex like I did. I needed to be on this case.

"I should tell you that if I catch you doing anything involving this case that I'm going to handcuff you to my desk so you won't get hurt, but I know how much you care for him. The truth is you're too close to this, Poppy. Can you honestly say you'll be able to accept it if Alex is guilty? I can't have someone impeding a case because they don't want the truth to come out."

"I wouldn't do that, Derek. I won't hide anything I find out. It will be just like the Geneva Woodward case. Whatever I find out, I'll bring to you. I need you to promise me you won't disregard it just because it doesn't fit into your preconceived beliefs about him, though."

Derek's eyebrows shot up in surprise. "Preconceived beliefs? You sound like his defense lawyer."

I smiled and tried to soften my attack, knowing that being too strident wasn't going to get me far. "Please just keep an open mind. Even with what happened in Alex's past, give him the benefit of the doubt until you can't anymore. He's been a good cop for you and this town, so don't give up on him just yet."

Nodding, Derek seemed to see I was right. "Okay, but I want you to be careful. We have no idea what's going on in this case yet, and if it's not Alex, then we have a murderer on the loose who killed your friend. I don't want to see you as his or her next victim."

For the first time since I woke up that morning, I smiled. "See, that's the spirit. At least I got you to admit it might not be him. We're making progress. I'm going to go inside and start to figure out who did this to Bethany. I'll let you know what I find out, and I hope you'll do the same for me."

Derek didn't have to do anything to help me prove Alex wasn't Bethany's killer. I knew that, and still I asked all the same because while he was chief of police, he was also my friend for as long as I could remember. That counted for something.

He smiled and I knew it meant something to him too. Gently touching my forearm in a gesture he rarely gave me unless he was protecting me from some bully on the school playground, he quietly said, "Be careful. I don't want to see you hurt in this."

"I will. I promise."

For all his faults, Derek Hampton was a good man, even if he was completely wrong about Alex. As I watched him pull away from the curb and saw the first hint of the sun rising on the horizon, I hoped I could do as Alex had asked. I didn't know how I'd do it without him, but I had to, and from the looks of it, I'd be doing it basically alone.

I RETREATED TO my house and my comfy chair to curl up under my chenille throw and try to get a handle on all that had happened that day. My world felt like it was spiraling out of control. Bethany was dead. Alex was the prime suspect. And I didn't know what was true or false. I didn't want to believe what Derek had said—I couldn't believe it.

But who had murdered Bethany and why?

The urge to talk to Alex pressed down on me, but when I called him, his phone rang the four times before sending me to voicemail. The sound of his voice telling me to leave a message in that way anyone who knew him understood was his serious tone made me smile, but I didn't leave one. How would I put into words how much everything I'd seen and heard that morning had devastated me?

I had to talk to someone, so I tried my father again and quietly rejoiced when his phone rang. Even hearing his voicemail message would make me feel better.

"Good morning, honey. How are you this beautiful day?"

The weight of the past few hours finally crushed me underneath it, and I began to sob. "Dad, it's horrible. I don't know what to do. Alex is the only suspect so far, and I don't know how to help him."

"What? What's happened?" my father asked in a

voice full of worry.

I wiped my eyes and tried to stop myself from crying. "Bethany was murdered, Dad. Someone slit her throat as she sat in her car. It was horrible. So much blood and the look on her face. I don't think it will ever leave me."

"Oh, Poppy. I'm so sorry. Bethany was your friend. But what's this about Alex being a suspect? That's crazy."

"I know," I answered as the tears fell harder. "Derek thinks he did it because he went over to see her last night after he left my house. I guess they had a fight. I don't know. I don't know why he'd go over there in the first place. Nothing's making sense, Dad."

"Shhh, I know what you're thinking, Elizabeth, and you're wrong. He cares deeply about you, honey. He wouldn't be dating Bethany behind your back. That's not the kind of man Alex is. And as for him murdering her, that's insane. The only way I'd believe that would be if I saw it happen right in front of my eyes."

"I know! Derek says because Alex's wife died the same way and there were rumors he did it that it's suspicious. But I just can't believe he could be that person."

As I told my father all that had happened, my emotions began to run amok. I didn't know what to do to fix any of this, and I felt like I was the only one who could.

My father tried to soothe me, like he always had when I unraveled like this. "Don't cry, Poppy. I know this will all turn out to be a big mistake. Just breathe and don't forget you know Alex."

"Do I?" I asked, unsure of everything in my life it seemed. "What do I know? What he likes to drink? That he was a cop in Baltimore before he came here? How he takes his coffee?"

"Stop it right now," my father scolded. "Don't belittle everything you two have become. Maybe six months ago that's all you knew, but now you know him like no one else does in this town. Don't let your insecurities trick you into thinking you don't know him because you do."

He was right. I knew Alex as well as anyone could know another person. "Thanks, Dad. I needed someone to remind me of that. I better go now."

"If you need me for anything, you know where I am, honey. If I can help, I will."

"Okay. I just need to figure out where to begin. I'll talk to you later. Thanks for setting me straight."

"That's what fathers do. And Poppy, be careful. Whoever killed Bethany is still out there and my guess is they want Alex to take the fall for this. They aren't going to be lining up for you to show the world what they did."

"I will, Dad. Love you and I'll talk to you later."

Feeling a little better after my talk with my father, I tried Alex once more and got his voicemail again. I pressed END and pulled my throw over me, curling up under its warmth as I wished I could talk to him, even if it was just for a minute to say I believed him.

More than anything, I felt lost without Alex. For almost a year, he and I had been a part of each other's lives every day, and since October, even my nights had been spent with him. Derek's idea about Alex being some kind of Jekyll and Hyde type of man who could be rational and caring in public and a monster who slits women's throats in private bounced around my brain as I sat there, and each time I soundly dismissed it as complete and utter nonsense.

Alex was no more a murderer than I was, but how would I prove it? Without him to flash his badge, I had limited avenues of investigation. At the time when I needed him most, it was him I had to do my best to clear.

At times like this, I wished my mother was still alive so I could talk to her and hear her tell me it would all work out. Siobhan McGuire always knew how to make a situation better. All she had to do was give me one of her beautiful smiles and softly kiss my forehead and I believed her when she said I'd be okay. Closing my eyes as my tears began to fall, I wished I could ask her what to do now.

I AWOKE A few hours later, thankful my dreams hadn't been of me running and eventually being buried under a mound of sand but of my mother telling me how important the search for truth was, no matter how bleak things looked. Feeling rejuvenated and determined to find Bethany's killer so everyone else could see Alex was innocent, I headed to my laptop to begin the investigation.

As I read through page after page of news articles on Helena Montero's murder, a thought came to me. Derek naturally saw Alex as a suspect because both his wife and Bethany had been killed in exactly the same manner, but what if the killer was someone who knew the details of Helena's death and copied them to make him look guilty? People had whispered back then that Alex had been his wife's murderer, so they'd naturally jump to the same conclusion with Bethany's death, especially since he had a past that involved the same crime. He was the perfect scapegoat.

My forefinger tapped on the pad at the bottom of my laptop to go to Helena's obituary. I scanned it and felt as if it read like a love letter from a bereaved husband. Every word seemed filled with his agony from losing her. He'd told me once that writing her obituary had been the hardest thing he'd ever done in his life. As I read it over again with Bethany's murder so fresh in my mind, I had to believe there was no way Alex could have been Helena's killer or Bethany's.

I needed more information. The problem was how to get it. Usually Alex was my way into official records, but that wasn't an option now. Asking Derek was certainly a possibility, but I had a feeling even as he'd promised me to keep an open mind, at that very moment he was far too sure one of his own men was guilty.

Then it came to me. If I wanted details on a murder in Baltimore, who better to call than a coroner who worked for that very city? I'd only met Ken Bryer that one time on the phone when Alex had called him for his expertise on knives, but I got the sense that he'd do anything to help his old friend.

And if Alex needed anything, he needed help.

After I found the coroner's office number, I took a deep breath and called Ken. I didn't like being the bearer of bad news and if there was some way to gently ease into what had happened, I would have. But there wasn't. Time was of the essence since no doubt Derek had already begun his official investigation and with all the resources he could bring to bear with just a phone call or the click of a mouse, in no time he'd be building a case against Alex that would make my efforts look meager in comparison.

So when Ken Bryer finally got on the phone, I began the sad tale of what had happened to his friend that morning and hoped he could shed some light on Helena's case that could help me with this one.

"I don't know if you remember me, Ken, but I'm Alex Montero's partner Poppy McGuire. We spoke once on a call between the three of us about knives. Alex needs your help now, but he can't call you."

The phone remained silent for a long moment before he said, "I remember you, Poppy. What's wrong? What's happened to Alex that he can't call me himself?"

I took another deep breath. "The woman he was dating, Bethany, was murdered last night in the same way as Alex's wife was and he's the prime suspect in the case. I don't believe for a second that he's guilty, but the local police here are currently considering him the only person of interest."

"Really? A second murder? I can't believe this has happened to Alex for a second time. No wonder the police there are looking at him."

"I know, but I think if you can tell me about Helena Montero's murder I might be able to find something that can help me show them they're looking at the wrong person for this murder."

"Why do you think they're related, other than that Alex was involved with both women?" he asked, clearly confused.

"Because Bethany's throat was slit just like Helena's. It's almost the same exact method of killing."

"Oh. No wonder they think he did it. What do you say to meeting me in my office at one this afternoon? If I can help you clear him, it's the least I can do for my old friend."

Relieved and hopeful that Ken could give me some lead I could run with, I thanked him. "I knew you'd help. Alex thinks the world of you, so I'm not surprised to find out the feeling is mutual. I'll be there at one sharp."

"My pleasure, Poppy. Anything to help my friend. See you then."

I thought about trying Alex again but decided a text might be better since I wasn't sure I could keep my emotions in check. The last thing he needed at that moment was me blubbering to him. But I wanted to let him know I believed in him and would prove he wasn't the man Derek thought he was.

No matter what, I know you didn't do this. I won't stop until I find out who did.

Setting my phone on the small table next to the chair, I closed my eyes and tried to imagine a time when this was all behind us and we were back to solving cases together. Oh, how I wanted that time to come soon.

My phone buzzed as it vibrated across the table to alert me to a new text, and I looked down to see Alex's message back to me.

Follow the facts and help me prove I'm innocent, Poppy. Please.

I typed my answer and pressed SEND.

Trust me. I won't let them do this to you.

As I set my phone on the table again and he

messaged back that he loved me, I realized that I'd never told him the truth about how I felt about him. I'd loved him for months before that first kiss, but I'd never said a word to him about it, even after we began dating.

It was about time I did. He needed to know this wasn't just Poppy his partner helping him but the woman who loved him.

So I typed out my message and sent it on its way, hoping it made him as happy as it made me to finally admit the truth.

I love you. I promise I'll find out what happened.

His message back to me told me he was okay, at least for the time being.

I know. I've known for a long time. Nice to see you admit it finally.

Typical Alex. Even in the middle of everything he was going through, he still had a way of making me smile.

Chapter Four

KEN BRYER'S ASSISTANT escorted me to a seat outside his lab to wait while he finished his twelve o'clock meeting. As I sat there alone in that dimly lit and cold basement hallway, I read Alex's texts and smiled at how cute he could be. Not usually a man anyone would think would be sweet, he had a way about him when it was just the two of us that I couldn't help but love.

I hadn't told him about my appointment with Dr. Bryer. On the chance that he had nothing to tell me that would help the case, I didn't want to get Alex's hopes up if all I'd end up doing was dashing them.

Stuffing my phone back into my bag, I looked around at where Ken worked and saw little to relate to. Even my tiny office at *The Eagle* had more ambiance than the basement of the old building I sat in. The white painted concrete walls gave the place a sense of coldness and forced sterility, and the stark white marble tile floors only added to the feeling. I'd seen old hospitals like this in movies. Never once was the setting part of a happy scene.

A chill ran down my spine as every horror movie set in an abandoned hospital ran through my mind. I rubbed my hands together to warm them but had no luck. Finally, I stuck them back in the pockets of my black wool coat to take advantage of some of my body heat.

After about fifteen minutes of sitting there and imagining every dreadful possibility that could happen in that empty hallway, Ken Bryer poked his head out of his office and waved me in.

"Poppy McGuire, I presume?" he asked with a broad smile as I rose to join him.

"In the flesh."

I followed him into his office and immediately noticed it looked every bit as desolate as the hallway outside. No pictures hung on the wall, except a single diploma, leaving the white painted concrete surface like some unfulfilled opportunity to show something of the man who inhabited the office.

Ken Bryer sat down behind his desk that had not a scrap of paper on top of it. I didn't know if I'd ever seen a tidier desk. I'd personally always considered anyone who could keep their workspace so clean a psychopath, but I had to reconsider that judgment with Ken.

Not exactly the complete opposite of Alex, he definitely looked different than our mutual friend. Quite thin for his over six foot frame, his look was best described as jagged. The cheekbones jutted out from under his skin like they strained to escape. Dirty blond hair hung ever so slightly too long in his eyes, forcing him to push it off his face frequently, like doing so was a nervous habit. When the hair was moved and his eyes were visible, I was struck by how blue they were. Almost what I'd call a sky blue, they appeared almost translucent. In another, they may have been jarring, but in Ken, they gave him a very Nordic look.

"I'm so happy to finally meet you in person, but I wish it was under better circumstances," he said in a pleasant voice I'd instantly liked the first time I heard it months earlier on the phone. Something about it just put me at ease.

As I wriggled my arms out of the sleeves of my coat, I nodded. "Me too. Alex speaks very highly of you. I don't know why he didn't formally introduce us in person already."

The eyebrow over Ken's right eye twitched slightly, and he pursed his lips. "I'll have to tell him about that because he shouldn't be keeping such a delightful creature all to himself up there in the hinterlands."

My cheeks warmed at his compliment. "That's so nice of you. I hope you get the chance to talk to him very soon."

He didn't continue our exchange of polite pleasantries, leaving the silence between us to awkwardly hang in the air. It felt strange that he should be so much the flatterer one minute and then silent as a stone the next, but I chalked up his strange behavior to the fact that he probably spent very little time with the living. Working with the dead all the time likely had made him socially awkward.

After a long minute of neither of us talking, I finally said, "So, I'm hoping you'll be able to help me, Ken. I need to know whatever you know about Helena's death."

Frowning, he said, "I've never really shaken the sadness from her death, you know that? I knew her as well as I knew Alex, and my heart was broken when I first got the news."

"I'm so sorry. I know how it feels to lose someone

you care so much about."

He stared across his bare desk like he was trying to judge the truthfulness of my apology and asked, "You've lost someone dear to you too?"

I nodded. "My mother a few years ago. I'm still not sure I've gotten over it."

"You and Alex are two of a kind then because I don't think he's ever gotten over the death of Helena. They were what everyone calls soul mates. I never believed in that kind of sappy nonsense until I saw those two together. They were two parts of one soul, no doubt."

A twinge of jealousy stabbed at me as I listened to Ken describe Alex and his wife in those terms. It was silly and very possibly juvenile, but I'd always wanted to have someone I could call a soul mate. I'd never found that person, even in Alex, but it seemed he had in Helena and it had been clear to everyone around them.

"That's a rare thing to find in this world," I mumbled as I searched my bag for paper and a pen.

"They were a one-of-a-kind couple. He fell hard and quick for her. Not that he didn't have reason. Helena was the type of woman men loved from the first time they laid eyes on her."

I scribbled on the piece of paper to get the ink flowing in my pen and nodded my understanding. Helena was stunning. Men loved her. Alex fell hard from the minute they met. Got it.

With my pen working, I tried to direct the conversation to her murder. "You said you didn't perform the autopsy on her, right? Does that mean you can't get the records about it?"

Ken seemed stunned for a moment at my sudden

changing of the topic, his pale blue eyes opening wide and then returning to their normal state, but it didn't last for long and then he was back to reminiscing about Alex and Helena and their epic love story and ignoring my interest in the findings from the coroner who examined her.

"She was beautiful, but it was a beauty that came from within. She had long black hair. I remember it being so glossy you could almost see your reflection in it. And big brown eyes like doe eyes. So full of kindness. That's how she and Alex met—because she was helping some homeless guy who had decided to make the area behind the restaurant where she worked his home."

"Really? What did he do that got the attention of the police?" I asked, my mind jumping on the notion that perhaps that homeless man had played a part in her murder.

Ken hesitated and looked up toward the ceiling as he tried to jog his memory. "Let me think. I want to say he was shot or stabbed. Whatever it was, something had happened to him that brought Alex and his partner to the restaurant and that's where they met, right in that back alley among the trash bins and everything else that was thrown back there."

I couldn't miss how even though he remembered every minute of the relationship between Alex and Helena, he seemed to have a lapse in memory as to what had happened to that poor homeless man that warranted the police come to investigate. I wanted to ask more about it, but I had the feeling he wouldn't be able to give me much more than something had happened to him that magically brought two people together.

Changing tactics once again, I encouraged him to

talk about Alex and Helena's relationship and hoped I could glean some sliver of a clue that might help with figuring out who had murdered Bethany.

"Is it possible that Helena had enemies who would want to see her dead?"

Ken frowned and shook his head. "Enemies? No. She was a sweet person who would help anyone, even those who often didn't deserve it. She worked as a chef at Manger. What kind of enemies could someone like that have? Once a person ate one of her meals, they were crazy about her. That's what happened with Alex."

I looked up from jotting down where Helena had worked and wondered if I'd heard him correctly. "He ate one of her meals and fell in love?"

Talk about knowing the way to a man's heart. No wonder I was still single. I barely knew my way around a kitchen, and even the crock pot presented me with challenges that made a good meal almost impossible.

"Yes, that's exactly what happened. She fed him her Coq Au Vin and that was it. He told me he had never tasted food so incredible in his life. He had to get to know the woman who could make a dish like that. Six months later, they were married in a ceremony over-looking the Chesapeake with family and a few friends."

Six months? The man I knew had taken six months to even realize he liked me enough to kiss me. Then again, he still was haunted by the ghost of his wife. Now I understood why.

"Sounds like a whirlwind romance, especially considering what I know of Alex," I said, hoping my jealousy wasn't obvious.

"It was. They went from the best meal he'd ever had to 'I do' in a sunset ceremony in a heartbeat. I have to admit I wondered if they were rushing things, but they both said it was true love when any of us dared to ask if they were moving too quickly."

I couldn't help but be enchanted by the story of Alex and Helena, even if it made me jealous for my own happily ever after. They sounded perfectly happy, and I couldn't shake the feeling that if some monster hadn't taken her away from him, they'd still be living their fairytale.

"Well, it's good to know that true love exists in the world. Here's to the rest of us finding a love like they did."

Ken shifted in his seat at my pronouncement of Alex and Helena's romance as one the rest of us would want. He began tapping the point of a pencil on a notepad that I noticed had hundreds of little dots from when he'd done the same thing at some earlier time.

"Did I say something wrong?" I asked, curious as to why his mood had changed so suddenly.

His pale eyes narrowed, as if what he had to say caused him pain, but he shook his head no. "I'm afraid this love story wasn't entirely happy."

"I don't understand. They fell in love over Coq Au Vin, had a whirlwind romance, and got married a few months later overlooking the Chesapeake Bay. Sounds pretty happy to me."

"It's what happened after the wedding that makes it a not-so-happy love story."

Alex had told me very little of his marriage, but everything he'd said had indicated that he and his wife had been happy up to the day she died. Ken's character-ization seemed entirely at odds with how Alex had always portrayed his life with Helena. I didn't want to think that he'd intentionally lied, but the thought did occur to me that how he saw their life together was likely colored by the love he felt for her.

Ken's judgment of their relationship, however, was from the standpoint of an outsider looking in, so he may not have truly understood everything the way it truly was. Still, I thought it worth hearing his opinion on what troubles they had experienced.

"They hit a hard patch that made things change. Alex was promoted to detective two years into the marriage. He began to work more and more hours and was always on the job. Helena wanted them to start a family, but that was impossible with Alex never being at home. I think they began to drift apart because he was so dedicated to his work."

I could certainly see Alex getting wrapped up in his cases. He'd given every one we worked, from the simplest robbery of someone's terra cotta planter taken from their porch to each murder, all his attention to the exclusion of everything else in his life. I'd just assumed he acted like that because he lived alone and loved his job, but Ken's memory about him being a workaholic made me think that's just who he was. The problem was if his wife wanted him to be someone else.

"Didn't he want to have children?" I asked as I thought for the first time about Alex being a father.

"I think the problem was every day he saw such ugliness in the world that he wasn't sure bringing a child into all that was a good idea. I'm not saying he wouldn't have been a great father or didn't love Helena enough to have a child with her, but it wasn't a priority for him like it was for her."

As I wrote down details I knew probably wouldn't

help me much with proving Alex was innocent, I felt sad for him, knowing that if he had made different choices he might still have a piece of her with him today that could give him solace like only a child could. My father had told me so many times that he didn't how he would have continued to go on if he didn't have me after my mother died.

"Then he got shot and it convinced him that he couldn't father a child he might not get to see grow up," Ken said in a voice full of sadness. "Helena didn't understand why he felt like that since the wound wasn't that bad."

I sat stunned at the news that Alex had ever been shot. He'd never told me. I wondered if I knew him as well as I thought I did because it felt like he'd intentionally kept an important detail about his past from me.

But why?

As my brain processed all this, I tried to keep my surprise at what Ken had said at bay by commenting as casually as possible, "Well, taking a bullet can certainly make a person look at life differently, as I'm sure you know, no matter how bad the wound is."

Ken didn't look impressed by my idea and continued. "Helena was devastated not only by the shooting but also by his announcement when he came home from the hospital a couple days later that he didn't want children. From that point on, nothing was ever the same. She couldn't let go of the desire to have a baby, and he wouldn't budge. All of us who were friends with them watched as their perfect love story disintegrated in front of our eyes."

Although he appeared saddened by having to tell me this story, I had the sense there was a hint of blame underneath his words. For me, the unraveling of Alex and Helena's relationship just made me wish things had turned out differently for them. I could only imagine how terrible his life was after her death, so full of what could have beens since that fateful day.

Leaning forward toward me, Ken lowered his voice. "I hate to have to tell you this, but I feel like you should know everything that went on back then. It's better to know than not know. They fought a lot after he made that decision. They fought like cats and dogs, sometimes even in front of me. When Alex is angry, he has quite a temper."

Without even thinking about it, my defense of Alex came right out of my mouth. "I can't believe that. I don't think I've ever met a calmer, more rational person in my life. If anything, the way Alex is makes others want to lash out, not the other way around."

Ken held his hands up to calm me down. "Oh, no, I wasn't saying he ever hit her or anything like that. He wouldn't do that. Alex isn't that kind of man. But ask anyone and they'll tell you when he's really angry, his temper can get the best of him."

I didn't know what to say to that. Whatever Alex Montero was, he wasn't violent or the type of man who would ever lay a hand on a woman. But Ken had known him a lot longer than I had, so maybe he had seen evidence of that supposed temper I'd never seen in all the time I'd spent with Alex.

"Then things got really bad when he accused her of cheating on him. She came to me nearly hysterical asking me what to do. Her marriage was crumbling around her, and she didn't know how to stop it."

I saw by the look on Ken's face that my surprise was

evident. "You look shocked, Poppy."

Stunned by what he'd said, I stammered out, "I guess…I just don't know him that way."

The person he was describing was so foreign to the one I thought I knew so well. The truth was, though, that I didn't know Alex as a man madly in love. Perhaps the man he was with Helena was more prone to emotion and losing her had made him close off that part of himself.

"People change, but who they really are stays with them," he said in an attempt to calm me, but all he succeeded in doing was making me think I didn't know much at all about the man I loved.

I didn't want to talk about them anymore. I'd come here to get information on her death, not their life together. Everything I'd heard only made what Derek suspected more likely. That didn't help me prove Alex's innocence at all.

"I think I'd like to hear some details about the actual murder, if you don't mind."

Ken nodded, as if he had nothing else to share about the love story of Alex and Helena. "She was found murdered behind Manger in the very same spot where she and Alex met that first night when he answered the 911 call. Someone had slit her throat and left her there to die. The homeless man she fed every night found her and called Alex directly because she'd given him both of their cell phone numbers."

And with that, my sadness for what Alex had gone through grew even worse. The place where his life had begun with Helena was the very place where it ended. I could only imagine the pain he lived with because of that still to that very day.

Chapter Five

WHILE KEN LOOKED through a stack of file folders on the side of his desk for the information on Helena Montero's autopsy, I sat silently wishing Alex was there by my side. Questioning witnesses and suspects I could handle. I'd actually gotten pretty good at figuring out exactly what to ask someone and how to ask it to elicit a truthful answer from them. This was nothing like that skill. Researching how someone died made me feel ghoulish, especially since the person's death I had to learn about was Alex's wife.

I'd never truly admitted how much I depended on him for virtually every step of our investigations. Obviously, he had ways of finding out information only the police could obtain, but it was so much more than that. His quiet way of making people want to bare their souls to him far outsmarted my more direct way of questioning, even when I asked the right questions in the right way.

And as much as he always liked to say I had great instincts, it was his gut feelings I relied on more than anything else. I knew the citizens of Sunset Ridge. He knew what made people tick. The difference wasn't lost on me.

Now when I needed his guidance and support as a partner the most, he couldn't be there with me. I didn't want to let him down. Never before in any of our cases had everything ridden on what I could do, and part of me feared I wasn't ready to take on a case alone, much less a case that could end up robbing him of his freedom if I didn't find out who the real killer was.

"You look uncomfortable, Poppy. Something wrong?"

I focused my gaze on Ken's face and forced a smile. "No, I'm fine. I've just never been anywhere near where dead bodies are kept."

Ken chuckled. "It's strange for civilians, but for those of us who work with the dead, it's just another day at work. I've had my hands in so many dead bodies that I can't even give an accurate count anymore."

I flashed him another half-smile while my skin crawled a little at the idea that anyone's day-to-day job involved putting their hands on the dead. More and more as I got to know him, I saw Ken Bryer's look fit the man and his job perfectly.

"I don't think I could ever do what you do, but you're an integral part of murder cases, so thank God you love your job."

Throwing his head back, he laughed louder this time. "I need you to talk to the cops in this city. You're great PR for the coroner's office, Poppy."

I couldn't help feel strange joking and smiling while he thumbed through the stack of brown folders full of autopsy details of murder victims. It felt disrespectful and unfeeling, but I had to imagine for him it was just another day at work. Chalking up his ability to be so lighthearted to gallows' humor, I hoped he'd find

Helena Montero's file soon because as much as he had tried to make me feel welcome there, all I wanted to do was get the information I'd come for and get back home.

"I'm sorry it's taking so long," Ken said as he continued to look through the files. "My assistant is new and I'm afraid she mixed up the contents of all these folders this morning. I'm almost to the bottom of the pile, so it won't be much longer. While I'm doing that, why don't you tell me what you and Alex have been up to in that little town you two live in? Other than dealing with the murder of his girlfriend, that is."

Ken flipped open each folder and quickly scanned the top page briefly, each time returning his gaze to me as if what I had to say was far more important than the contents of those files. Certainly flattered, I wished he would focus more on what I'd called him about and less on the boring goings-on in Sunset Ridge. But since I didn't want to offend him, I tried to think of what the two of us had been doing before the horrible news of Bethany's murder had turned our lives upside down.

"You know how small towns are. There's not much to do, so people spend a lot of time indoors in the winter watching movies. We live very exciting lives up in Sunset Ridge."

A file slid out of his hand and fell to the floor. He didn't make a move to pick it up, oddly enough, but since he'd scanned that one, I figured he'd checked it and saw no need to stop his search for Helena's file.

"I often wonder how Alex handles that since he's a born and bred Baltimore boy used to the city," Ken said with a chuckle.

As he continued to scan each file, I explained how his friend seemed right at home in Sunset Ridge. "I think he's gotten used to the slower pace up there. All we do is work during the day and watch movies at night now that the weather has gotten cold. I have to say I'm looking forward to spring coming and us having a chance to get out of the house after we get done for the day."

Ken's hands stopped shuffling the file folders, and he stared at me across the desk like I'd just given him some disturbing news. "What do you mean you watch movies at night? I thought Alex was dating the young lady who was murdered."

"No, they stopped dating a while ago. I want to say sometime in August maybe?"

He shook his head and knitted his brows. "That's not possible. I met her when he brought her to the city in September."

I thought back to the early fall and realized he might have been right. "It could have been in September. I know by October they were definitely done."

My answer pleased him, and the smile returned to his face. "I was beginning to get worried I'd forgotten the last time I saw my friend. I'm sorry to hear he and Bethany broke up. They seemed like such a good couple. She looked like she made him happy."

Whether or not Bethany had made Alex happy I couldn't say without my jealousy clouding my judgment, so I gave Ken my best polite smile and a noncommittal shrug. He seemed to want more than that from me, though, so I reminded him of her demise and hoped he'd find the file so we didn't have to make this awkward small talk about Alex and my social life.

"It's still sinking in that Bethany's gone. I just can't imagine why anyone would want to do this to her."

Ken stopped rifling through his files and looked at me with an expression of disgust. "Murderers have a code of ethics all to themselves. I don't think anyone so nice like yourself could ever understand the mind of one of them."

"You're probably right. I can barely kill a bug, much less look someone in the eyes and end their life, no matter what my reason might be."

"Here it is at the bottom of the pile," Ken said shaking his head as he opened the folder on his desk. "I'm going to have to talk to that assistant of mine so I don't have a replay of this kind of thing."

Instead of immediately telling me the details of Helena Montero's death, he turned to the pile of file folders on the right side of his desk and tapped them into a neat pile before placing them in a basket on the cabinet a few feet away. He really was a neat freak.

"Does it say anything about what weapon Alex's wife was killed with?" I eagerly asked as he turned his focus back to the open file just waiting for him to examine it.

Unlike when he was looking for the file, now that he had it right in front of him, he seemed intent on reading every single word before answering me. I sat there on the edge of my seat desperate for any details I might be able to use in the case against Alex.

"Well, it looks like it was a hunting knife, a Krear 550."

He sounded impressed by the murderer's choice of weapon, so I asked, "Is that a good knife for these kinds of things? Not to be indelicate, but you seemed to like that model."

After a few seconds, he lifted his gaze from the page and shook his head. "I don't think I've ever seen a hunting knife outside of work, so I don't know if it's a particularly well-chosen murder weapon. I can say that it's efficient, if this report is any indication."

I leaned forward to catch a glimpse of what he had read but couldn't see anything clearly on the upside down page. "Efficient? What do you mean?"

"It nearly cut her head off."

He said those words so calmly, like it was a normal utterance coming out of his mouth. As the horror of them settled into my brain, a thought came to me. "I thought no one had ever been arrested and tried for Helena Montero's murder? How did the coroner know what knife was used to slit her throat?"

"It's actually quite easy to figure out what kind of weapon was used since knives have particular cut patterns. The Krear 550 has a jagged edge that leaves a very distinctive mark on the skin. It wouldn't have been difficult for the medical examiner on the case to determine this."

Feeling somewhat deflated by his easy dismissal of what I'd thought was a very clever question, I sat back in my chair and waited for him to continue reading the report.

"From what it says here, the coroner believed the killer came up from behind, and with one swipe, cut her from ear to ear."

"Is it really that easy to cut human flesh and bone?" I asked, my stomach turning at the thought of Helena and Bethany suffering through that.

Ken nodded and lifted his chin to show me his neck. Running his fingers up and down, he said, "Feel your neck. It's skin and muscle, so a sharp knife applied to the area with enough pressure would slice through easily since there really is no bone to cut."

I tilted my head back and mimicked his motions with my own fingertips, astonished at how delicate it was considering it had to hold up a head. "You're right. I never realized how soft this whole area is. So it wouldn't necessarily have to be a large attacker. It could be a woman, for example?"

"Oh, definitely. The knife wields all the power in this type of situation. A female could certainly be strong enough to slit another female's throat."

"What happens after the knife begins cutting?"

With a twinkle in his eye I guessed came from having the chance to talk shop with someone, Ken said, "Blood. Lots of it. You've got major arteries and veins running up and down the neck. If the attacker cuts the victim's throat from the front, they're going to be hit with jets of blood, at the very least. I've seen instances where someone cut a person when they were standing facing them, and the guy was drenched in blood."

I jotted all these details down on my sheet of paper and looked up to see him waiting for me to continue. "What if someone was attacked from behind? I mean, what if the killer slit their victim's throat while they were standing behind them? Would they be covered in blood the same way as if they did it facing them?"

Shaking his head, Ken pursed his lips. "No, they wouldn't. It's possible if an attacker came up behind someone and slit their throat that they wouldn't have blood on them at all."

The idea that someone had lay in wait in Bethany's back seat until she got in and without even looking into her eyes slit her throat from ear to ear made a chill run up my spine. I couldn't imagine the level of rage that someone would have to feel to want to kill like that.

Hoping to hear some detail that would be less gory, I asked, "Does it say anything else that I might be able to use to help Alex?"

Ken narrowed his eyes and began to read the report again, but soon he looked up and I saw disappointment on his face. "I'm having a hard time reading the coroner's notes."

"You guys still hand write notes in this day and age?" I asked, surprised to hear anyone other than Alex and I still wrote notes on paper like that.

"Sometimes. It's up to the medical examiner on staff for the case. I don't because my handwriting is terrible, but some do. Their report is still complete, but the handwritten notes can have details they didn't include in the official autopsy. I'm having a hard time reading this one."

I stood from my seat and leaned over his desk. "Can I take a look? I'm pretty good with deciphering even the worst handwriting. Doctor's notes are no match for me."

"I wish I could, Poppy, but you're not an officer, so by rights, I shouldn't even be telling you about this, except I want to help my friend," he said as he pulled the folder away so I couldn't see anything.

"Yeah, I understand." I sat back down in my seat feeling helpless yet again that day. "Too bad you weren't the medical examiner on Helena's case."

He nodded and said in a sad voice, "I know. I can't tell you how many times I wished I was instead of being out of town for a medical conference in West Palm Beach the day she was murdered. I can't believe it's been so long since she died. I remember the moment I first heard the news. I was sitting on the beach relaxing between conference sessions. It was a gorgeous sunny day. And then I heard those terrible words telling me she was gone from this world and it was like the sun had been stolen from the sky."

I felt awkward asking him to give me any other details after hearing his sorrow over losing his friend, but I had to. Alex couldn't afford for me to be sensitive or socially polite.

"Is there anything else you can tell me from the report on her death? Anything that could show who may have done this to Helena? Did the homeless man say anything to the police about seeing who the killer was?"

Ken opened the file once again and scanned the information it held. Without looking up, he said, "The officers on the case weren't able to get anything definitive from the homeless man, unfortunately. As for the coroner's findings about who may have done this crime, he believed that it was a man at least six feet tall who was right handed."

With every word he said, Alex remained a viable suspect, even as I told myself that was impossible. Just over six feet tall, he was right handed. Discouraged, I asked, "Why would he or she have to be right handed?"

"By the way the knife cut her, the medical examiner determined it started under her left ear and came across the front of the neck until it stopped under her right ear. That indicates a right handed killer."

"Oh," I mumbled as I hung my head.

"I wish I could have been more help, Poppy. I'm sorry. Nothing would make me happier than being able to help find Helena's murderer. It's been years and every day I think about her."

"Helena's murderer? I came here hoping to prove

that Alex had no part in Bethany's murder."

Ken nodded and closed the file, pushing it away from him off to the side. "I know, but I thought you wanted details on Helena's murder because it's likely the same killer."

"I know, but the problem is that nothing in her autopsy doesn't exclude Alex. I was hoping to hear some clue that would help me show he wasn't part of Bethany's murder."

I stood and extended my hand over his desk to thank him. "I appreciate you taking the time to help me, Ken. I'll be sure to tell Alex how great you were to fit me in this afternoon."

"Do and be sure to tell him I'm thinking of him."

"I will."

Turning to leave, I walked toward the door, but Ken stopped me. "Poppy, one more thing. I want you to be careful as you look into this."

His face told me he feared for my safety, but why? Did he know something he wasn't telling me?

"I will. I'm just looking for the truth."

"The problem is that with now two murders of two women associated with Alex, I worry that your life may be in danger from whoever is guilty of these heinous crimes."

"What are you saying?" I asked as I wondered if he'd just implicated Alex in both Bethany's and Helena's murders.

"Within months of her death, Alex moved away from Baltimore and bought a house in Sunset Ridge where he basically lived like a hermit until you came into his life. Then poor Bethany came into it too and look what happened. I'd hate to see you get hurt, Poppy."

Defiant even as he listed so succinctly how entwined Alex was in both murder cases, I tilted my head up and said, "I'll be fine. Thanks for all your help, Ken. Time for me to go look for clues so Alex isn't unjustly blamed for either of these terrible crimes."

He merely nodded, understanding that whatever would happen, I wasn't going to back down from finding out the truth. Alex deserved that from his partner, and I wouldn't disappoint him.

Chapter Six

A LITTLE OVER an hour later, I returned to Sunset Ridge and drove directly to the police station. Although I hadn't found out anything from Ken Bryer that could show conclusively that Alex wasn't his wife's killer or Bethany's, and in truth hadn't found anything at all that could help him, I worried that Derek had more luck than I had and may not have been in a hurry to let me in on what he'd learned. Better for me to stay on top of him because if I planned on waiting for him to come to me with information, I may be waiting a long time.

I found Sunset Ridge's chief of police sitting in his office staring at the far wall with a look that said he was either deep in thought or sleeping with his eyes open. That he was just hanging out in his office gave me hope he hadn't found any more neighbors willing to claim that Alex and Bethany had been fighting like cats and dogs last night, or even better, hadn't found actual evidence to tie Alex to the crime at all.

Derek sitting and staring usually meant he had nothing to go on and the case had stalled. As I stepped into his office, I could only hope.

"Hey, Chief, what's new?" I asked, trying to remain as upbeat as possible so as not to make him think I'd found anything that would incriminate Alex.

Turning his focus toward me, Derek shook his head and frowned. "Nothing. I have a few leads I want to follow up on, but in general, nothing's new.

As I sat down in the chair in front of his desk, I asked, "So you don't have any more evidence in the case?"

He leveled his gaze on me and said nothing for a few seconds. I had no idea what was going through his head as he stared at me, but I hoped it wasn't that he had changed his mind and decided to ice me out of the investigation. I didn't want to, but I wasn't above begging to get him to let me stay on. Without the ability to know what the police knew, I'd be working blind and have little chance to help Alex.

"If you're asking if I found the knife with Alex's fingerprints on it, the answer is no."

I sighed, my head already hurting from Derek's pigheadedness on this issue. "Why is it so easy for you to believe one of your officers killed someone? It's like you aren't even considering anyone else could have done this. I swear, Derek, I can't figure out why you became a cop if you have no interest in finding out who really committed crimes and prefer to just jump to ridiculous conclusions."

My insult stunned him, and his mouth hung open for a moment before he sat straight up in his chair and snapped, "I don't have to let you work on this case, Poppy McGuire, average citizen with no badge, no training, and no ability to do much other than muddle things up."

Ouch. It was true I'd been a little harsh in my comment to him, but he didn't have to slice and dice my feelings like that. Ordinarily, I'd simply brush him off if he acted like that, but this case had my emotions all jumbled, so I didn't stop the tears when they filled my eyes. Also, I knew Derek Hampton well enough to know that making a woman cry was one of those things he hated doing.

It was his Kryptonite, and I wasn't above using it to stay on this case.

Burying my face in my hands, I let the tears flow. They came because I missed Bethany. They came because of my fear that I wouldn't be able to show the world that the man I loved wasn't a killer. They came because of the frustration building inside me from finding nothing at Ken Bryer's office that would exonerate Alex.

They came because as I sat there, I was little more than a wrung-out emotional dishrag after the past few hours.

"Christ, Poppy, stop crying. I didn't mean it. You don't have to stop looking into the case."

I dropped my hands from my face and looked up at him through tear-filled eyes as my emotions continued to unravel. "Does that mean you think I muddle things up?"

He shook his head and handed me a tissue. "No. I shouldn't have said that. I'm sorry. This case has me has on edge and I took it out on you. I know you're just trying to help Alex."

Thanking him for the tissue and his apology, I dried my eyes and sniffled the last of my sobs away. "It's just so hard, Derek. I'm trying to find something that can show he would never do this—something other than my just knowing deep down in my soul that he would never hurt Bethany like this. I know that's not enough."

"No, it's not. I like him, Poppy. I do, but I can't ignore the facts here. He and Bethany had dated, and from what her next door neighbor saw, they'd rekindled their relationship recently."

"That's not possible, Derek! That, at least, I can prove."

Curious, his eyebrows shot up into his forehead. "Really? How's that?"

"Because he's been at my house almost every night since October."

Derek knitted his now angry eyebrows. "What are you saying, Poppy? Are you two more than just partners who work on cases?"

As much as I preferred my private life to stay just that, I wasn't going to lie about what I felt for Alex. Nodding, I told Derek the truth. "Yes. We're dating and have been for months, so whatever Bethany's nosy neighbor thinks she saw is nonsense. Alex wasn't back with Bethany because he's with me."

Sunset Ridge's police chief had liked me since grade school when he would walk me home from school every day, and as he sat there gaping at me in surprise at what I'd just told him, I saw hints of that same young boy who still liked me in his eyes. I also saw disapproval, but I didn't know if that was because he had feelings for me, as I'd long suspected, or because there was an unspoken sense between him, Alex, and me that when he agreed to let us work together that it meant that was all it could ever be.

"You and Alex are together?" he asked in a quiet voice full of shock.

"Yes, so you see, Mallory Michaels was wrong. Alex

may have gone over there last night, but he and Bethany weren't back together."

Derek remained silent as he processed what I'd told him and then announced, "You can't work on this case, Poppy. You're too close to it. I thought you were too close before when I thought you and Alex were just good friends and partners, but if you're lovers, that's definitely too close."

"What?" I screamed as I jumped out of my seat. "Don't do this, Derek. I need to be able to work on this case to help him. Don't push me out."

He stared up at me, and as the surprise faded, I saw resignation fill his eyes. It was one of the best parts of Derek. He hated a hassle, and if I could be anything, I could be a huge hassle for him and he knew it.

"Sit down before one of my officers comes in and puts you in handcuffs for acting this way toward the chief of police."

I leaned my hands against the edge of his desk and lowered my head so we were just about eye level. "Tell me you're not going to force me off this case and I'll sit down."

He remained silent for a long moment and then blew the air out of his lungs. "Fine. Now sit down and get yourself together. First, you're crying, and then you're jumping all over the place. You won't be able to help your boyfriend if you're an emotional mess."

I took my seat again and tried to compose myself. "If we could just stick with calling Alex by his given name, I'd appreciate it. Oh, and if the word lovers ever comes out of your mouth in regard to my personal life, Derek Hampton, I won't care if you're the chief of police of this town or not. I'll tell anyone who's willing to listen about how Kristy Baumburger left you standing without your pants in the woods out past the Hotel Piermont in the middle of the night in senior year and how you called me begging me to get clothes for you so nobody would see. Got it?"

A smile spread across his face, and he nodded. "That's low, Poppy, but message received. I'm worried you're going to have your heart broken on this, though, and I won't be able to do a thing about it."

"Don't worry about me. I'm a lot tougher than I look, but it won't matter. Alex didn't do this, so there won't be any hearts breaking. So can we get back to the case and where we're at with it?"

My outburst behind us, he returned to his usual all-business way. "The coroner won't have his report until tomorrow, but the knife nearly took poor Bethany's head off. Other than that, there's Mallory Michaels and her eyewitness testimony."

The thought of Bethany's last moments being so unbelievably awful made my heart contract, but I had to keep focused on getting Derek to see the murderer could be anyone. "We need to begin looking at the clues to find suspects because Alex can't be the killer."

"I want to believe that, Poppy, but Mallory's statement about Alex and Bethany having a fight makes it look bad."

"What about her cell phone? What did you find on that? Bethany was never without her cell phone."

Derek opened up his notes and read from them. "She only called one person last night. Alex at right around nine. Her last call before that was to *The Eagle* on Friday around four."

That didn't sound right. Like most people, Bethany

was always on her cell and her last call was to her workplace on a Friday until she made one call Sunday night? Something wasn't right.

"So you think a woman with an active social life like Bethany didn't call a soul from Friday afternoon until Sunday evening? How likely does that sound, Derek?"

He shrugged, clearly not seeing the problem. "I don't know, but that's what her phone said. Her sister had been in town for the past few weeks, so it wouldn't be surprising that she wouldn't be calling many people with family around and her active social life, as you call it, could have slowed down a lot so she could spend time with her sister."

"What about incoming calls?"

Derek looked down at the paper in front of him and shook his head as he looked up at me. "A few from work. That's all."

That didn't sound right either. Bethany wasn't some lonely hermit. But maybe he was correct and she was spending a lot of time with her sister.

"Have you found Mariah yet?"

"No, she hasn't been heard from and we don't know her whereabouts yet. I called her from the number on Bethany's phone, but the phone was turned off and I couldn't leave a voicemail. We found none of her belongings in Bethany's apartment. It's like she wasn't there Sunday."

"There's something wrong with all this. She was supposed to stay for three weeks, and that would leave a week more. Bethany told me herself about the visit and said three weeks. Why would she leave early?"

Derek shrugged again. "For a million reasons we might never know. Maybe she got homesick. Maybe she and her sister had a fight. Maybe she had to return to work early. I don't know. I'm just hoping whoever killed Bethany didn't harm her sister too."

He might have thought the whole Mariah facet of this case was next to meaningless, but I sure didn't. Bethany and her sister had been estranged for a few years, and this was the first visit between the two of them in a long time. She'd told me how happy she was to have her sister coming to town and how she hoped to truly mend the rift that had come between them after their mother died, so the idea that Bethany would let anything happen to ruin their planned time together to me sounded like something we needed to investigate.

But it was clear that until Derek found Mariah he didn't intend to do much with that line of inquiry, even though Mariah was likely an integral part of this entire case.

"So what's your theory of the case then?" I asked him, hoping to hear something other than Alex did it.

A sheepish look crossed his face. "Well, until about ten minutes ago, I thought it was very possible that this was a case of a jilted love. Bethany broke up with Alex and he didn't take it well. He snapped and killed her."

I felt my face twist into a look of pure disgust. "Well, now that you know that's complete and utter nonsense, do you have a different theory of the case?"

"No, but I'm sure you have one, so let's hear it," he said with a similar look to mine marring his usually attractive face.

In truth, I didn't have a theory of the case, other than Alex wasn't the murderer. I knew Bethany well enough to know that active social life of hers had included some winners in the boyfriend department, but she hadn't told me about anyone since she and Alex had stopped seeing each other. Part of that was surely because she knew he and I had grown close, but I had the sense that she hadn't moved on to anyone worth mentioning.

So I admitted the truth to Derek. "I don't have one. I can't imagine why anyone would want to do that to Bethany. Everyone loved her."

As I thought about how true that statement really was, Stephen walked into the office to deliver a piece of paper to Derek. He walked past me on his way out and shot me the same snarky look he had at the crime scene. Unnerved, I opened my mouth to ask what his problem could be, but Derek began talking about what he'd given him.

"Speaking of everyone loving her, did you see that bouquet of red roses on the kitchen counter in Bethany's apartment this morning?"

I thought back to walking through there earlier and couldn't recall seeing any flowers. "No, but I wasn't exactly focused since I'd just heard one of my good friends had been murdered."

"Well, the card on the dozen of red roses said, 'I know I messed up but forgive me, my love.'"

"And? Was it signed by someone?"

"No, and there weren't any fingerprints on the card either."

Confused as to where he was trying to take me with this, I asked, "So you're taking time to focus on a card with no signature or fingerprints why?"

Derek looked down at a sheet of paper to his left and handed it and the card to me. "See anything similar?"

I scanned the report sheet he'd just handed me and

saw only one place where there was handwriting. At the very bottom of the form Alex had handwritten his signature. I looked at the card from the bouquet of flowers and understood why Derek had given this any thought at all. The handwriting on the report and on the card could be seen as similar, although I didn't think they were from the same person.

"So you think this is Alex's handwriting? No way. And can I mention that this doesn't even sound like him? 'I know I messed up but forgive me, my love.' I don't think so. He wouldn't write something like that. It's just not him."

Derek took the card and piece of paper back and shook his head. "I think you're being swayed by your feelings, Poppy. The handwriting on both of these is very close."

"Do we know where the flowers came from? The card didn't have any florist's name on it."

"Carson's Floral Shop right here in Sunset Ridge."

Refusing to believe that mattered, I defiantly stood my ground. "That doesn't prove anything. They could have been ordered anywhere and just delivered by Carson's. It isn't like in the old days when you could only get flowers from your local florist. Anyone in the world could have ordered those flowers and had Carson's deliver them."

"And the handwriting on the card? How do you explain that?" Derek asked sharply.

"I have no idea, but why don't we ask them? Feel like a little field work, Chief?" I asked as I stood to head over to Carson's Floral Shop. With or without Derek, I was going to find out who ordered those flowers and if they delivered them.

"Why not?" he said with a smile as he rose from behind his desk. "Maybe we'll find something that will help us figure out what the hell was going on between the two of them."

I shot him a nasty glance, and he quickly added, "If anything. It could turn out that Carson's helps us crack this case wide open."

Before we left, I stopped him with my finger in his chest and angrily said, "Do you think you could put away the nails for the crucifixion until you actually have some real proof that says Alex had anything to do with this? You are the chief of police, Derek, and he is one of your officers. Don't you think a little of that innocent before being proven guilty thing could be extended to Alex?"

He glared down at me for a moment but then softened his expression and nodded. "You're right. I don't mean to convict him already. You could be right and he could be innocent."

Looking up into that cute face, I smiled. "Try to remember that, okay? I know what's behind this personal witch hunt you have going with him, but can you push your jealousy aside so a man's life isn't ruined?"

"Jealousy? What do you mean?"

"Don't bother putting that confused face on, Derek. I know what your problem with Alex is. You're jealous because I like him. Admit it."

He rolled his eyes and pushed past me to leave his office. "Ridiculous. I'm no more jealous of Alex because you're with him than…"

His sentence drifted off, likely because he couldn't come up with an appropriate comparison, but I knew the truth. Like everyone else in Sunset Ridge, Derek had become accustomed to me being single and forever available, and now that had all changed. As flattered as I was that he liked me in that way, I couldn't let his interest in me hurt Alex.

Chapter Seven

C ARSON'S FLORAL SHOP stood as the only florist in Sunset Ridge, but its lack of competition hadn't affected the charm of the store that had first opened back in the sixties by the current owner's grandfather, Mitchell Carson. Always a place to find unique gifts and floral arrangements, it remained a favorite of folks in town even with the advent of online ordering and the ability to never step foot in the actual store while still buying flowers.

A line of three young men all wanting a dozen red roses waited ahead of us, making me think that some kind of strange wave of disagreements had come over the couples in town. Young enough to be the type of customer who would choose to order online instead of coming into the store, the three each explained as they reached the counter that they needed a special bouquet for their girlfriends to appease their anger.

Finally, after nearly ten minutes, we took our turn at the counter to speak to the store's owner, Maria Carson. With her dark brown hair styled in a pixie cut that only reinforced how truly short she was at just over five feet tall, Maria perpetually looked like a little girl, even though she was in her mid-thirties. Derek and I had known her from school, and I remembered he'd dated her for a brief time right around the time of prom in their junior year. As with all of Derek's ex-girlfriends, there was no bad blood between them, even if they weren't close anymore.

She recognized both of us and flashed us a smile. I pointed toward the door as I joked, "What's going on in Sunset Ridge? Three boyfriends needing makeup flowers?"

"It's the January rush. I see it every year. The holidays can be killers on relationships. Too many family events, too much alcohol, too many chances for guys to mess up. So flowers help them get back in their girlfriends' good graces. I don't complain. Let them mess up all the time."

I elbowed Derek in the ribs and chuckled. "Hear that, Derek? It's a thing with your entire sex."

He rolled his eyes as Maria asked, "What can I do for you two this afternoon?"

The way she asked made it sound like she thought we were together in a romantic sense, so I quickly corrected her. "We're here on police business, not personal."

I realized it was probably the place of the chief of police to explain that and looked up to see Derek smiling at me.

"Thanks, Poppy. I guess they just give me the title because it sounds good."

Apologizing for my eagerness, I let him take over and do the talking, and he asked Maria about the flowers that had come from her shop to Bethany. "We don't know when they were purchased, but I can tell you they looked fresh this morning."

Maria's eyes opened wide in horror. "Oh my God! You mean that girl who was murdered in her car? That's so horrible! Let me see what I can find out because I don't think I took the order. I'd remember if I did."

She turned around to type in a few words into her computer and then walked away into the back room where they designed the flower arrangements. A few seconds later she returned with one of her employees in tow.

"I didn't take the order but Cynthia did. She can tell you what she knows."

I studied Cynthia and surmised she couldn't have been more than twenty, if that. Unremarkable in every way save the way her one eye turned ever so slightly outward while the other one stared forward, she seemed eager to help.

"Cynthia, I'm Derek Hampton, the chief of police, and this is Poppy McGuire. We need to ask you some questions about flowers that were sent to Bethany Lewis on Main Street in town. Can you tell us who ordered those flowers? Was it online or in person?"

Without missing a beat, she answered, "In person. I remember because I mentioned to the man that I thought the name Bethany was very pretty and he said he thought so too."

"Do you remember what the man looked like?" I asked with my heart in my throat as I silently prayed to hear he was short and fat with blond hair.

"Tall with dark hair. And he had a deep voice," she said without thinking about it.

My heart sank.

"Are you sure?" I asked, my shoulders sagging under the weight of lost hope.

Derek then showed her the card that had come with the flowers and asked, "Did he write out this card?"

Cynthia shook her head. "No, that's my handwriting. He told me what to write, though."

My hopes buoyed, I quickly asked, "Do you remember anything else about him?"

She took a moment to think and shrugged her shoulders. "Not really. It was really busy that day. It took all of five minutes, so I didn't really pay attention to him. He was nice enough, though. Said he wanted them delivered to his girlfriend on Sunday, which meant he had to pay extra. He didn't seem to be bothered by that, though."

"How did he pay?" Derek asked as I tried not to hate the way she referred to Bethany as the man's girlfriend.

Cynthia turned around to look at the computer and then back to face us. "Cash. I had to look because I remember it got really busy right after he came in."

"Do you remember anything else about him? Had you ever seen him before that day?" I asked, silently praying she wouldn't say she'd seen him all the time since he was one of Derek's police officers.

"You know, now that I think about it, I had seen him before, but I can't remember where."

Then Derek did what I knew he had to and handed her a picture of Alex taken at a picnic the police had held last summer. Smiling and happy, he looked like he didn't have a care in the world as he waited for his turn at bat in the baseball game in which he'd scored the winning run.

"Is this the man?" he asked as I continued to remember that happy day at the park.

She looked at the picture for nearly a minute and then looked up at us. "I'm not sure, but it could be. I was so busy that day I can't say for sure."

Derek took the picture from her and said, "If you remember anything else, please call me at the police station. Just ask for the chief, okay?"

Cynthia agreed and said she'd think about it to try to jog her memory. We left Carson's to head back to the station, but I knew what Derek was thinking. Even though she hadn't been able to say it was Alex she'd waited on, she hadn't been able to say it wasn't either. He was just as much a suspect now as before we walked into the flower shop.

We silently walked the few blocks back to the police station where I decided I needed to step up my efforts in the case. Grabbing his arm, I looked up into his eyes with a pleading look and said, "I want to see Bethany's apartment, Derek."

"I'm not sure that's a good idea. It's still a live crime scene, Poppy."

"Please, Derek. I need to get in there and look around for myself. Don't tie my hands. Please."

He frowned and shook his head, but I could tell he would relent. "I need to have dinner, but I'll pick you up at your house at eight."

"Okay. Good."

Derek took hold of my shoulders and stared down into my eyes so intently I leaned away from him, frightened. "Do not go over there without me, or I swear to God, Poppy, I'll make sure you don't see another thing in this investigation. Do you understand me?"

"Yes, I understand, Derek."

Relief washed over me that I'd get the chance to

look through Bethany's apartment and not have to rely on Derek's guys and the state police crime scene unit to find a clue. I knew they were highly trained, but they didn't know her like I did and I was sure I'd find something there to show Alex was innocent.

I threw my arms around his middle and hugged him close. "Thank you, Derek. Thank you!"

"Yeah, yeah. Do you want a ride home now? I know it's been a long day for you too, so you must be exhausted."

Stepping back, I shook my head. "No. I'm good to walk. It will give me time to clear my head and focus on what I need to do. See you at eight!"

As I headed down the street toward my house, I took out my phone and texted Alex to let him know I was doing everything I could to prove he couldn't have done this terrible thing. I didn't tell him what I would be doing in just a few hours because I didn't want to get his hopes up, but mine were already soaring.

After the day I'd had and the lack of luck with both Ken and Cynthia, things had to get better.

Chapter Eight

J UST BEFORE EIGHT as I stood waiting for any sign of
Derek's car turning the corner onto Barn Street, my
phone vibrated against my hip. I dug it out of my pocket
to see Alex had messaged, and a tiny part of me didn't
want to read what he'd written because I'd found
nothing to help him. The first day of the investigation
had nearly ended and still everything seemed to point to
him.

Frowning, I swiped my fingertip across the screen
and his words lit up in front of me. In each one, I heard
the anguish he'd suffered all day, and my heart nearly
broke.

**Tell me you've found something. Has Derek checked
her phone and laptop? I feel like a caged animal here.
Give me anything to hold onto.**

I couldn't let him languish out there in his house all
alone. A text back telling him some nice lies wasn't what
he deserved, so even though I had nothing to report that
would give him any solace, I called him. It was more for
me than him, in truth. I needed to hear his voice. I
needed to hear him say the words that would make me

believe in myself again.

He answered after only one ring, like he was sitting on top of the phone waiting for some word to put his mind at ease. "Poppy? What's going on?"

Tears threatened to choke me and trap my words in my throat, but I swallowed hard and said, "Alex, I wanted to call and see how you're doing. Are you okay?"

All I heard was a heavy sigh. I hated to hear him so torn up like this. Finally, he answered my question. "I don't know. I've been going out of my mind here all day waiting to hear from you or to see the police pull up to my door to arrest me. I don't know how much more of this I can take."

Quietly, I admitted the truth. "I didn't call because I haven't found anything out yet, Alex. I swear I'm working on it. I won't let them railroad you on this. I just haven't found the evidence that will clear you."

My words didn't sound as optimistic as I'd hoped they would, instead coming out like some sentence my brain had passed. I believed him when he said he didn't kill Bethany, but nothing I'd found so far proved that.

"You have good instincts, Poppy. I've told you that since the first day we talked."

Smiling as I remembered our first real meeting, I joked, "Actually, that was the second day we talked. The first day you pointed a gun at me, but I know what you're saying."

He surprised me with a witty comeback that told me the Alex I knew and loved was still alive and well inside him. "Actually, that was the first night we met as you were sneaking around my house, and I still stand on the claim that I was justified to point a gun at you. I didn't know if you were a burglar come to rob me."

"Well, we've come a long way since then, thankfully. It's an interesting first meeting story, though, don't you think?"

He chuckled, and I heard the forced happiness in his voice when he said, "It is. I'm hoping it's not going to be replaced by one about how you had to stand there and watch Derek arrest me for your friend's murder."

"Alex, I won't let that happen. Derek has nothing but suspicions that you had something to do with this, and that has more to do with things other than this case than what he really thinks you may have done."

Another chuckle and then he said, "You mean his jealousy over my seeing you?"

Surprised he knew about that since I hadn't thought Derek knew about us before I told him that day, I said, "Wait a minute. He acted like he had no idea we had begun to date each other when I said something about it today. You're saying he's known? Since when?"

"We never actually talked about it, but a few months ago he started being difficult with me. I started getting more overnight shifts, remember? I think that was his way of dealing with his jealousy over us."

Alex had been scheduled for the overnights more than ever before after we started seeing each other. I hadn't thought anything of it since he was the second to last hire on the force. I just figured being a lower man on the totem pole meant he had to pay his dues, regardless of how much experience he brought to the job since he'd been a detective in Baltimore.

Now it all made sense, though. Derek was jealous and had been for months.

"I don't know how I didn't pick up on that. I'm sorry you're paying for his silliness, Alex. He and I have never been anything more than friends, so I don't know why he's acting this way. It's not like he's asked me out every week for years and I said no only to say yes to you the first time you came calling. It's not like that."

"I don't think it is, to be honest. I just don't think he likes us together. I don't care what he likes, though. Do you?"

The insecurity in his question came from what he'd been through that day. I knew that. Never before had he bothered to think about what anyone else thought of us together. That wasn't the kind of man he was.

"You know the answer to that. He better stop this nonsense, though, or he's going to lose me as a friend if he isn't careful," I joked halfheartedly, hoping Alex understood how much I'd give up for him.

"Poppy, I want you to keep close to Derek," he said, his voice suddenly deathly serious.

A sudden gust of wind roared across my porch, sending chills through my body. Huddling under my coat, I lowered my head. "Why? What's wrong? Why do I need to stay close to him?"

"I just want you to," he answered, his voice somber.

Now I needed to know. "Why are you saying it like that? You're frightening me. What is it?"

Another sharp gust of wind bit at the tips of my ears sticking out of my collar as I listened for his answer to my questions. I wasn't going to let him just give me some vague, spooky response.

"Poppy, do you believe me when I say I didn't kill Bethany?"

I'd never heard him so serious in all the time I'd known him. Without even thinking how best to answer, I said, "I believe you, Alex. You aren't a murderer."

"Then there's a murderer walking free out there. They're not above killing someone, especially someone who's trying to prove their patsy didn't do it. I don't believe for second Bethany's killer didn't know I'd be the prime suspect right off the bat. They knew. I'd bet they banked on it. You trying to find proof that I didn't do it puts them in danger. It threatens to expose them. I wouldn't be able to live with myself if you got hurt trying to clear my name."

The dread in his voice settled into my brain, suddenly making me realize I might be a target if I got too close to the truth. I couldn't let that scare me off, though. With Alex branded the main suspect, the only person committed to seeing him keep his freedom was me.

"Okay, I'll stick close to him, but I'm not giving up just because this might get dangerous, so don't even think of asking me to."

The phone fell silent for a long moment, and then he finally said in a low voice barely above a whisper, "As much as I hate possibly putting you in harm's way, I can't ask you to give up. You're all I have, Poppy. If anyone is going to show that I didn't do this, it's you."

"I promise you I won't let you down, Alex."

"I just wish I wasn't stuck here instead of being out there helping you find the evidence we need. Did Derek check Bethany's phone and laptop?"

As much as I knew he was going stir crazy waiting out there for something to happen, good or bad, I knew he needed something to hold onto, so I said, "I'll be sure to ask him about them. I want you to know I went to see your friend Ken in Baltimore to see if there was anything he could tell me that would help with this case."

"Why would Ken be able to help you? He's not the coroner on Bethany's case, for sure, so what would he have to say that could help?" Alex asked sharply.

I didn't know what I'd said to upset him. Trying to diffuse his anger, I said, "I just hoped to find out something that would help."

"You went to him because Bethany's case is just like my wife's, didn't you?" When I didn't answer, he barked, "Didn't you? You think there's something to this. You weren't sure the two murders weren't too close to be connected. Oh my God, you aren't sure I'm innocent, are you, Poppy?"

Derek's car pulled up to the curb in front of my house, and I waved to him. "It's not like that, Alex. I was just hoping he might be able to tell me something about either case to show you didn't kill Bethany."

"You think I killed my wife and now Bethany, don't you?" he roared into the phone.

"No! Alex, I would never think that. Why would I be helping you prove your innocence if I thought for a moment that you were guilty?" I pleaded, hoping to fix the mistake I'd made by telling him about my visit to Ken Bryer.

But it was no use. He said nothing, and when I pulled the phone away to make sure he was still there, he was gone.

I slowly walked to the car and got in as my tears threatened to spill down my cheeks. I'd done the one thing I had never intended to do. All I wanted was to hear his voice, but now as he sat out at his house waiting for something to happen, he thought I believed he was a killer.

"I want you to know I shouldn't be doing this, but I

know that if I don't, you'll just keep nagging at me until I do, so I figure I might as well give in sooner than later," Derek said with a smile as I slipped the seatbelt around me.

Nodding, I turned to look out the window so he couldn't see me crying, but it was no use. As my tears came, so did my sobs shaking my body. After a full day of everything being terrible—my friend murdered, the man I loved the prime suspect, and my efforts amounting to nothing—I couldn't hold my emotions together anymore. All the sadness and fear I'd been carrying around all day poured out of me right there in the passenger seat of Derek's car.

He gently touched my shoulder. "Poppy, what's wrong? I was just trying to lighten things up a little. I didn't mean anything by that."

Wiping my eyes, I willed myself to stop crying like some foolish girl. I turned to look at him staring at me with so much concern written all over his face, and I almost burst into tears again. God, I was a mess!

"I'm okay. It's just been a long day. I don't have to tell you that, though, right?" I said, hoping my attempt to downplay my emotional outburst would work. I really didn't want to sit there with Derek and discuss the mess I'd made of my relationship with Alex.

He said nothing for a long time, so long that I wondered if I should fill in the dead space with more of my pretending to be okay. I knew he was probably thinking taking me to Bethany's apartment was a huge mistake, compounded by the fact that I clearly wasn't in the right emotional state to do much of anything tonight. I couldn't let him think that, though.

"Really, I'm good, Derek. Ready to go?"

"You don't look it."

I seized on his proclamation to change the subject to something far less serious. Sure I could get him to focus less on how I was feeling, I smiled and joked, "That's a lovely thing to say to a girl. You don't look good. Nice. I can't imagine why you're still single, Derek."

For a second, he looked worried, like he thought I'd really interpreted what he said that way. Then it dawned on him that I wasn't being serious, and he rolled his eyes in typical Derek fashion.

As he put the car into drive and we began rolling down Barn Street, he said, "You're going to drive me to drink, you know that? You look beautiful, like you always do. I just meant…forget what I meant. Let's just go. Any chance you want to tell me what you're looking for when we get to Bethany's?"

I remembered what Alex had asked about finding anything on her phone or laptop, so I casually said, "I was thinking that we might be able to find something on her computer. Has it been checked yet?"

"Been talking to your boyfriend, huh?" he said with a sideways glance as he stopped the car at a stop sign.

"You don't think I'd naturally ask about that? I'm not a newbie, Derek."

That I hadn't thought about Bethany's laptop not once all day I chalked up to the fact that my brain had been preoccupied with about a million other ideas and emotions whirling through it for hours. I didn't want Derek to know that, though.

"Well, you didn't ask me about it all day, so I just figured he was prompting you just now when I pulled up."

We turned onto Main Street and headed toward the

apartment complex where Bethany lived as I silently pledged to pay more attention to the case. The laptop detail shouldn't have slipped my mind.

"So did your guy find anything on it or not?"

Derek parked in front of Bethany's front door and shut the car off. Turning to face me, he shook his head. "Nothing of note. Her recent search history included some sites about clubs in Baltimore and some employment recruiting site, and there was a search for florists. It looks like she was thinking of switching jobs. That might be an interesting lead."

I sat stunned at Derek's ability to be so completely obtuse. When my brain could function without sending a stream of insults flying out of my mouth, I said in my calmest tone, "So you think it's perfectly normal that a woman who has lived in this town for years would go searching for florists when we have one right here in town? That doesn't sound a bit strange to you?"

"Well…"

"Well nothing, Derek! Bethany wouldn't be bothering to look for florists online since Carson's is less than a mile away and she'd used them before. She sent me flowers when I lost my job last spring. Trust me, she knew all she needed to know about Carson's. And why the hell would she be looking at all? Are you thinking she sent those flowers to herself?"

His face sort of fell, like what I was saying to him had ruined a perfectly formed theory and now he had to start back at square one. "Now that you mention it, I guess it doesn't make a lot of sense for someone who knew about Maria's shop to go online for information about it, but what if she wanted to send flowers to someone? Maybe she wanted to ask for details on the person who sent her flowers. Either of those seem pretty likely."

Sometimes the way he made things more difficult than they had to be could frustrate me to the point where I wanted to smack him. As my blood pressure rose, I tried to slow walk him to where he should be. "I'm sure your guys have checked out her credit card purchases recently. Did she order flowers online at any point?"

Frowning, he shook his head. "No. All we've found that she bought within the past month or so were a few new outfits at some shop in Baltimore and new tires for her car."

"So she didn't buy flowers online, but you think she'd be searching for florists on her laptop within the last few days of her life? This doesn't sound odd to you?"

Clearly frustrated himself, Derek turned away and opened his car door as he mumbled something about this case being a monkey on his back. I wanted to shake him since he obviously hadn't made it to where I had already gone.

That it wasn't Bethany who had been searching online for florists at all.

My bet was her sister had been the one to check out where to get flowers on Bethany's computer. Mariah wasn't from Sunset Ridge and had visited only a few times in all the time her sister had lived here, according to what Bethany herself had told me when she mentioned Mariah was coming to visit. Practically a stranger in town, she'd have to either ask someone like her sister where to find a florist or search online.

Now I just needed to find some proof to back up my theory. Without being able to get my hands on that laptop, it was going to be difficult, but maybe I'd find something inside the apartment.

Chapter Nine

I CAUGHT UP to Derek as he opened the front door to Bethany's apartment, still grumbling about our conversation in the car. Knowing I had to keep on his good side if I wanted to remain in the loop on this case, I tapped him on the shoulder just before he pushed the door open and apologized.

"I'm sorry, Derek. I didn't mean to sound so overzealous about the whole florist thing. Are we okay?"

He raised his eyebrows as if he didn't believe a word of my effort to be contrite, but he smiled nonetheless. "You would have made a great lawyer, Poppy. There's no denying you're smart. Just try to remember not everyone's brain works the same as yours. I get to the truth the same as you. It's just that I might take a little longer and get there by a different route."

I looked up into his brown eyes and saw that I'd offended him. "I know, and I'm sorry. It's only that I feel like I'm fighting against you on this case. You've suspected Alex since the minute Mallory Michaels, the nosy neighbor there, told her story. It's like you want it to be Alex who killed Bethany."

Derek looked over my head toward Mallory's apartment and grimaced. "It's not that, Poppy. I just can't overlook the fact that a suspect in this case has had the same thing happen to another woman in his life."

Nodding, I chose not to suggest what had popped into my head more than once that day. That the same person had killed both Bethany and Helena, but it wasn't Alex and whoever it was, they chose those women intentionally to hurt him. That theory sounded great, but the possibilities of who could have been behind both crimes immediately became staggering in light of how many criminals Alex had been responsible for putting away in his time working as a cop in Baltimore and then Sunset Ridge.

I knew it was a longshot, but so far, it was all I had. I didn't have a choice. I had to believe it was possible, no matter how outrageous it all sounded every time the thought entered my mind.

He opened the door and flipped on the light switch, turning back to say, "The crime scene team has been through here, but try to keep from touching things, okay?"

With a smile, I pulled out the gloves I always wore when Alex and I investigated a scene. "Again with the newbie insults. Man, a girl can't get any respect with you, can she?"

We stepped into the apartment, and Derek took his place by the door after closing it. "Remember your promise to tell me about anything you find, although I can't imagine you'd stumble upon anything that the guys who are trained to do this didn't."

I walked toward Bethany's bedroom shaking my head. "No respect. No respect at all."

Making a beeline to her closet, I set to checking for any hint of where Mariah had gone to. I pushed hanger after hanger to the right side of the metal bar, checking the pockets of every pair of pants and each coat, until there wasn't a piece of clothing left. I found nothing, but even more interesting, I found nothing to indicate Mariah had ever been there.

Had something happened to change her plans and she had to cancel her trip? I hadn't spoken to Bethany since before Christmas, so it was possible.

"I think you rummaging through her clothes might be disrespectful to the dead," Derek said from the doorway. "What are you looking for?"

I closed the closet door and walked past him into the living room. Looking around, I asked, "Derek, have you ever been here before Bethany was murdered?"

He smiled and took a seat on a red upholstered chair. "Once when she first moved to Sunset Ridge years ago. Why?"

The memory of Derek with Bethany for about fifteen seconds right after she came to Sunset Ridge raced through my head, and I smiled at how she'd told me she decided not to see him after only one date because he was too much a player.

"That's right. You two got together. Well, tell me, does it look like anyone but Bethany was here recently?"

He looked around and shrugged. "I don't remember what the place looked like when I was here then. I'm not sure what you're going for, Poppy."

I walked into the kitchen and didn't find even a dirty glass in the sink. The place looked like no one, including Bethany, had been there recently, even though her next door neighbor claimed she saw not only her but a man here.

Turning back to join Derek, I said, "I have no basis

for this, but something tells me her killer was in here."

The look of surprise on Derek's face told me how ridiculous my claim sounded. Not that I needed him to tell me that. I already knew before I said it that even the mere thought was bizarre. The murderer killed her in her car, not in her apartment, so why would they have any reason to come inside?

There was only one reason—to make sure there was nothing to tie them to the murder. And at that moment, to my mind only one person seemed to fit that description.

Mariah Lewis, the sister of the victim and a woman whose whereabouts were currently unknown, and someone who had means, opportunity, and if she didn't feel the same way as Bethany did about patching up their differences, motive too.

Derek merely shook his head and stood from his seat. "I think you're crazy, Poppy. Are you done here?"

"I am. I can't say I found anything useful, but if any of my hunches pan out, I'll be sure to tell you everything, just as I promised."

I knew Mariah didn't fit with my theory about the same person being the killer of both Bethany and Helena, but for the moment, she worked as someone who could be considered a suspect so Alex wouldn't remain the only person who seemed to work as the murderer.

Not that I intended to tell Derek one word of any of this. It was too messy and I couldn't prove a thing. But whether my first theory or this one had any merit, at least I had something to work with and a direction that didn't point to Alex.

Pleased that he could leave and get back to whatever

he did at night, Derek headed out the door back to the car. I followed him, and as I approached the door, I caught a glimpse of a paperback stuffed into the cushions of the couch. Curious that the crime scene investigators wouldn't have dislodged it from its home, I quickly reached down and pulled out a self-help book on how to turn off negative thoughts to improve your work life.

I had no problem imagining Bethany subscribing to the author's ideas, and smiled at the thought of her using the techniques to get ahead at her job at *The Eagle*. She always was a go-getter.

Flipping through the first pages and wondering if I should consider following some of the ideas, I saw a single bloody fingerprint pressed into one of the pages. It was only a partial print, but it was clear.

My mind began to race, and I looked around to see if Derek had seen me pick up the book. I heard the car running, so he likely hadn't. I took a hard look at the fingerprint and instantly worried because of its size that it had come from a man's hand.

Without thinking, I stuffed the book into my purse as the horrible thought that it could be Alex's fingerprint tore through my brain and closed the apartment door behind me before heading to the car. Derek seemed utterly unaware that anything had happened after he left, and even though I couldn't help but feel guilty about going back on my word to share everything I found with him, I had to keep this from him if there was the slightest chance that the fingerprint could be Alex's.

We drove back to my house, the two of us not saying a word the entire time. As he stopped the car and put it in park, he turned to look at me and I knew what he what on his mind.

"Poppy, once I get the coroner's report, if there's anything that points to Alex, I'm going to have to bring him in and very likely arrest him. I know you're in contact with him, so please tell him to make this easy on everyone and not cause a problem."

I felt my world begin to spin out of control. Grasping for any semblance of his feelings for me, I begged him to put it off as long as possible. "Alex isn't going anywhere and I need some time to find more clues. I can't believe Mariah's disappearing is a coincidence. We need to find her and hear what she has to say before you arrest him. Please, Derek."

He hung his head and sighed. "Poppy, Mallory Michaels said she wasn't even sure Bethany had anyone staying with her. You seem to be the only person who thinks her sister was there."

"Please, Derek. She's important to this case. I know it."

He looked at me and shook his head. "I can't promise anything. If the coroner's report is damning, there will be nothing I can do to help him. I have the report from his wife's murder, so I'll be using that to consider if I should arrest him for this one."

There it was. As he'd believed all along, Alex was guilty of not only Bethany's murder but his wife's all those years ago.

And there was nothing I could say that would convince him otherwise until I found some real evidence to prove he was dead wrong.

Nodding my head, I silently got out of the car as the wind picked up and pushed me toward my porch. I didn't look back to wave goodbye but hurried inside to the safety of my warm house. Maybe if I crawled under the covers and closed my eyes, the nightmare of the past day would go away.

At least for a few hours until the morning when I'd get up and start all over again trying to find a way to prove Alex wasn't the man Derek had made him out to be.

Chapter Ten

A BAG OF pretzels left over from the holidays sat on the kitchen counter calling to me and threatening to ruin my attempt once again to lose weight. I stared at it trying to deny its siren song as some part of my brain had already given in to temptation, giving the command to my hand to grab the bag and satisfy my craving for carbs. I did just that and closed my eyes as the salty tang hit my tongue and whatever pleasure center inside me associated with junk food kicked into overdrive.

I couldn't help but notice this was my first truly happy experience all day since Derek woke me up all those hours ago. Every other experience, even talking with the man I loved, had ended up as nothing but bad and more bad.

Taking a seat at my kitchen table, I tried to unravel the mystery less than twenty-four hours old that had taken over my life. I'd last spoken to Bethany before she took off work to spend time with her sister for vacation. I wasn't going crazy when I thought that she said Mariah would stay for three weeks, was I? I remembered her saying she'd be coming a few days after Christmas, and then she'd be there until at least the second week of January.

Three weeks. Then why wasn't she at the apartment when her sister was being brutally murdered just feet from her front door on the night of January 10? And why was there no evidence that she'd ever been there at all?

My brain jumped to the possibility that Bethany had been having problems with someone, maybe a new boyfriend. It had been a few weeks since she and I had last talked, so maybe she'd met a man over the holidays.

I fumbled around inside the bag for another pretzel rod and stuck it in my mouth, letting it hang like a cigar from between my lips as I tried to imagine who might be able to help me find out what Bethany had been doing in the weeks before her death. She had a few other friends, but she hadn't mentioned them to me in ages. One had moved away a while ago, and another had gotten married last year, so they'd drifted apart as often happens when a husband comes into the picture.

No, the key to finding out what was going on with Bethany was her sister, who had somehow seemingly dropped off the face of the Earth. Until Derek and his men found her, an integral piece of this mystery would remain unknown.

I grabbed a glass of water and sat back down, my brain consumed by the idea that there was something about Bethany's life I didn't know about that could help me unravel who had lay in wait in the backseat of her car and so viciously murdered her in the middle of the night. Where was she going at that time dressed in jeans, a sweater, and her favorite black suede boots?

Those boots had been such a find for her last summer. When the rest of the world was shopping for flip flops and swimsuits, she'd snagged those knee-high black suede beauties for seventy-five percent off at the Hagerstown outlets. I still could see the proud look on her face as she slid the oversized rectangular box out of the shopping bag to show me her awesome find the next day at work. The box nearly knocked over much of the knick-knacks on my desk, and she apologized profusely even as she told me she had to show me those great boots.

Never in my wildest nightmares had I thought she'd be wearing them when some madman slit her throat less than a year later. When I looked into the car and saw them, all I could think about was how happy she'd been that day over finding those boots, and now she was gone and they were covered in her blood.

Shortly after buying those boots, she began seeing Alex. I remembered her happiness then too, but as I sat there at my kitchen table absentmindedly eating one pretzel after another until the delicious saltiness they provided made my tongue numb to their taste, I couldn't avoid remembering how I'd felt when she was so elated back then.

The jealousy had practically eaten me alive for the first few days after I found out they'd begun seeing each other. While she chatted on and on about how much she liked him and how great a time they had together whenever they went out, it was all I could do to keep my mouth shut and a smile plastered on my face because if I had opened it to speak, that same tongue that now sat numb from too much salt might have spewed all those horrible, hateful things seething in my mind.

How she wasn't right for him. How he wasn't right for her. How they were total opposites and would never work out because of their differences.

And worst of all, how I wanted their relationship to fail since I liked him because he and I weren't total opposites. Because I didn't go through men like water and then discard them when they became inconvenient.

I cringed at how terrible a friend I'd been to her then. I had no excuse. I secretly hoped and prayed for Bethany and Alex to crash and burn, and when it did, I had to pretend to be upset for her. I'd thought after a little while that I had come to accept him with her, but it never truly happened. Every day they were together I harbored that jealousy and knew full well how petty it made me.

And even knowing that, I couldn't stop myself from wishing they weren't together.

Then when he and I began seeing each other after they'd broken up, the reality of how awful I'd been to my friend became clear. Brokenhearted by the split, Bethany never once acted spiteful or jealous. I knew she probably felt like I had, but it never showed when she asked me how we were doing or if I was happy.

She'd simply reacted like a friend should have and smiled as she told me she was happy for the two of us.

Like I hadn't.

Regret choked my thoughts and made trying to tease out the truth about this case impossible, at least for the time being. For now, I'd have to live with what I'd done and hope that somewhere Bethany saw that I hated myself for the person I'd been to her.

I'm sorry, Bethany. I wish you were here sitting in my kitchen tonight with those cool black suede boots so I could tell you how truly sorry I am.

I pushed the now almost empty bag of pretzels away from me, disgusted and sick to my stomach, although I wasn't sure if that was because I'd eaten too many or because I'd finally admitted the truth of the horrible person I'd been to my friend too late for her to ever find solace in my apology.

A knock at my door startled me out of my misery, so I forced myself to cheer up and shuffled over to answer it. I wasn't in the mood to explain to my father or Derek, who were the only two people I expected to see standing on my porch when I opened the door, how awful I felt at that moment. That would only bring out their sympathy, and I didn't deserve that.

Feeling the chill of the cold January air as I approached the door, I opened it and stood in shock at the sight of Alex standing there shivering in just a sweatshirt and jeans. He looked like he hadn't slept in days. His face was unshaven with substantially more than a five o'clock shadow to prove how little time he'd spent on his usually impeccable appearance, and that face that always seemed to wear a stoic expression now looked like it would never be rid of the deep frown that showed his sadness. Worst of all, the look in his eyes screamed how lost he felt.

"Alex! Come in! You'll freeze out there without a coat on," I said as I grabbed his arm and pulled him into the house.

His lips were practically blue from the cold, but his cheeks were red raw, like he'd been out in the wind for hours. I cradled his face to warm them and felt the ice cold skin against mine as he silently stood staring at me with that sorrowful look that had made my heart clench as I saw him standing there on my porch.

"What are you doing, Alex? You look like you're half frozen to death."

"I couldn't stay in that house any more, Poppy, but I couldn't think of anywhere else I should go but here," he said quietly as he lowered his gaze.

Pulling him into my arms, I held him to me. "I'm so happy you thought that."

His body slowly warmed while I hugged him close, but he didn't say another word the whole time we stood embracing in my kitchen. He didn't need to tell me how he felt, though. I knew. The man who rarely spoke had taught me to focus more on his eyes and his expression to understand what was really going on with him, so it had only taken one look into those deep brown eyes filled with sadness to know how torn up this day had made him. Added to that was the strong scent of alcohol on his breath, and I knew what he'd done to himself to try to forget.

Although I could have been happy standing there with him in my arms for hours more, after about five minutes I pulled away and asked, "Would you like something warm to drink?"

He simply shook his head, but the frown that seemed permanently etched into his face didn't budge. I kissed him softly on the lips and smiled, hoping I could coax out some tiny bit of happiness I knew still existed in him.

"Why don't we go into the living room and get you warm?"

I took him by the hand and we walked to the same place where we'd had our first kiss all those months ago. He sat down on the couch with a rush like the world was pressing down on him and he couldn't fight it anymore.

Staring off toward the opposite side of the room, he began talking, the words coming out as if each one was forcibly pulled from his throat. "I'm sorry about what I said on the phone before, Poppy. I didn't mean it."

I brought his still ice cold hand to my lips and kissed the red skin. "Don't, Alex. You don't have to apologize for anything you said."

"I was just afraid you were turning on me. I couldn't deal with that if you did," he said, still refusing to look at me.

"Never. I would never turn on you." Gently turning his face toward me, I kissed him. "I know you're not the person who did this. Not to Bethany and not to your wife. Don't ever think I doubt you because I don't."

He closed his eyes. "I never felt the way Bethany did for me. I couldn't. I feel bad about that, but I wasn't ready. Or maybe it just wasn't right between us. I don't know, but no matter what, I would never hurt her like that."

"I know. You don't have to explain yourself to me. You're a good man, Alex. A good man who never led her on. She knew what you were capable of giving her. Don't beat yourself up about that."

His eyelids slowly lifted to show the pain he felt. "At one point today, I sat there in my house wishing I had never gone over to her house last night. If I hadn't, none of this would be happening. I'd be working this case and looking for the bastard who killed her instead of being the one Derek and the rest of the force thinks is guilty."

Stroking his cheek with the pad of my thumb, I shook my head at the thought that he wouldn't go to someone in need. "That's not the kind of man you are. Of course you went to her when she asked you to."

"I saw the look on your face when you found out I stopped over there after leaving here last night. You looked so hurt, so betrayed. It made me feel like someone was squeezing my heart in their fist. I'm sorry you had to find out that way. I didn't intend on hiding it from you. I just never got the chance to tell you before everything happened."

"It's okay, Alex. I was thrown for a second there, I have to admit. Probably more my petty jealousy than anything else, but I know you. You wouldn't lie to me."

His eyebrows knitted, and he shook his head. "I wouldn't. I swear to you I didn't do this, Poppy."

I pressed my forehead to his and whispered, "You don't have to say that ever again. I know you didn't. I believe in you, Alex. Don't ever doubt that."

He sighed, letting out a breath full of liquor that made my eyes tear. I'd never seen him drink more than one or two, but clearly from the smell of him, he'd spent the last few hours downing far more than just a couple drinks.

I leaned back against the arm of the couch and let out my own sigh. "You're going to have to stay here tonight because I can't let you drive after how many you've had."

Alex had never stayed the night, even though I had the sense that he wanted to as much as I did. A sheepish look crossed his face as I knew he realized that.

Hanging his head, he said, "Hell of a way for the first time I finally spend the entire night here. I didn't drive, though, so I can walk home, if you want."

That's why his cheeks had been so red raw. His house was miles away, and in the cold he'd walked all the way here to find me. Inching across the couch to be closer to him, I cradled his face once again and kissed him sweetly on the lips.

"You're not going anywhere. You can stay here on

the couch, if you like, or with me upstairs. Whatever makes you happy. I just want to see that frown leave your face."

"I love you, Poppy. I can't imagine what it must feel like to suddenly have me be tied up in something like this. I wouldn't blame you if you didn't want to be around me until this is all over."

I certainly hoped that was the large amount of alcohol talking because if not, he had lost his mind if he thought I'd leave him now. "You're crazy, Alex Montero. I'm sorry to inform you of this, but you're stuck with me."

For the first time that night, I saw a hint of a smile form on his lips. I wished it would blossom into more, but I'd take that for now and do whatever I must to ensure that charming smile of his returned soon.

"She used to say that, you know? She used to say I was stuck with her, like it was some kind of hardship," he said in a faraway voice that threatened to break my heart.

"Your wife?"

Alex nodded. "Yeah." He hesitated for a moment and then continued. "Helena. Her name was Helena. I've never felt right saying anything about her to you. I don't know why. I just didn't. Until now."

Emotion flooded his face as he winced like he was in pain from his admission. I didn't want him to feel like he had to defend his marriage or how much he loved her to me just to prove he couldn't have killed her. I didn't need that.

I gently squeezed his hand. "You don't have to talk about this tonight, Alex. You've been through hell today. Let it wait for when things aren't so bad."

He shook his head, determined to say what was on his mind. "No, I want to. I haven't told a soul this, and it's time."

Bracing myself for what he was about to say, I prayed for the strength to be supportive and not petty as I had been when he was with Bethany. I didn't want to be jealous of a ghost.

Alex took a deep breath and closed his eyes as he slowly released the air from his lungs. I wasn't sure what to expect, but all I knew was whatever he said, I was the one person fortunate enough to hear those words he hadn't uttered to another human.

"I adored her. She was everything to me."

In those eight words, I heard how painful her loss still was to him all this time later. I remained silent and waited to hear more from him about the couple Ken Bryer described earlier that day. His view of them had been from the outside. Now I'd hear from the only person left who could tell me who Alex and Helena really were.

"We were happy. I never thought I'd be happy as a husband because I'd always tended to be a loner. The man you know is who I've been most of my adult life. I was perfectly content to be single for the rest of my life, and then one day I answered a 911 call to a restaurant and all that changed. I met Helena and suddenly I didn't want to be alone anymore."

He stopped for a moment and he squinted his eyes as he looked past me. "If I'd only known that we'd have so little time together maybe I would have done things differently. I don't know."

I didn't ask, but I wondered if he was referring to what Ken had told me about Alex not wanting children.

After a few seconds, he turned back to face me, the memory of whatever had bothered him passed.

"Life was good. I got promoted to detective after a few years, and she had her success at the restaurant. I couldn't imagine us being happier. I mean, we were both working long hours, but at the end of the day, we were both happy. I keep saying that word, but it's true. We were."

Unsure if Ken had misunderstood the relationship or if Alex's memories were clouded by the wish of what could have been, I decided to gently probe him about children to find out.

"Did you and Helena ever plan to have any kids?"

He nodded while the frown he'd worn for nearly all our time together that night deepened. "We tried for months, and then finally when she did get pregnant, she miscarried before she even made it through the first trimester. We didn't have a chance to celebrate and tell our friends before it was all over and we were back at square one again."

I hated seeing him relive that terrible sadness after enduring the shock of Bethany's murder and then the realization that yet another person he'd cared about had been taken in such a similar way. I would have stopped him from continuing, but he seemed to want to tell me, so I listened even as my heart broke for him.

"We had a fight right after the miscarriage. Our emotions were so raw after trying for so long, and I told her I wasn't sure we should try again yet. I just didn't want to see her heartbroken again, but she thought that meant I didn't love her or want to have kids."

He covered his face with his hands and I heard him say in a tortured voice that was just a week before she died. "I stormed out that day to go to work, and we never talked about the fight again. And then I didn't have the chance to."

His shoulders sagged from the weight of his sadness. I took him into my arms and held him as he quietly swore he wasn't the man people thought he was. He didn't have to tell me. I knew who Alex Montero was, and he was no killer.

"I didn't do this to Bethany. I know it's similar to the way Helena died, but I didn't do this. I can't believe it's a coincidence either, though. I can't imagine how this happened."

As I softly stroked his back, I broached the idea that had crossed my mind more than once that day. "Do you think it's possible you're being targeted? You were a cop for years, Alex. There has to be any number of people who bear a grudge against you."

He slowly leaned back away from me and thought about what I'd said. "You mean the same person who murdered Helena has now murdered Bethany five years later? I'll tell you what I'd say as a cop. It's highly unlikely. In fact, I know what I'd say about this case if I were investigating it. I'd be looking at me."

"Then it's good that you have me around to throw some other ideas into the mix. So far I have Bethany's sister Mariah having something to do with it and someone killing both women."

He didn't look hopeful as I explained my theories, and I didn't blame him. He'd entrusted his freedom to me and believed I'd show he was innocent, and so far I'd only come up with the obvious and the unlikely.

Leaning back against the couch, he looked over at me and asked, "Have you told Derek about either of these theories of yours?"

"No way. He thinks it's you, so I've been pretending to just try to prove you had nothing to do with the murder, not coming up with my own ideas. He underestimates me all the time anyway, so it's pretty much how this works with us."

Alex smiled, closing his eyes as he said, "Like your new partner more than your old one?"

"You're my only partner. Derek is just someone I want to convince of your innocence," I said as I ran my hand through his dark hair. "I'm hoping to make some headway on that tomorrow."

He didn't respond, and after a minute or so, I realized he'd fallen asleep. After the day he'd spent and the amount he'd drank, everything had finally caught up with him. I watched as the frown he'd worn faded away to reveal his usual stoic expression he wore awake or asleep, and I couldn't help but smile.

I covered him with my chenille throw to keep him warm and curled up next to his side to put my head on his shoulder. He wrapped his arm around me, instantly making me feel protected, and murmured something I didn't understand, but it didn't matter. Whatever he had to say could wait until tomorrow like everything else that had turned our lives upside down in the last twenty-four hours.

Until then, it was just him and me there on the couch where we'd first told one another how much more we meant to each other than just work partners.

Chapter Eleven

THE NEXT MORNING, I sat at my kitchen table holding the note Alex left me and wishing he was still there. He'd slipped away during the night, careful not to wake me up as he left my side, and walked home or wherever he felt he had to go to. I ran my fingertip over his signature as I read over the words he'd written.

> Thank you for taking care of me tonight. You're the only person I trust now, Poppy.
>
> Love,
> Alex

As always, he was a man of few words, but what he said in those words meant the world to me. I needed to attack this case like I knew he would if he could and figure out who the killer was and why this case felt more and more like an attempt to railroad Alex.

First, though, I needed to know he'd gotten home safely, so I called him. His phone rang for the usual four rings and then sent me to voicemail. I ended the call and quickly texted him, my concern growing after not being able to speak to him.

Are you ok? I need to know you got home safe.

I sent it off and waited for his answer. If he didn't text back to me before I finished my morning coffee, I'd drive out to his house and find out if he was all right for myself before heading to Derek's office to see what progress he'd made, not that I thought he'd have much to tell me at nine in the morning.

But Alex did text back just as I reached the bottom of my cup. Anxious to know how he was doing, I grabbed my phone as soon as it began to vibrate and read his text.

I'm okay. I didn't want to leave last night, but I didn't want things to go further with me like I was. Forgive me.

That he wanted me to forgive him for some slight he thought he'd shown me was so typical Alex. A gentleman through and through, even when he was looking at the real possibility that Derek would arrest him at any moment, he still worried about me. It was no wonder I loved him.

No forgiveness needed. I was disappointed not to see you when I woke up, but I'll get over that. My only concern is how to prove to Derek that you're innocent. I'll make sure to let you know what I find out. Will I see you later?

Barely half a minute passed before his answer came back to me.

I trust you, Poppy. You'll find a way to show him the truth. Talk to you later.

I couldn't help but notice he didn't answer my question about if I'd see him later that day, but I didn't repeat it in another text. I knew as well as he did that it was very possible he may not be able to see me by day's end if the coroner's preliminary report came back showing there could even be a tangential connection between Alex and Bethany's death.

And knowing the pressure our chief of police was liking receiving from the town council about the possibility that one of his officers was involved in a murder, Derek would likely be dragging Alex in for questioning so anyone in town wondering would see how serious he was taking this case.

Finishing the last of my coffee, I washed my cup and slipped my coat on to make the walk to the police station. The winds from last night had died down and the sun even seemed to want to poke its head out from behind the grey clouds that filled the sky. I hoped this was a sign that today would be a better day than yesterday.

I didn't make it a block away from my house before my cell phone rang in my purse. Digging it out just as it hit the third ring, I saw it was my father and remembered I hadn't spoken to him since my call yesterday. Swiping a gloved finger across the screen, I answered it with an apology for being so forgetful.

"I'm so sorry, Dad. I meant to call, but everything got so crazy that I didn't get to."

He worried about me, especially when it came to solving crimes with Alex, so I wasn't surprised when he expressed how concerned he'd been waiting all day to hear some news about what had happened.

"Have you found out anything? You know I don't

like you working without Alex. And don't start with that independence business you always throw in my face when I tell you I worry about you, Poppy."

At least he hadn't called me by my given name. Then I'd know he was truly worried or angry since those were the only two occasions which called for the use of my birth name, as far as I could tell.

I inhaled a deep breath of cold air and felt the inside of my nose freeze. "It's okay, Dad. I like that you worry about me. I haven't found out anything yet, but I'm not working alone. Derek and I are checking into things with Bethany's case."

My father paused for a long moment before he said, "That's what I was calling you about, honey. He was at the bar last night, and I overheard him talking to the mayor. He all but promised him he'd be bringing in a suspect today. I had a feeling it was Alex he was talking about."

"How? Did you hear how he was going to find enough evidence against him to bring him in?" I asked as I hurried across Main Street toward the police station.

"No, I'm sorry I didn't. We had a good crowd in last night and I didn't get a chance to pay any attention to him at all until the end of the night. It was after he'd had a few beers and the mayor had joined him at the table near the dartboard. I got the sense that he thought he had his suspect and now he just had to tie up some loose ends before moving on him."

Panic raced through me as I broke into a run to get to Derek before he did something stupid. "I have to go, Dad, but thanks for the head's up. I'll talk to you later, okay?"

"Okay. Be careful and don't let our chief run

roughshod over this case. You show him you're as good a detective as he is."

"Thanks, Dad!"

I pressed END and nearly tripped over a raised concrete slab in the sidewalk in front of the station as I tossed my phone into my bag. My father's news had me frazzled, and I hadn't even spoken to Derek yet that morning.

Not a good sign.

The chief of police sat behind his desk drinking a coffee from The Grounds and dressed in his officer's uniform, something odd since he hadn't been seen in it much since getting his promotion nearly a year ago. Something about it made him look smarter, like the clothes sharpened his detecting abilities. I knew that was merely appearances, but it made me think that I should approach him differently today.

Perhaps the buddy thing wasn't my best plan. I didn't want to trade on what I was sure were his feelings for me, so that left me with being a professional, something Derek had never responded to from me.

There had to be a first for everything, though. With that thought in mind, I unbuttoned my black wool coat and knocked on the door to his office.

"Excuse me, Derek. I didn't mean to interrupt. Can I come in?"

He looked up and smiled at me, but I saw his confusion over my change in tactics settle into his face. "When did you start knocking before you come into my office?"

I stepped in and took my usual seat in front of his desk as I slipped my coat off. "It isn't a big deal. You are the chief of police, so I just figured you deserve the respect accorded to someone who has achieved that position."

Derek leveled his gaze on me across the desk. "The respect accorded to someone who has achieved that position? What the hell is going on with you, Poppy? Did you get hit in the head after I dropped you off last night?"

So far, treating him with that respect I'd mentioned wasn't getting me very far, but I wasn't ready to give up just yet. Flashing my best and confident smile, I folded my hands in my lap and asked, "How are things going today, Derek?"

Still suspicious about the change in me, he leaned back in his chair and took a sip of coffee. "You mean how are things going with the murder case, I assume."

"Not necessarily. I mean, yes, I am here to discuss that with you, but that doesn't mean we can't talk about other things first. I have to say you look very striking in your uniform, for example. Are you having your picture taken today?"

That didn't sound as professional as I'd hoped it would. The problem was I'd known the man since we were both children, so whatever I said to him always seemed to have a ring of familiarity that superseded whatever else I intended. Acting like he wasn't practically the brother I'd never had wasn't easy for me, and I suspected whatever he felt for me made seeing me as a fellow professional next to impossible for him.

"Poppy, what do you say we forget this dance we're doing and you ask me what you want to know? That's the kind of respect this person in this position would like most."

The jig was up. Out the window went profession-alism to be replaced with our usual friendly familiarity. I just hoped it didn't hurt what I was trying to do for Alex.

I let out a sigh and nodded my agreement. "Fine. I just wanted to try to approach this as two professionals, but you're probably right. Being straightforward like two people who've known each other forever is really the only way we can play this. I hear you are planning to bring in a suspect today. Is it Alex?"

Derek gave me one of his funny grins and shook his head. "You've been talking to your father, I guess. That's what I get for having one too many last night. I really should find somewhere else to drink."

"That doesn't answer my question. Is it him?"

"See, there's the bulldog of a woman I know and love. The answer to your question is a truthful I don't know yet. I'm hoping to hear from the coroner with his preliminary report any time now. If there's anything in it that makes it wise to speak to Alex more in depth than last time, I will."

His calling me a bulldog of a woman didn't make my self-confidence in my looks soar, but it did make me feel like he knew he wasn't going to shake me off this case. At least there was that.

"I would have preferred a more appealing breed of dog, Derek. Maybe one with long flowing hair," I joked. Maybe if I succeeded in lightening the mood I might have a chance at changing his mind about Alex.

"You're like a dog with a bone is all I was trying to say, Poppy. I will tell you this. As I was downing too many drinks last night trying to put yesterday out of my mind, I had to admit I don't want it to be him who did this. I really don't. In the end, he's one of my officers, and I don't want that to change, but if the evidence points to him, I don't have a choice. I hope you know that."

I slumped in my seat as my worry returned in full force with every word he spoke. Maybe he was telling the truth about not wanting to think Alex was the murderer, but he wouldn't be able to shirk his responsibilities if even the tiniest piece of evidence pointed to him, especially if the mayor was already pestering him for an arrest.

"Okay, Derek. I know you're a decent guy who has to answer to people I don't have to. I get that. I only wish something would come to light that would show there was no way Alex could have done this."

"I do too. Believe me. I do."

His office phone rang, interrupting what had begun to feel like a wake for the man we both knew, and I suspected things were about to get a lot worse.

Derek's face twisted into a grimace as he listened to the person on the phone. "Okay, tell him I'll be waiting in my office."

He said nothing, which told me whatever he heard wasn't good, so I asked, "Was that the coroner's office? Is Donny coming?"

"That was his assistant. He said he got called out early this morning for an accident in Frederick but he'd be here soon. He said he's got cause of death and DNA."

"Her head was nearly cut off, Derek. I don't think we need Donny for cause of death."

My gallows' humor fell flat, so I quickly changed the subject to Mariah and if they'd heard anything about her yet. "What about Bethany's sister? Do we know where she is or has that line of inquiry disappeared from the Sunset Ridge police department radar?"

He rolled his eyes and sighed in frustration. Whether

it was toward me or this case I didn't know. "We haven't found her yet, but we heard back from the police in Peninsula, Ohio where she lives that she hasn't been seen at home for over two weeks and her next door neighbor says she's supposed to collect her mail for another week until she gets back. If they hear she's home, they promise to give me a call. That's all we know as of right now."

I was sure when we finally got to speak to Mariah that this entire case would take on a new light, and Derek's complacent attitude toward her potential part in her sister's murder was nothing less than exasperating. I was just as sure that blowing up at him to press my point about her being more important than he thought would get me nowhere, so I forced a smile to appear on my face and kept my mouth shut.

We sat there in silence waiting for Donny to show up with his initial report as the minutes ticked by. While I studied the nearly bare beige walls of Derek's office surrounding us, I prayed to God that whatever the coroner had to say showed us a different potential suspect. I really wanted Donny to say there was no way Alex could have done this horrific crime, but I'd take him offering something that would point us in a different direction if that's the best I could get.

A knock on Derek's office door startled me out of my daydreams of being able to give Alex the good news that he was no longer a suspect, and I spun around in my chair to see Donny standing in the doorway waving a brown folder in front of him.

He stepped into the office and handed it to Derek as he said, "Remember what I said about this being purely preliminary. You're in a hurry, but I can only say what was done to your victim and what I think was the weapon used."

Derek opened the file and scanned the information for a few seconds before closing it and tossing it on the desk. "Just cut to the chase and tell me so I don't have to sift through all that, okay?"

Shrugging, Donny looked unhappy about having to give him a verbal rundown after just handing him the official preliminary report. "Fine. Your victim was attacked by a right handed person from behind. They came around with a knife and jammed it into the left side of her neck cutting her clear over to the other side. She bled out in minutes."

"Can you tell if the person who did this was taller than her?" I asked as my heart slammed into my ribcage.

Both Derek and Donny turned to look at me with narrowed eyes as if I'd asked a question they thought I shouldn't have. Shaking his head, Donny said, "She was killed as she sat in a car. That makes the killer's height pretty much a non-issue."

"Continue," Derek ordered. "Is there anything in this report that I can use to focus on a single suspect?"

Donny's body language screamed his defensiveness at Derek's pressing for something definitive. With his arms folded across his chest, he answered him. "As I told you yesterday, I believe a hunting knife was used. I don't have the company name and model, if that's what you're looking for. There was some skin I scraped from under her fingernails, and I found two dark hairs behind her right ear to go with one the crime scene guys found in the backseat. I don't know if they're from the same person, though. I'll know more in a few days, so that's really all I can give you for now."

Looking thoroughly dissatisfied that Donny couldn't give him anything more, Derek thanked him and waved him out of his office like a king tired of the person trying to please him. As I sat replaying everything the coroner had reported, I had to think Derek's plan to bring in a suspect today had been quashed, thankfully. Nothing he'd told us pointed to Alex, so at least there was that.

I had an idea, though. While the crime scene unit had already scoured Bethany's car, I wanted to see it for myself. I didn't think I'd find anything they hadn't, but maybe by seeing it firsthand in the light of day I could get a sense of how the crime had happened. Also, it would keep Derek busy for a few hours if he had to escort me on my field trip.

"I'd like to see Bethany's car," I announced to Derek and instantly saw a look of confusion cross his face.

"Why? It's been checked over by the state police crime unit. What do you think you're going to find that they didn't?"

"Please just humor me this one last time," I pleaded, knowing this wouldn't be the last time I asked him for a favor.

He looked unconvinced. "I can't figure out what you want to see it for is all. Aren't you the one in the partnership who likes to focus on the behavior and psychology of people instead of actual physical evidence?"

"I just want to see it. How long is it going to take to ride out to the barracks and have a quick look-see? You'll be back before it's time to take your mid-morning coffee break."

"And if I say no can I assume you're going to badger

me until I change my mind?"

"Badger is such an ugly word, Derek. Admit it. You have nothing more than you did yesterday to warrant questioning Alex or anyone else, for that matter. It might do you good to get out of this office, and at the very least you'll be able to tell the mayor you're actively working on the case."

Derek's eyebrows shot up into his forehead. "I think you're going to lose your father a customer at this rate."

I stood up and put on my coat as I continued to cajole my way into a trip to the state police barracks where Bethany's car was being held. "Come on. What's an hour out of your life to satisfy your curiosity?"

He smiled and grabbed his coat. "I'm satisfying your curiosity, Poppy. At least try to keep it straight as you're manipulating me."

I chuckled as I followed him out into the hallway to leave. "Manipulating is such an ugly word, Derek. So ugly."

"Uh huh. Let's get this moving." He stopped midway to the car and turned to look at me. "Remember the chances are just as good that you'll find something that hurts your partner as helps him."

I didn't need to be reminded of that. The mention of dark hairs found on Bethany's body had made my heart sink, and it hadn't recovered yet, even if my playacting like nothing the coroner had said was successful.

DEREK LED THE way to the trooper on duty in charge of evidence and warned me to hang back while he got permission to see the car. Unlike usual, I listened to his command, afraid if I didn't that he might recant on his agreement to let me take a look at the inside of the car. While I assumed I was grasping at straws, I needed to believe what I was doing might result in something to give me hope.

He stormed back toward me after speaking to the trooper for nearly five minutes. I hadn't overheard much since I'd been lost in my own thoughts of how I was going to tell Alex I didn't find anything yet to help him, but by the furious look on Derek's face as he approached me, what he'd heard hadn't been good.

"What's wrong? Did they say we can't examine the car? Why? Is it because I'm here?" I asked in Gatling gun fashion as he walked past me out the door. I followed him and repeated my questions in case he hadn't heard me in his rage.

By the time we reached his squad car, he'd calmed down enough so there wasn't smoke about to pour out his ears. Leaning against the driver's side door, he said, "The car has been moved, and no one seems to know where and all the records associated with the case are gone too."

Stunned, I struggled to find the words to say and finally just asked, "What?"

He ignored me and instead took out his cell phone to call someone. Furious, he barked into the phone, "Donny, we're going to need to rely on the DNA off Bethany because the goddamn crime scene is gone."

Before the coroner had the opportunity to say anything in response, Derek jammed his fingertip onto the END on his cell phone screen and jammed the phone back into his coat pocket. I didn't know what to say or what to think. Was the fact that the car was missing going to help Alex? I wasn't sure of anything anymore.

"Derek, what's going on? The state police don't just lose a whole car. What did they say happened to it?"

Once again, he ignored me. He opened his car door, and as he got in, he mumbled, "Maybe Alex really is the killer. If he had a friend in the Maryland State Police, maybe he could get them to hide the evidence to give him time to flee."

I grabbed a hold of the door as he moved to close it, shaking my head as I stared down at him in disbelief at what I'd just heard. "What are you talking about? Fleeing? What makes you think Alex had anything to do with this? You act like he's some all-powerful super villain who can just make evidence like a car disappear. He doesn't have that kind of pull with the state police. No one does."

Derek looked up at me and said, "Get in the car, Poppy."

"No! I want you to listen to me now!"

He tore the door from my hold and slammed it in my face. I hurried around to the other side to get in before he drove away and left me standing there, and as I sat down next to him I heard him say into his phone, "Bring Alex in for questioning. Have him there when I get back."

Once again he angrily ended the call and then started the car without saying another word to me. My mind spun with questions I knew he wouldn't or couldn't answer, but I had to try to convince him that he was making a mistake jumping to those conclusions.

As we sped down the highway back toward Sunset Ridge, I did my best to change his mind. "Derek, you know Alex isn't the type of person to kill anyone, and he's not the type of cop to destroy or hide evidence or have someone do it for him. Please listen to me!"

The emotion drained from his face, and he stared straight ahead as he shook his head. "I want to believe he's innocent, but every time I let myself think that, something comes up to point to him. Bethany's neighbor's claim that she heard him fighting with Bethany. The florist who pretty much described Alex to a T. The missing evidence. The fact that this murder is just like the murder of his wife."

"Those are all just coincidences. Think about it. They're just coincidences. That's all."

He stopped the car as we got off the exit and turned to look at me. "Just when do these coincidences begin to add up for you, Poppy? Because they're adding up for me."

I didn't know how to answer that question, but for me, none of those things added up to Alex being guilty of murdering Bethany. No matter what Derek thought, they didn't mean he was a murderer.

Chapter Twelve

ALEX SAT ALONE in the interrogation room when Derek and I returned to the police station after what may have been the most tension-filled car ride I'd ever experienced. I'd utterly failed in my attempt to persuade him to see any side of this case that didn't involve Alex acting like some criminal mastermind, forever one step ahead of the law and mocking them the entire time.

I followed him toward the room, but Derek turned and stopped me with a stiff arm to my midsection. "I think I'll be doing this alone, Poppy."

God, I was tired of this with him! Pushing his forearm away from my body, I poked him in the chest and every ounce of professionalism in me disappeared. "I'm sick of you constantly threatening to cut me out of this investigation. I'm his partner and I'm going to be there when you question him. And don't tell me you can have me hauled out of here in handcuffs because I have threats of my own that I can use on you, and they're a hell of a lot worse than me being seen in handcuffs. So stop with this nonsense and let's get in there so you can ask your questions and hear him answer them."

Derek's eyes opened wide in surprise at my outburst,

and I waited for him to bark right back at me, but he didn't. Instead, he took a deep breath in and puffing his cheeks, let the air out as he shook his head. "You must really care about him. I hope you're ready for what he might say because it may not be what you're hoping for."

Still standing toe-to-toe with him, I stared up into his eyes, confident in my knowledge of who Alex truly was. "I know what he's going to say because he didn't do it, Derek. So ask all the questions you want. The answers aren't going to change from yesterday. He's not your killer."

Derek's steely gaze remained locked on mine in a battle for who believed in their side more. "Fine, but when this all falls apart, don't come running to me crying because he wasn't who you thought he was."

He turned before I could tell him that first, I wouldn't be running to anyone crying, and second, if I did, he'd be there for me like he always had been because that's what friends did for one another. Even if they disagreed like never before and couldn't understand the other's point of view no matter how hard they tried.

The door opened, and my eyes met Alex's. They were filled with so much sadness. There he sat in the very room where he'd questioned suspects, and now he was the one on the opposite side of the table being accused. I smiled as I sat down wishing I could sit beside him so he wouldn't feel so alone.

Derek didn't waste any time on niceties and got right to work. With his eyes set in a hard stare, he asked, "Are you sure you wouldn't prefer to have your attorney join you for this, Mr. Montero?"

Alex's expression twisted into a grimace before he

croaked out, "Mr. Montero? You can't even call me by the name you've used ever since the day we met?"

I touched Derek's sleeve, and he turned to look at me with a face that made me yank my hand away from him. Hoping to change the tone of this interrogation session, I gently said, "This doesn't have to be acrimonious, does it? I know you see him as a suspect, but you do know him."

"Poppy, you can either remain quiet or you can remove yourself from this room. Your choice."

His harsh tone surprised me with how much it hurt. Derek had never spoken to me like that before. I backed away to nurse my injured feelings, but Alex came to my defense immediately.

"You don't have to speak to her like that, Derek. Whatever you think of her opinion about me, she's your friend. Try acting like she is."

The look in Derek's eyes made me fear for Alex's safety, and when he snapped his head around to face him, I worried he might go over the table at him. Instead, he merely barked, "I'll treat her as I see fit. She's in my house now. If you don't like that, too bad. You don't get a say in how I run this investigation."

And then Alex said what he and I had thought from the very beginning but hadn't said a thing about to anyone but each other. "Investigation? Why don't you call it what it really is? A vendetta against me because you've got some small town jealousy thing going with me. It's not like you've actually bothered to look for anyone else who might have done this crime, other than when Poppy has forced you to. No, this is your own personal revenge on a professional rival. Or is it a personal rival, Derek? Is that what this is?"

His words came out so fast I couldn't jump in and stop them. Derek heard about half of them before he jumped out of his seat and leaned toward Alex like he wanted to hit him. By the time Alex had finished speaking, Derek's right arm was cocked and ready.

I leaped out of my chair to try to get control of the situation before the two of them began to pound each other's faces into the concrete floor. Standing on the side of the metal table as they glared across it at each other, I gently spoke up and hoped what I was about to say wouldn't make things worse.

"Please, don't do this. Stop before this gets out of hand." As if they didn't hear me, they continued to exchange glowers, Derek's blue eyes full of fire and Alex's dark brown eyes full of hatred.

After a few seconds, I knew my nice girl act wasn't going to end this standoff, so I raised my voice to as loud as it could get and yelled, "That's enough! The two of you aren't getting anything done here but showing everyone how much testosterone you have. Derek, sit down and do your job, and Alex, try to remember he has to do this, no matter how much you hate it. Okay? Or do I have to get nasty here?"

They didn't move for a long moment, and then at the same time, they both looked over at me with surprise in their eyes. I rarely unleashed that side of my personality, so I could understand why it had shocked them to hear me snapping at them like that. I just hoped it didn't mean Derek would now refuse to let me stay while he asked his questions.

He sighed and slowly sat back down in his chair while the corners of Alex's mouth crept up ever so slightly to give me a tiny smile that told me he approved of my gambit. I took my seat again too but held my breath as I waited for Derek to tell me whether I could stay or had to go.

"Okay, things got a little heated there for a minute, but Poppy's right. We both have to do this, no matter how much we don't want to. Once again I have to ask, though, Alex, you don't want your attorney present for this?"

Alex shook his head. "No. I don't need a lawyer to tell you I'm not the person who killed Bethany. I'm fine by myself."

I smiled at him to let him know I was there for him. I wasn't sure not having his attorney by his side was the best choice, but I believed in his innocence and his choice. I just hoped talking like this wasn't a huge mistake that would come back to haunt him.

"Okay. Let's get started. I need you to trace your movements Sunday night. Where were you in the hours before the murder?"

Alex looked over at me with sadness in his eyes, and I knew he hated telling Derek our personal business. I didn't have a problem with being dragged into this, though, so with a silent nod I let him know he should tell him everything we did that evening.

"I was at Poppy's that night, but I didn't feel well, so I left to go home a few minutes after eight o'clock. I drove home and Bethany called me on my way there. I talked to her and then after spending a few minutes at my house, I drove to her apartment."

Derek turned to look at me and then looked back at Alex. "I guess I don't have to ask if Poppy can vouch for what you're saying regarding when you left her house. Okay, now about that phone call from Bethany. What did she want?"

"She wanted me to come over so we could talk."

"Why? Why not just talk on the phone?"

Alex shook his head. "She said she wanted to talk and asked if I'd come over. She sounded upset, so I told her I would."

"Did you know what she wanted to talk to you about?" Derek asked as he jotted down details from Alex's answers on a sheet of paper in front of him.

"No."

"So you drove over to her place to talk to her at what time?"

"It was right around nine."

I listened as Alex gave answers that offered the most basic of details and couldn't help but wish he'd give more. I wanted to know why she'd felt like she could call him to come over when she knew full well he was with me. I wanted to hear him describe how she acted so I could know everything about why she'd invited the man I was seeing to her house.

Derek didn't seem frustrated by the lack of details, though, and continued to ask his questions more methodically than I'd ever seen him. "Okay, so you get to her apartment and she acts how? Happy to see you? Hugs you? What happened?"

Swallowing hard, Alex thought about the question and then said, "She acted like she didn't even know why I was there and screamed at me to stop toying around with her feelings."

"And where exactly was this? Outside the apartment? Inside? Where were you two standing when she started screaming at you?" Derek asked, clearly remembering how Mallory Michaels had described

Bethany fighting with a man just outside her front door that night.

"Outside. Well, sort of outside. She answered the door and immediately she asked what I was doing there, like she didn't remember calling me just a few minutes earlier. I stood outside, never going in, and I think she eventually came outside with me as she continued screaming at me."

"What did you say to her?"

"I told her I'd come over because she asked me to, and she kept saying I was toying with her feelings."

Derek looked up from his notes and asked, "Did she hit you at any point in that exchange between the two of you?"

A sheepish look came over Alex's face, and I thought back to Mallory's claim that Bethany had gotten physical with whoever the male she was fighting with. "She was flailing her arms because she was upset, but I wouldn't say she hit me. And before you ask, I didn't hit her either. I merely put my hands up to stop her."

Mimicking what he'd just heard Alex describe, Derek put his hands up in front of his face like he was shielding himself from an attack. "Like this?"

Alex nodded. "Yeah. She wasn't trying to hurt me or anything like that. She was just upset."

"Okay. Then I'd like you to push up your sleeves, if you will. I want to see if she left any marks."

A rush of emotion tore through me as my mind flashed back to that afternoon when we'd been together. Had I jokingly tickled him and in the process scratched his forearms in the same way Bethany may have that night when she was so upset? Part of me sat terrified at what I might see if he lifted up his sleeves, but another part of me needed to see the evidence that what had happened between them was exactly as he'd described.

Not hesitating for a moment, he pushed up the sleeves of his black thermal shirt past his elbows and displayed his muscular arms for us to see there wasn't a scratch on either one. Just as he'd described.

A feeling of relief washed over me, followed by a feeling of guilt for doubting him. As Derek wrote down the details of what Alex's arms looked like, I took the opportunity to ask a question that had plagued me since I'd first heard how upset Bethany had been when she saw Alex there to talk to her. I just hoped it didn't get me thrown out of the room.

"Did she sound strange on the phone, like she had been forced to call you?"

My question made Derek stop writing, and he looked over to me sitting on his left with an expression that told me he wasn't happy I'd decided to be a part of the questioning. I smiled and looked over at Alex, who sat thinking about what I'd asked.

Finally, he answered, "Not like she'd been forced to call me, no. She didn't sound like herself, though."

"What do you mean?" Derek asked, seeing some use for my idea after all. "How would you describe how she sounded on the phone?"

"I don't know. She didn't sound right. That's the only way I can describe it. She didn't sound like herself."

Wanting more than that, Derek began talking with his hands, waving them around as he pressed further. "Like what? Was she talking unusually slow or fast? Did she sound upset? Frightened?"

Alex's face showed his frustration as he tried to remember exactly how Bethany sounded nearly forty-eight hours earlier. "I don't know. I can't really describe it. She just didn't sound right."

His voice louder now, Derek continued to ask, "What do you mean? How did she sound, Alex?"

Finally, his frustration overwhelmed him, and Alex exploded. His eyes flashing his exasperation, he shouted, "Don't you think I'd tell you if I knew? She just didn't sound like she always had when I spoke to her on the phone. She sounded different. That's all I know!"

Derek and I sat stunned at Alex's outburst, and as he leaned back in his chair after the final word had left his mouth, he looked exhausted like he'd run through all these same questions over and over in his mind since the moment he found out Bethany had been murdered and he was the prime suspect.

I'd never seen Alex so emotional in all the time I'd known him. Even when we were together in private, he'd never shown me that side of him. I'd come to rely on how even his mood had always been, and now I saw this whole thing had already begun to take its toll on that balance I so admired.

Turning his attention back to the exact time when Alex saw her last, Derek asked, "Okay, what time did you leave her apartment?"

"Just after nine. I wasn't there more than five minutes before I left."

"Did you see her sister in the apartment?" I asked, eager to find out if Mariah had been there at that point Sunday night.

Alex shook his head. "No, I didn't. I only saw into the apartment for a second or two, but I didn't see her. Only Bethany. Did you find her sister yet?"

Quickly, Derek snapped, "I'll be asking the questions

here, even though Poppy here seems to think she's part of this too. Don't forget you're not on this side of the table now, Alex."

I saw the hurt in his eyes from Derek's icy rebuke, and it was evident in his voice when he asked, "Do you really think I did this? After all those months we've worked together, you think I could kill someone?"

For a moment, I couldn't hear a sound in the room as I wondered if Derek would finally answer that question I'd asked him half a dozen times since the investigation began. Did he really think Alex could kill Bethany in cold blood like that? Or was his insistence on Alex being his main suspect borne out of something else that had nothing to do with Bethany's murder?

He didn't answer the question, though, and continued on with his own. "How would you char-acterize your relationship with Bethany?"

Alex glanced over at me and then away. "We were friends."

Derek wrote down the word friends with a question mark and looked up to face him. "I meant before you two broke up."

"A typical relationship," Alex answered flatly. "We dated and then broke up."

"Was it physical?" Derek asked.

"Yes."

With just one word, all that jealousy I'd harbored when they were dating came rushing back. I knew it was silly, but I felt my cheeks warm at the thought of him with Bethany. I didn't want to face him, so I looked away as Derek continued to probe into the nature of their relationship.

"Did you love her?"

I listened with desperation to hear what he'd never told me about her. In all fairness, I'd never asked about anything concerning his time with Bethany, so it wasn't like he'd hidden anything from me. But now as I waited along with Derek to hear how he'd honestly felt about her, I wished I would have asked when it was just the two of us and I didn't have to dread his answer.

He hung his head and quietly said, "No, but I don't think she felt that way for me either."

"So you didn't love her, but do you think she loved you?" Derek asked, strangely referring to something already answered. What did he know that I didn't?

Alex raised his eyes to look at him and shook his head. "No, I think she cared about me, but I don't think it was ever love."

And then I saw what Derek had kept from me when he lifted the piece of paper he'd been writing on to reveal photocopies of handwritten journals. I didn't have to guess whose they were.

Tapping them into a neat pile, he looked across the table at Alex and said, "Let me read you a few passages from her diaries. Here's one from late August where she says, 'Alex isn't like anyone else I've ever met. So silent usually, but sometimes I see a side to him that's so intense. I haven't told him how I feel about him yet because I don't know which side will respond.' That's from the 29th of August."

With every word, I wanted to run out of the room so I didn't have to hear what she thought of the man I loved. Alex simply kept his eyes fixed on a spot above Derek's head and didn't react at all.

Turning the page over, Derek said, "Here's another one from early October. 'Alex is slipping away and I don't know what to do to stop it. Is it her or another woman that makes him so able to just brush me off night after night? I love him and I'm losing him.'"

I watched for Alex's reaction and saw him wince like hearing she cared for him more than he cared for her hurt. For me, the jealousy that had flooded my brain with her first diary entry had been replaced by guilt. I didn't know if I had any part in why they'd broken up, but that she mentioned me as a possible reason for why he didn't care about her as she wanted him to made me feel sick. For as much as I hated him with her, I never consciously acted in any way to see their time together end.

Derek turned another page and asked, "Now you say you two broke up in October, right?"

Alex pursed his lips, nodding yes to answer his question. By the number of entries still left in that pile of papers, I had a feeling what Derek was about to ask would make me feel even sicker.

"Then why did she continue to mention you in her diary even up to the day she died? This is from not even a week before her murder. 'No matter if I see him every day or not, he never leaves my mind. Sometimes I press my lips together and I can still remember how they felt when he last kissed me. I don't ever want to forget that.'"

For a while, Alex sat speechless as Bethany's words hung in the air around the three of us. What was he supposed to say? What would anyone say hearing another's deepest thoughts about them?

"So I ask you again. Did she love you?"

His voice low as if answering in his normal tone would be disrespectful, Alex said, "I didn't think so. I had no idea she felt this way about me."

Either did I. Yes, it was true that I had a sense when they broke up that Bethany had been hurt by it, but it didn't take long before she was back to her normal self. Had she been hiding this secret love she still felt even recently from everyone but her diary?

Or maybe I hadn't seen it because I didn't want to.

Alex continued, "We hadn't seen each other in months, other than in passing at The Grounds or at the diner and once on the street while her sister was visiting. She gave me no indication that she felt that way about me after we broke up. I mean, I knew she wanted to continue seeing me, but I never thought she loved me like she said in those diary entries."

"Well, it sounds like it would have been hard to miss. So let's get back to that night. What did you do when you got home from going to talk to her?"

"I drove home and went to bed. I planned to wake up early, go for a hike, and then meet Poppy by nine at The Grounds."

Derek added to his answer, "Like you do every day, right?"

For the first time since he'd avoided my gaze during Derek's questions about his relationship with Bethany, Alex looked over at me and smiled. "Yeah, like we have since almost the first day we began working together."

"And you didn't leave your house after you returned home from Bethany's that night? Can anyone vouch for you on that?"

Shaking his head, Alex sighed. "I didn't leave, and no, nobody can vouch for my whereabouts. You know where I live. There's not a soul around for nearly a mile. The next time I saw another soul was when you and Poppy showed up at my house at five the next morning."

"You seemed to be asleep for a long time then since you say you were back at your house by ten. Was it usual for you to sleep that much?"

I wanted to interrupt and explain that he'd left my house early Sunday night because he'd felt sick, but I kept my mouth closed since the reality was Derek didn't care about those hours Alex had been with me. All he cared about were the hours after he'd seen Bethany at nine.

"It wasn't usual or unusual, but I'd been feeling sick earlier in the evening and I was pretty worn out when I returned to the house."

"Why?"

"Because Bethany's outburst had shocked me and I felt bad about her being unhappy."

"Why would it bother you so much if you didn't love her, like you said?"

"Because I'm a decent human being, Derek. I don't know what you want me to say. Yes, I had a relationship with Bethany, but no, I didn't love her. I feel bad about that. I broke it off with her because I knew I never would be able to feel like that for her."

"So what you're saying is while you were sleeping, someone else with some hatred for the woman you'd been sleeping with for months until you broke up with her surprised Bethany as she got into her car and with a hunting knife dug into the left side of her neck and then dragged it across to the right side under her ear, nearly cutting her head clean off. Someone we haven't been able to find in her personal life. Someone who coincidentally murdered her just like your wife was murdered. That's what you're saying?"

Alex said nothing, but his deep frown and the

sadness in his eyes told the story Derek didn't want to hear. He hadn't hurt Bethany or Helena, and just hearing what happened to them devastated him.

"Is that what you're saying, Alex? That this person with a hunting knife like the one that slit your wife's throat did the same thing to Bethany but it's not you? That—"

I jumped out of my chair and ran around the table to stand next to Alex. "Stop it! Stop describing it like that! You're not a heartless person, Derek. Can't you see what you're doing to him?"

He looked up at me with no expression at all and then lowered his stare to Alex, who sat with his shoulders hunched over like he'd just been punched in the gut. "I can't hold you because I don't have proof yet, but once the coroner gets the DNA results back from the lab, I won't have a choice."

"Even though I showed you I had no scratches on my arms, and even though I had no motive to kill her, you have me guilty and convicted already. Everything Poppy has tried to tell you, you've ignored because you had your mind made up by the time you came to see me that morning," Alex said sadly as he weaved his fingers through mine at his side.

Derek gathered up his notes and papers and shrugged. "I'm no different than your partner here usually is. That should tell you something."

He left, and I crouched down beside Alex. I looked up into his eyes and saw how much what Derek had done had hurt him. "Don't listen to him, and if I have ever been like that on any case, I apologize. Let's get out of here."

Alex nodded and brought my hand to his lips for a

kiss. "I hope you don't mind, but I'm tired of sitting on the sidelines on this case. I think it's time for your partner to jump into the game before Derek sends me up the river."

My emotions a wreck, I went from wanting to cry after watching Derek practically torture him to wanting to cry in happiness that Alex was finally going to be by my side again on a case.

"It's about time. Your partner has missed you so much."

For the first time in public, he kissed me. "And he's missed you too."

Chapter Thirteen

W E WALKED OUT of the police station together as we had so often in the past, but this time it was different, even if only the two of us understood how. After that interrogation, it truly was Alex and me working together because Derek clearly had no interest in pursuing anyone but him. If we wanted to find Bethany's killer, we'd need to do it on our own.

Heading down Main Street toward my house, Alex stopped in the middle of the block and turned to face me. "He was wrong back there. I hope you know that."

"Of course he was wrong," I said as I stopped next to him. "You could never kill her, Alex. I know that."

He hung his head. "No, I mean when he said he was like you. He's not. When you jump to conclusions, it helps me see another side to the case. It opens my mind, no matter how wild and crazy your idea may be. Derek's not like you."

I took hold of his hand and smiled up at him. "He's just doing his job. The problem is he's not as good at it as you are."

Those brown eyes I could get lost in for hours filled with sadness once again. "I'm sorry for all the times I chastised you for jumping to conclusions, Poppy. You really do have great instincts. I forget that sometimes, but seeing how misguided Derek is on this case made me realize how good you are."

Shivering from the cold, I waved off his apology as I tugged him in the direction of my house. "You don't have to be sorry for anything. My type of detective work is an acquired taste. It's just good that you've acquired it. Let Derek get mired down in his DNA and everything Donny has to offer. We've got better things to do. Science isn't how this case is going to be solved."

Alex chuckled at my anti-science attitude. "He's banking on that to break this case."

"He can bank on whatever he likes," I said with a wink. "He can keep all those beakers and gizmos that kind of police work can give him. We'll stick to our usual way of solving cases. We're going to find out who killed Bethany by figuring out why someone would want to see her dead. That's why Derek doesn't figure things out. He doesn't ask why."

We crossed Main Street and made our way up Barn Street to my house, each step another one toward us finding the truth and Alex proving his innocence. We'd take our methods and untangle this mystery before Derek and his guys did and show how wrong they'd been.

As I thought about that, I remembered what had happened at the state police barracks and grabbed hold of Alex's arm in excitement. "I didn't tell you! The car and all the case files are missing. We found out when I convinced Derek to let me take a look at Bethany's car earlier this afternoon. So that science he's banking on is mostly missing at the moment."

Instead of making him happy, hearing my news

made his face twist into a grimace. "The state police don't just lose evidence, Poppy. It's next to impossible for that to happen."

"I don't understand. I thought this would be good news. Now Derek only has the DNA Donny and his guys collected for the preliminary report to go on."

Alex shook his head as worry settled into his features. "Derek thought I had something to do with this, didn't he? That's why he brought me in for questioning, wasn't it?"

"Yeah. He called Craig the minute he found out about the evidence being missing."

"Of course. He's sure not only that I killed her but also that I'm calling in favors from my time as a cop in Baltimore to hide my crime."

"I told him that was nonsense, Alex. You aren't some super villain from a comic book. He didn't want to hear it, though, so he called Craig and told him to have you at the station for questioning when we got back from Frederick."

Alex grabbed my hand to hurry me up the sidewalk to my house. "Something's very wrong here, Poppy. My gut is telling me this case is far more than what we've been thinking."

I practically had to run to keep up with him. When we reached my back porch a few seconds later, I stopped to catch my breath and asked, "What does all this mean? We aren't investigating Bethany's murder anymore?"

As I fumbled for my keys, he explained, "No, we are, but we can't ignore the fact that something strange is happening. If the state police lost the file and her car, then they were intentionally sent somewhere. Only someone in law enforcement could do that. That's why

Derek naturally said I did it."

The whole idea of someone manipulating this case like Alex was talking about sent a chill down my spine. Opening my kitchen door, I turned to look at him and saw he was serious. "So if it wasn't you who did something with the evidence, then who?"

Alex quickly closed the door behind us and locked the deadbolt. "What other person in law enforcement do we know who would want the evidence gone?"

I slid out of my coat as his question rambled around my brain. I couldn't think of anyone who would want it to go missing. How could that help anyone?

"I'm not following you. What are you saying?"

He sat down at my kitchen table and took his coat off. Draping it over the chair, he sat back and folded his arms before answering my question. "I'm saying that if the evidence doesn't point to me, then losing it would be a convenient way to frame me."

I stood there leaning against my counter staring at him in shock as my mouth dropped open. When my amazement at what he'd said subsided and I could wrap my head around it, I said, "If what you're saying is Derek did this, I have to say I think you're overestimating his abilities and influence. Trust me, Alex. He's not that clever. He never has been. I think he became a cop because he thought he could get more women because of the uniform. He couldn't do this."

"Really? Why? He's a police chief, Poppy. He has more power than you think."

Talking about this made me need a drink. I grabbed a beer from my refrigerator and downed a gulp to give me time to get my thoughts straight before they all spun out of control. I sat down next to Alex and touched his arm to calm him down since clearly he was seeing things in this case that just weren't there.

"Alex, I know this has been hard. I can't imagine what it was like to go through what Derek put you through back there. The whole time he was describing it I hated him. But he's not capable of framing you for this murder. Police chief or not, he doesn't wield the kind of power necessary to get the state police to do anything he says. Being chief in Sunset Ridge comes with a few perks, I guess, like free drinks at my father's bar and a good table at Diamanti's, but that's about it."

"You don't know, Poppy."

I didn't know what he meant, but I thought it best not to focus on the murder at that moment. I didn't know if he could handle it after what Derek had done. "There's a reason he's always felt intimidated by you, Alex. Even as chief here, he still feels like nothing compared to someone who was a detective in a big city. He's a little narrow-minded and sees only what he wants to. Add that to his inferiority to you and it isn't surprising that he wants to believe you did this. But that's it."

He turned away to hide his face from me and said in a low voice, "You think I'm going crazy, don't you? The one person I had on my side and you think I'm losing my mind."

Squeezing his forearm, I tried to get him to look at me, but he wouldn't. I couldn't let this case do this to us. To him. "No matter what happens, I'm on your side. Don't think some crazy theory talk is going to change that, Alex Montero. Look at me. I want to tell you something."

"I can't. If I see doubt in your eyes, it would crush

me today, Poppy."

I gently tugged his collar to make him face me and saw how worried he was that I had given up on him. Leaning in, I kissed him softly on the lips and whispered against them, "There's no doubt here. I'm one hundred percent Team Alex and nothing's going to change that. But just like when I offer up theories that you're sure are a bit off the mark and you let me know, I'm letting you now that Derek isn't trying to frame you."

Alex pressed his forehead to mine and confessed what I knew had been on his mind all day. "If we don't find out who did this, it won't matter what the DNA says or doesn't say. My past is going to get me convicted, Poppy."

"Then we can't let that happen," I said, my heart breaking for him as I cradled his face and looked into those beautiful brown eyes so scared as they stared back at me.

He sighed and then closed his eyes. "I don't know what I would do without you. I love you."

"And I love you." Leaning back away from him, I took his hand in mine. "Why don't you rest for a while? It's been a long day already, and we have work to do, but you won't be any good if you're exhausted. I'll make us dinner and when you're rested and fed, then we'll start to figure out this case."

For a second, it looked like he wanted to fight me about resting for a bit, but whatever opposition he had to the idea faded away. With a smile, he said, "Okay. Just for a little while, though. I don't know how much time we have to solve this before Derek arrests me for real next time."

I knew Alex wasn't exaggerating. For all his less than

wonderful traits, Sunset Ridge's chief of police had one that had never failed to impress me—his tenacity, even when he was dead wrong. He wouldn't give up until he had just enough evidence to see Alex in handcuffs.

We just had to make sure we solved this case before he could do that.

LESS THAN THIRTY minutes later, Alex's eyes flew open. He stared in terror at me next to him but said nothing. I smiled, happy to see him awake again, even if his nap had been all too brief, and quietly said, "Hey, sleepyhead. You okay?"

The fear in his eyes slowly abated until I saw he recognized me and his surroundings. One of his smiles I never saw unless we were in private lit up his face, and he nodded. "Yeah. Just a nightmare. Nothing new, except this time I got to see you when I woke up."

I pressed my lips to his in a soft kiss and ran my hand through his thick, dark hair. "Glad I could be the first thing you saw when you opened your eyes. I just wish you slept a little longer."

"No time for sleep. We need to get to work," he said as he sat up next to me. "You ready?"

"I was born ready. Well, actually, I was born a few weeks premature and wasn't really ready for anything, but I am now," I joked, hoping to see that smile of his again.

He shook his head like he always did when I said something silly and gave me my wish. "Thanks for being the only light in a world of darkness. I can't tell you how much that means to me."

"Probably as much as you mean to me, so we're

equal."

He stood from the couch, but I grabbed his arm to stop him. While he'd slept, I'd thought about what he said about Derek framing him. I still didn't believe it, mainly because of who I knew Derek to be, but maybe someone else would be able to pull it off.

Looking down at me, he asked, "What's wrong, Poppy?"

"I was just wondering if you know of any enemies you have here in Sunset Ridge. You know, anyone who would want to see you found guilty for Bethany's murder."

"Here, in Sunset Ridge? I can't think of anyone but Derek. I'm only known to the local people as one of the Sunset Ridge police. Nothing more. I think they see me as an outsider, although hanging around with you has lessened that perception, though."

He was right. Other than Bethany, few people in town knew Alex at all, except for those who had been involved in our cases. Perhaps one of them was behind this?

"Alex, do you think anyone you've arrested here in Sunset Ridge could be the one who did this?"

He shook his head dismissing the idea out of hand. "The problem with that is the way Bethany was murdered is almost exactly the same way Helena was killed. Most people in town don't know about my wife's murder, so I doubt it would be anyone here. No, I think if this is meant as something against me, it's got to be someone like Derek who can manipulate the case."

"And if it's not and just a coincidence that Bethany and Helena were killed the same way?"

Alex gently pulled his arm from my hold. "I don't

believe coincidences like that happen, Poppy. Whoever's behind this knows the details of Helena's case and intentionally killed Bethany the same way."

So who would want to see him sent away for this crime?

I followed him into the kitchen and saw no matter how strong he wanted me to think he was back in the living room, when he thought he was alone the fear he hid in front of me was obvious. As I stood in the doorway watching him look out the window, the frown he'd worn nearly every moment since finding out about Bethany deepened. He wasn't sure we'd solve this case and show the world he was innocent.

"We're going to take care of this, Alex. I won't let you down."

"I don't doubt that, Poppy. You are the one thing in my life I can rely on. I know you believe in me. I'm just worried what we do might not be enough."

I crossed the room and slid my arms around his waist to give him the hug we both needed. "I believe in an innocent man. That's all I need to know. We're going to find Bethany's killer and when we do, I'm going to make Derek listen to me say I told him so for months."

Turning his head to look at me, he smiled and shook his head. "He's going to hate that, but he'll still be crazy about you."

"I don't care what he's crazy about. I have the man I want right here. All joking aside, though, I think we need to consider Mariah Lewis a suspect, even though she never really knew you. Her being missing tells me she's involved in this."

Alex let the air out of his lungs with a whoosh. "I can't see it, but if I've learned anything about your hunches, I know not to discount them out of hand. Why do you think she's involved?"

I sat down at the table to get my ideas together so what I meant made sense when it came out of my mouth. "I think Mariah searched online for a florist. I know it wasn't a woman but a man who went into Carson's to order the flowers Bethany thought were from you, but my gut says Bethany didn't look online for flowers. That leaves her sister, but why?"

"I think we need to talk to the clerk at Carson's then. Since I had the courtesy of being brought to town in the back of a police cruiser, it looks like we're taking your car. You ready to get some answers?"

"I've been ready since this case started. Let's go talk to Cynthia at Carson's Floral Shop and see if we can't figure out who bought those flowers for Bethany."

WE WALKED INTO Carson's to find it empty, except for Cynthia standing behind the counter. She recognized me from earlier and flashed me a smile as we approached her.

"Hi! Here for flowers or more questions?" she asked. "I see you have a different partner this time."

I looked over at Alex on my left and smiled at her comment. "This is my partner. The other guy was just someone I was working with. We do want to ask you about those flowers again, though."

Cynthia studied Alex for a moment and then turned her attention back to me. "Okay. Shoot."

"I remember you saying before that a man came in to order the flowers that were sent to Bethany Lewis on Sunday. Can you tell me anything else you may have remembered?"

"The biggest thing was the flowers were scheduled by the man who came in who insisted they be delivered on Sunday. He even paid extra for Sunday delivery since that's not something we usually offer. He told me they absolutely had to be delivered on Sunday."

I moved behind Alex and looking around his right shoulder, I asked her the question I needed answered, even though my heart was pounding against my chest at just the thought of what her answer might be.

"Cynthia, would you look closely at him? Is this the man you waited on who ordered those flowers to be delivered to Bethany Lewis on Sunday?"

Alex's body tensed while Cynthia took a good hard look at him. I didn't know what his expression looked like, but I felt his fear radiating off him as he held his breath waiting for someone to say he wasn't the guy.

Finally, after what felt like forever, she shook her head. "No. You're not the man. The man who came in to order the flowers to send to Bethany wasn't as tall and his eyes were different. His dark hair was shaggier too."

Letting himself breathe again, Alex thanked her for her honesty and asked, "Do you remember anything else? You looked like you might have when you were just looking at me."

Cynthia nodded. "You're good. Yeah, I did remember something else. He had some kind of bracelet or something around his wrist. Not silver. I can't remember exactly what it looked like, but it caught my eye."

"He wasn't wearing a coat?" I asked, curious how she saw his wrists since winter coats generally covered them.

"No, he was, but when he went into his pocket to get

his wallet, his sleeve moved and I saw that thing on his wrist."

I thanked Cynthia for her help again, and as we left the shop, I wondered if Mariah and some accomplice were working together. Walking to my car, I asked Alex, "Do you think Bethany's sister had someone helping her with this who was the man who ordered the flowers?"

He thought about it but didn't answer me. Closing the passenger side door, he looked over at me with a worried gaze that made me uneasy. "If that's the case, then this isn't about framing me so much as killing Bethany, so instead of looking for my enemies, we're going to have to look for hers."

Shifting the car into drive, I thought about Bethany and who would want to see her dead. I couldn't imagine anyone in the world who didn't like her.

"That's going to be a much harder task than finding your enemies. You know as well as I do everyone loved Bethany."

His voice low and somber, Alex said, "Not everyone, unfortunately."

Chapter Fourteen

ALEX HANDED ME a glass of soda and sat down beside me on his couch as a thought came to me about everyone loving Bethany. I'd always seen her as the girl who loved to have a good time, whether it was at *The Eagle* or after working hours. With her smile that could light up the gloomiest room and her unique way of looking at life, always so full of fun, she'd enchanted others anytime I was around.

But there were hints of darker things in her life. She and her sister hadn't been on speaking terms until just a few weeks ago, refusing to talk to one another after a disagreement over something about their mother's death or her will. Bethany had mentioned it only once to me right after she passed away a few years back, but she'd never said another word about it, even when she told me about Mariah coming to stay with her for the holidays.

In addition to the problem with her sister, there had been a relationship that had turned sour while she worked at *The Eagle*. I remembered her mentioning that he was a married man and she regretted ever starting anything with him.

"You look a million miles away. You okay?"

Alex's deep voice shook me from my thoughts. I took

a sip of soda and set my glass on the coffee table in front of me. "I was thinking about what I said in the car about Bethany. To me, she was the golden girl. It seemed like everyone loved her."

I stopped talking for a moment, feeling like I was about to trash the dead, and saw Alex look away. Touching his arm, I broached the subject neither one of us had ever really talked about. "Look at me. I want to say this, but I need to see your eyes when I do."

He turned to face me and waited while I found the right words. I didn't want to make him feel like he'd done anything wrong when he dated her. My jealousy was my problem, not his.

"I don't want to pretend you and Bethany were never together. She deserves better than that, and trust me, I know."

He narrowed his eyes to squints as his face showed his confusion. "What do you mean you know?"

I took a deep breath, and finally after all this time, I confessed the truth. "I was so jealous she was with you that I wasn't a very good friend to her when you two were together. I've been thinking a lot about that since I saw her sitting in that car. I feel terrible about it. I know what you saw in her. What everyone saw. She was fun and so full of life. And I wasn't like her and I was so jealous that she got to be with you and all I got was to work with you."

Now it was my turn to look away. As good as I was at being strong for others, when I had to admit my own failings, that strength disappeared and I was left with my insecurities for all the world to see. I felt so open, so vulnerable in a way that I'd never been comfortable with.

"I never knew, Poppy. If I had..."

I turned back to look at him and shook my head. "You never needed to know that. My feelings were my own, and just because you didn't share them doesn't mean you did anything wrong. Bethany didn't either. You two had every right to be together. You were two single adults, so why not? I don't want us to feel awkward about acknowledging the fact that you were together."

"I'm sorry, though. I wish I knew how you felt back then."

"Why? Would it have changed anything? You liked her. Maybe even loved her in some way. What I felt had nothing to do with that."

Alex hung his head and quietly said, "I didn't love her. Now that she's dead, I wish I could say I did, though, especially since she felt something like that for me."

Squeezing his hand, I brought it to my lips to kiss. "Not every relationship we have in life has to be love. Sometimes two people just feel better being with each other. Whatever you two were together, it gave you something you both needed. There's no shame in that."

I didn't admit that part of me was still jealous of Bethany, no matter how twisted I knew that was. She had known him in a way I hadn't yet, and although I didn't think about it all the time, I couldn't deny that his lack of interest in sleeping with me had made me wonder why.

"She made me feel like I could take a chance again, but it wasn't her I wanted to take that chance with. That's why I can't help feeling a sense of regret when I think about the two of us together. She wanted more than I could give her, and for that, I'm sorry."

Even as the urge to know if it was me he'd wanted to take that chance with made me want to ask him, I didn't. It felt wrong to press for that information as we sat there trying to figure out who had killed her.

I grabbed my glass of soda and stood from the couch to take it into the kitchen, even though I didn't need to refill it. Something about telling him how I'd felt made me feel more exposed than I could handle, and in that moment as I knew he sat there watching me walk away from him, why we hadn't slept together yet became all too apparent.

Unlike Bethany, who always made him and everyone else feel like they were the center of her world every minute she was around them, I spent much of my time around Alex keeping him at arm's length. Still haunted by my own past, I was as broken as I'd always believed him to be.

Walking up behind me, he slid his arms around my waist. He rested his chin on my shoulder, so I felt his newly sprouted stubble brush up against my jaw and whispered low in my ear, "I'm sorry if I said something wrong there. It's not the same with you as it was with her. You know that, right?"

I did, but that didn't matter. My jealousy had come out of my own insecurities, not anything he or Bethany had done, and it wasn't his job to take the blame for it.

Turning around to face him, I looked into those deep brown eyes and knew what I saw in them was something she hadn't, no matter how much she wished she could. And I understood why her diary entries sounded so full of love for him.

"I know. It's okay, Alex. You don't have to make

excuses for not wanting to be alone. Bethany was the kind of woman men loved to be around."

"You don't have to feel bad, Poppy. Bethany and I didn't break up because of you. She knew that."

I didn't want to keep talking about this because there was no escaping the rest of that answer—that he'd stopped seeing her because he was haunted by the love he still had for his wife. Even though he'd told me he loved me, I wasn't a fool. Just as he'd been unable to give Bethany what she wanted, it was just as likely he'd never be able to give me what I wanted either.

And as much as I loved him, I didn't want to think about that on top of everything else this case had brought up. So I let it go for another time.

"I remembered that Bethany mentioned to me that she was seeing some guy from Baltimore. She regretted it when she broke up with him too."

Curious, Alex asked, "Why? She wasn't really a regrets kind of person."

"Because he was married and had kids. She said he didn't take it well when she broke things off either."

"When was that?"

I thought about that day she came into my office to talk about the problems she was having with the man. It had been right before spring the year before. "Around nine or ten months ago. Maybe March of last year? Bethany's job was to bring in more advertisers, and part of that included working with a firm in Baltimore that the paper used on a freelance basis. The guy worked at that firm."

"What did she say happened?" he asked as he headed back into the living room.

Following him, I sat down on the couch and took

another sip of my drink. "She got some weird phone calls a few times at work, and one time she told me that she realized too late that she'd made a mistake dating him. She didn't go into it, but I figured she understood that dating a married man was a road to nowhere, but now I wonder if the mistake was something less with offending her ethics and more with danger."

"How can we find out who this man is?"

There was only one way to find that out. I had to go to work, where hopefully my boss wasn't since I hadn't checked in for days even before all this terrible business with Bethany's death.

"I can check her office at *The Eagle* for anything that could point us in the right direction."

A slow smile crept onto Alex's face. "If it was me investigating this case, I would have been over that office with a fine tooth comb already."

I chuckled at the truth of his comment. "Then I guess we should be happy Derek is the one doing the investigating this time."

Alex stood from the couch and moved to get his coat. "I guess we should. Let's go then. We don't want to end up running into him if it ever dawns on him to check there."

I stood to stop him and kissed his lips to soften what I had to say. "I think it might be better if you stay here while I head over to *The Eagle* to see what I can find out. On the off chance that Derek shows up, I don't think I can handle another confrontation between you two today, okay?"

As much as I knew he didn't want to sit on the sidelines anymore, Alex begrudgingly nodded his head in agreement. "Okay. I want you to be careful, though, and if you have any problems, call me and I'll be there in a heartbeat."

"It's my workplace, so I think I'll be fine. I'm just going to do a little snooping and hope I don't run into my boss since I've been slacking off on the job."

Alex buttoned my coat, and smiling, planted a tiny kiss on the tip of my nose. "Then be careful with that too. Hurry back."

As I turned my collar up to brace me from the winter cold I was about to run out into, I gave him a wink. "Aren't I always?"

I didn't wait for his reply.

Chapter Fifteen

THE SUNSET RIDGE EAGLE buzzed with people scurrying through the hallways like someone had gotten the scoop of the century. I quickly made my way through the crowd of my fellow writers to Bethany's office and shut the door behind me to get some privacy for my investigating duties.

I looked around and still felt her presence there like it had been for nearly five years. The smell of her vanilla scented perfume. Her half-empty pack of sugar-free gum on the desk right where she kept it near the box of paper clips. The pencil holder full of dry erase markers in a rainbow of colors for her monthly calendars she kept hung on the wall so she knew what was coming for the next quarter. Her favorite black scarf she wore to keep her warm in the office she claimed never got hot enough lay slung over the back of her desk chair.

It all felt like she'd walk through the door at any moment and announce some great thing had happened to her that she couldn't wait to tell me all about. Suddenly, coming here seemed like a bad idea. It felt disrespectful, like grave robbing.

I couldn't do it. I ran out of her office and met one of her advertising teammates, Erika Simpson, just outside the door. A beautiful blond with great cheekbones I'd long admired, her upbeat expression I was used to seeing so often around the office was nowhere to be found, replaced by a look of utter sadness.

"Oh, Poppy, what are we going to do without her?" she asked as tears filled her green eyes. "The place won't be the same without Bethany."

Nodding, I struggled to keep my composure as my tears threatened to come again. "I know. It's terrible. I can't imagine who would want to do this to her. What's going on here today?"

Wiping the mascara that began to run under her eyes, Erika sniffled and shook her head. "I don't know, but the bosses all came in about an hour ago. Whoever did this to Bethany, I hope they hang them when they find them."

Gingerly, I probed for anything that might help to uncover the killer, even an office problem Bethany may not have thought much about. "Can you think of anyone who would have hated her so much? I've been racking my brain since I found out. Who could have done this? Everyone here loved her."

Erika's eyes grew wide, and she leaned in close to me. "Not everyone. I never had a problem with Bethany professionally, but she could be cutthroat when it came to getting an account, and more than once I heard her and one of the other ad execs arguing in her office. It got so bad that the woman left in a huff a few months back after telling the bosses that Bethany should be fired for how she conducted herself."

This was all news to me. Bethany had never mentioned anything about problems she was having with anyone at the newspaper. "Who? She never told me about this."

Grimacing, Erika whispered the name. "Samantha Cooper. She's a real barracuda. I didn't mind one bit when she left, and I'm not the only one. But she and Bethany had it out a few times because she claimed Bethany poached an account of hers."

"Really? What happened to this person?" I asked, suddenly wondering if that visit to Bethany's office wouldn't reveal yet another possible suspect.

"I have no idea, but it was good riddance to bad rubbish as far as I was concerned when she left in November. I better get back to my office, but if you hear about a memorial service for Bethany, let me know, okay? I'll want to be there for her."

With all the investigating of the case and dealing with my own guilty feelings about our friend, the idea of a memorial service had slipped my mind. She deserved to be remembered as the person those of us who cared about her knew.

"I will, Erika. Thanks."

When she and everyone else had gone to their offices, I quietly returned to Bethany's and began searching for anything on the married man and this new person I'd just found out about who sounded like she had an ax to grind with her. In the back of the top drawer of her desk, I found five envelopes with Baltimore listed on the return address and postmarks from last June. I stuffed them into my purse without even looking at the letters inside, and finding nothing else of note, hurried out of her office directly into a woman with long black hair and blood red lipstick coloring her harsh looking mouth.

And when she spoke, I knew I hadn't judged that

mouth incorrectly.

"Who the hell are you? What are you doing in my office?" she snapped as she pushed past me through the doorway.

"This is Bethany Lewis's office," I said defiantly, wanting whoever this intruder was to know where she was and who had occupied this space until a few days ago.

"Not anymore. There's a new sheriff in town, so if you don't mind, perhaps you can take all of this junk out of MY office now."

Stunned at her rudeness, I asked, "Who are you?"

Snapping her head to look at me so her long hair flew around her head like a fan, she shot out her left hip and announced, "I'm Samantha Cooper, the person who should have had this office in the first place." She threw a box from the floor at me and said, "Now if you want any of this junk, I suggest you take it now before I have maintenance clear it all out so all traces of her are gone."

I couldn't believe how heartless she was! "Her name was Bethany and she's dead. A little respect for her wouldn't kill you."

Samantha looked sideways at me as she sat down in her new office chair and sneered. "You have two minutes before I have whoever you are escorted out of here."

There was no point in continuing to speak to her since she was possibly the rudest person I'd ever met in my life, so I quickly gathered up Bethany's things into the box as she told someone on the phone how happy she was to be back at work where she belonged.

"Of course, this entire office will have to be changed

around since the bitch who had it before me had no taste
or class at all, but knowing that I'm back in my rightful
place again makes what I'll have to deal with until it gets
fixed at least bearable."

The word she used was the right one, but just not for
the correct person.

I left her a few minutes later without another word
as I promised myself if I ever had the chance I'd see her
put in her proper place for being so awful to Bethany's
memory.

As I drove back to Alex's with the box of her
belongings, I had to wonder if that venom Samantha
Cooper obviously had in ample supply meant she could
do more than just verbally attack someone. She hadn't
even tried to hide her hatred for Bethany, so maybe she
had done more than just taken her office.

Maybe she'd gotten her revenge first.

I opened the front door to Alex's house and saw the
surprise on his face when he saw the box of things in my
arms. Hurrying to my side to take it from me, he carried
it over to the coffee table as I sat down on the couch next
to him.

He picked up the scarf from the top of the pile of
things and held it up in front of him. "I didn't think
you'd be bringing back a whole box of things, Poppy. It
looks like you cleared out her entire office."

Sighing, I tried to push my encounter with
Samantha Cooper out of my mind. "Pretty much. I
didn't really have a choice, to be honest."

"Why? What's wrong?"

I sat back against the couch cushion and sighed
again. "It seems that the big bosses hired Bethany's
replacement. I ran into her at her office when she

ordered me to remove all of Bethany's things or she'd throw them out as junk. Alex, she was so rude. It was awful. The woman is dead for just a couple days and she acted like she was happy about it."

"I'm sorry, Poppy. I should have gone there with you."

"No, that would have only made it worse. This woman was perfectly wretched. She called Bethany a bitch! Talk about disrespecting the dead!"

"If she's her replacement, why would she be so nasty about the person who had the job before her?" he asked as he turned back to the box.

"She is her replacement, but Samantha Cooper used to work at *The Eagle*. One of Bethany's friends said she had a problem with her and she was the reason this Cooper woman left in November. Now that Bethany's gone, she's back and she's pretty smug about it."

Alex reached for his notepad on the table next to the box and opened it to a new page. Grabbing a pen, he began to jot down what I'd just told him and smiled. "I'd say she's our first suspect then. She certainly sounds like she had motive. Revenge."

"Make her suspect number two. Mariah Lewis is still top on my list. I know you aren't really sure about that, but until she's found, I think she's definitely a suspect."

He nodded his agreement and wrote down Mariah's name in the notebook. "Well, we have at least two suspects. Did you find anything on the married man Bethany told you she was having problems with?"

I pulled out the letters from the Baltimore address and showed them to him. "I found these. I don't know if they'll tell us anything about him, though, but if they don't, maybe something in that box will."

"Let's take a look."

I opened up the envelope dated first and began reading the letter as Alex looked over my shoulder. I didn't get through the first two lines before he said, "I think we've found our guy."

Aloud, I reread the line that had caught my eye. "I won't let you do this to me without making you pay."

Turning to look at Alex, I saw him pointing further down the page. "It gets even better or worse, depending on how you look at it. Take a look at the line where he comes right out and threatens her."

"What do you do? Speedread?" I asked as I returned to reading the part of the letter his finger pointed to.

"We're meant for each other, Bethany. I gave up everything for you. Your life can't go on like this was nothing but a few months of sex. I won't let you live that life." I stopped reading and looked to the bottom of the letter to see the name Michael.

The words made my stomach hurt. Had this person finally stopped waiting to fulfill his threat and murdered her Sunday night? Had she been going to meet him when she got into her car?

Alex took the letter out of my hand as the thought of Bethany having her life taken by some crazy boyfriend settled into my mind. "Let's keep reading, Poppy. I know it's hard, but we have to find out all we can about this guy."

We read the other four letters, but they all said basically the same things until the last one. At the very end of that letter, I read his words and knew he was obsessed with her. "I'll make you pay for the pain I suffered by losing my wife and children over my relationship with you. I lost everything to be with you.

Now you're going to lose everything too."

I dropped my hand into my lap, letting the letter fall. "Why didn't she tell me or anyone about these letters? This guy was crazy, Alex. He threatens to take her life right there in that last line."

"We need to find out who this Michael is who wrote this and talk to him. Is there anyone who would know his last name?"

"Maybe Erika. I can ask her."

Standing from the couch, he pulled me up to join him. "I'm coming this time because I want to get to Baltimore today, so we'll stop on the way out of town."

I leveled my gaze on him and said, "You just want to meet that horrible shrew, don't you?"

He slid his coat over his shoulders and grinned. "Well, by the way you described her, I wouldn't mind finding out she's the one who'll be spending the rest of her life in jail for this crime, but I'm in a bigger hurry to get to Baltimore to find this Michael. Samantha whatever her name is might be a shrew, but my guess is Michael is our far likelier suspect."

As we walked out the door, I turned to look at him and said, "I guess, but I'd much rather it be her. Something tells me she wouldn't be so nasty if she had to spend the rest of her life behind bars."

I wasn't kidding about that either. A jilted lover killing Bethany didn't satisfy my need for justice anywhere as much as finding out that the harpy who'd jumped into her office and claimed her job was actually the one who'd taken her from this world. Seeing that snarky bitch in handcuffs and being led away to prison for the rest of her days would be real justice.

Chapter Sixteen

B Y THE TIME Alex and I arrived at *The Eagle*, the excitement of earlier had calmed down since most of the office workers had left for the day. I hoped we weren't too late and had missed Erika because I didn't know who else might know who this Michael person was.

I hurried Alex into my office and quickly shut the door behind us. Sunset Ridge was a small town, and no doubt word had already gotten around that he was the main suspect in Bethany's murder. I didn't need my editor spying him there and demanding I get an interview with the man who would be her killer, and I definitely didn't need to deal with the gossip that would spread faster than wildfire right back to Derek if Alex was found questioning people about the case.

"Stay here and I'll be right back. I don't want anyone to see you here, so keep quiet."

He screwed his face into a frown and sat down at my desk. He didn't appreciate me being the one calling the shots. "Anything else? Maybe I can get you a coffee, boss?"

"Do you want Derek to find out you're investigating this case with me because if you do, feel free to walk up and down the hallway announcing your interest in talking to anyone who might know who Michael from Baltimore is. If you'd rather not alert our friend to what we're up to, stay here and I'll be right back."

Alex sighed and nodded, accepting if not entirely agreeing with my point. Hopefully, he'd see I was just trying to protect him from what I knew would be certain gossip if he was seen trying to figure out who Bethany's killer was.

I headed up the hallway to Erika's office and saw a light shining under the door. Happy she hadn't left yet, I knocked and waited to hear her call me in, but she said nothing. I knocked a second time, and when she didn't answer, I threw open the door and saw her sitting at her desk with her head in her hands.

"Erika, are you okay? I knocked, but when I didn't get an answer…"

She turned around and I saw the evidence that she'd been crying all over her tear-stained face. Wiping her cheeks, she said, "I didn't hear you, Poppy. I'm sorry. It's been a rough day."

"I know. Every time I think about her, I feel like crying." I closed the door behind me and took a seat next to Erika as she cleaned herself up. "Is there anything I can do?"

She shook her head and sniffled. "It's not Bethany I'm crying about now. You must think I'm a total mess. Two times you've seen me today, and both times I've been like this. I'm usually much stronger, but that woman—that woman makes me so angry I can't help it. When I get furious, I always cry. I'm such a girl."

"What woman?" I asked, even as I suspected I knew the one who had brought her to tears this second time.

"Samantha Cooper," Erika answered, her words coming out in a hiss. "I swear to God I need this job, Poppy, but that woman is going to drive me from this place. She's a shrew."

"Ah, yes. I met the lovely and gracious Miss Cooper the first time I was here this afternoon. Shrew is the nicest word I can think of for her."

Erika smiled at my characterization of her nemesis and blew her nose before telling me about her own run-in with Samantha Cooper. "She comes back after being away for months and even though she's no more my superior than Bethany was, she began barking out orders like I was some stupid underling who knew nothing."

She stopped for a moment as her face grew redder and redder by the moment and then continued. "I'm not usually one for confrontation, but I guess I was channeling Bethany's spirit today because I stood right up to her and told her what was what. And you know what she did? She ran to our boss, who then called me into his office and scolded me for not being able to get along with my co-workers! He actually gave me that whole team player speech, as if I haven't been a team player since the day I started working here."

I patted her arm to calm her, and even though I truly wanted to be there for her to commiserate about how rotten her new co-worker was, Alex and I needed to get to Baltimore so my time for being nice was limited.

"She's awful. You just have to be strong and stand your ground, Erika. I came back to see you because I have a question, though. I'm trying to find out who someone named Michael was in Bethany's life. He lives in Baltimore. Do you know who that could be?"

Erika's eyes lit up, but she didn't answer my

question. Instead, she asked one of her own. "Are you investigating Bethany's death, Poppy? I heard your partner was the only suspect in her case."

"Well, you heard wrong. Don't listen to the gossip about this. Trust me. It's totally wrong," I said, instantly launching into my defense of Alex.

Nodding, she smiled. "I thought it was nonsense myself. I saw Bethany and him out one night and he seemed like a really nice guy. And I know you two have worked together on police stuff for a while now, so if anyone knows he couldn't do that to her, it's you."

"Exactly. Now if I could just get Derek Hampton to see that," I said, thinking out loud more than continuing the conversation.

"I wish I could help with that, but I'm a married woman," Erika said with a wicked smile as she wiggled the fingers on her left hand to show me her wedding rings. "If I wasn't, though, I'd be all over that police chief of ours. I'd give him something better to think about than accusing one of his own cops of murder."

My surprise at her interest in Derek must have been written all over my face because she quickly added, "Not that I'd ever cheat on my husband. I don't want you to think that. I just know a good looking man when I see one."

As much as I liked seeing Erika happy again and wished we could dish about Derek more, I needed to guide her back to my question. "This Michael person was someone Bethany was seeing. He lives in Baltimore and probably works there. Do you remember her ever mentioning anyone who would fit that description?"

She shook her head sadly. "No, I don't know who that could be."

I hadn't wanted to give away Bethany's secret that the man she'd been seeing was married, but at least I hoped it wouldn't be for naught. "Erika, this Michael was a married man Bethany was dating. Do you remember her saying anything about him?"

Shaking her head again, she lowered her voice and said, "No, but I'd heard rumors that she was seeing some married guy from that firm the paper used as freelancers. I don't know if his name was Michael, but I do know the name of the firm he worked for."

Erika turned in her chair to grab her cell phone and opened up her contacts. Excited, I grabbed a pen and piece of paper from her desk and waited for her to say the name. At least if we had that, we might be able to find out who Michael was, although it was a very common name. At least it was something to go on, though.

"Asher and Mitchell Advertising," she read off her phone. "I think I might have their card somewhere in my drawer. Hang on."

I scribbled down the name as she looked, thinking if we drove fast enough we might be able to reach their office building before the end of the workday. While the newspaper routinely let us out before four, I knew bigger city businesses kept their workers often much later. With any luck, Asher and Mitchell Advertising was one of them.

She spun around in her chair holding a tiny white card in her hand. "Here it is! I hope this helps."

I took it from her hold and read the address. 15 St. Paul Street, Baltimore. I had no idea where that was, but Alex would. Thrilled to finally have a direction to follow in our search for this Michael person who had threatened Bethany just months before, I stood from my chair and thanked Erika for her help.

"Don't let that harpy chase you out of here, okay?" I said in the hope that she'd learn quickly enough to be strong in the face of Samantha Cooper's nastiness.

She smiled up at me and nodded. "I'm going to try to be like Bethany with her. With any luck, I'll chase her away like she did."

"Good. Thanks again, Erika."

As I opened the door to leave her office, she said, "Find out who did this to her, please. I know most people in town would look down on her for dating a married man, but whatever she did, she didn't deserve the end she got."

I knew how Erika felt. I wanted to find the bastard who had taken the life of our friend more than she could ever know.

"I will. I promise."

I just hoped I would be able to fulfill that pledge when the time came.

Hurrying back to my office, I found Alex rummaging through my desk drawers like I was a suspect he wanted to know more about. He didn't even have the decency to look guilty when I caught him either.

"Finding anything interesting, Officer Montero? Do you have a search warrant to be looking through my personal things?" I asked in mock anger, folding my arms across my chest.

He slowly closed the top drawer of my desk and stood up, his smile telling me he probably saw something he shouldn't have in there. "Miss McGuire, I find out something new about you every day, and thanks to my checking out your desk, I now know even more. Did you get anything we can use?"

I triumphantly held up the business card. "How does an address where our Michael very well may work sound?"

His smile grew broader, and he snatched the card from my grip. "It sounds like you succeeded. I think it's time for us to leave. With any luck and me driving, we might get there before they all go home."

I turned on my heels and headed out into the hallway. "You driving? Are you saying I can't get us there on time?"

Alex followed me, saying beneath his breath, "If on time is tomorrow."

Looking behind me, I saw him grin when he realized I'd heard what he said. "Well, Mr. Speed Demon, how about you just get us there in one piece, okay? That means we don't have to go Mach two."

Jingling the keys, he chuckled as he passed me out the front door of *The Eagle* building. "I'm a man, Poppy. Our goal is always to go as fast as possible."

Strangely enough, I hadn't found that always the case with him, but maybe he was only referring to driving.

Chapter Seventeen

WE WALKED DOWN the carpeted main hallway of Asher and Mitchell Advertising Agency past the multitude of awards that lined the walls and portraits of the firm's chiseled-jawed partners to the receptionist desk where a young woman with plain brown hair and black rimmed glasses that made her look like an old-fashioned librarian sat waiting to greet us.

"Welcome to Asher and Mitchell. Can I help you?"

I hadn't seen Alex turn on the policeman charm thing for a while since most people in Sunset Ridge had gotten used to him and simply answered questions without being cajoled. I wasn't sure why, but for whatever reason, he clearly believed he needed to turn it on for this woman, though.

Leaning forward on her desk, he smiled and said, "Hi, I'm Officer Alex Montero from the Sunset Ridge police. I need to speak to someone about one of your employees."

Her response was even warmer than her initial hello. "Of course. Let me get someone who can do that for you, Officer Montero. Please just wait here."

She trotted off on her search for someone to do as Alex had asked. I tapped him on his shoulder as he stood up from draping himself over her desk and shot him a glare of disapproval.

"Exactly what was that about? We aren't in our small town, so what's with the smarmy thing you had going on there?"

"I went with my gut. It looks like it worked," he answered smugly.

I rolled my eyes at his charm offensive and the all-too-confident look he wore. "Let's hope you get a female partner to help you because if not, I don't know how you're going to charm your way out of the fact that you can say you're a cop from Sunset Ridge all you want, but you don't have your badge to flash in front of them to prove it. Did you forget that?"

The smugness faded from his expression as he felt near his belt where his badge usually sat. "Yeah, I forgot about that. No worry, though. If all else fails, we could always tell the truth."

"That you're the main suspect in the murder of my friend and we're here to try to find someone else we're convinced may have done it?" I asked, framing the issue succinctly.

Alex smirked at my need to be that truthful. "That we're here to find someone who cared about their contact at *The Eagle*, who I'd bet money was loved by all here."

"Oh, that truth," I said as the receptionist rounded the corner and approached us again. "Thanks for clearing that up for me."

Whispering out the side of his mouth as he smiled for the girl with the thick black glasses, he said, "My pleasure. Now let me do the talking so your version of the truth doesn't come flying out of your mouth and we get thrown out of here."

"Please follow me," she said with a smile as she waved us over to where she stood. "Mr. Asher will see you now."

I had no idea what Mr. Asher would be like—old or young—but I had a feeling Alex's charm wasn't going to be of much help from this point on. He knew it too by the disappointed look he wore. Perhaps some version of the truth would have to do what that Alex charm couldn't.

Hopefully, something would work so we could at least find out how to locate Michael before Derek swooped in and hauled Alex off to jail.

She escorted us into his office where Mr. Asher stood behind an enormous cherry wood desk in a three-piece suit wearing a smile that didn't look genuine. Nothing but one of those executive toys with silver spheres that swung back and forth mesmerizing onlookers and a desk calendar I immediately noticed had nothing written on it sat on top of his very expensive looking desk.

A quick glance at how his blue eyes sparkled when he looked at his receptionist and then at his ring finger with a wedding band around it told me Mr. Asher was very likely guilty of infidelity, and I had a feeling his partner in crime was none other than the mousey looking girl with dark glasses who winked at him as she closed the door behind her as she left us with him. Whatever was going on between them, Mr. Asher's expression changed to one of mild irritation once she was gone.

He extended his hand to shake Alex's and then mine and offered us each a seat. "I'm Daniel Asher, one of the firm's junior partners. My receptionist tells me that you're here about one of my employees. You're a little out of your jurisdiction, aren't you, Officer Montero?"

"I just have a few questions, so we won't take up but a few minutes of your time, Mr. Asher. Do you have someone named Michael working for you who would have had a connection to your firm's work with *The Sunset Ridge Eagle?*"

"I'm not sure you have the right firm. The only Michael we've had working for us in the past few years was Michael Thompson."

Alex wrote down the name and asked, "Did he work with *The Eagle?*"

"I believe he did."

"Can you tell us where we can find him?"

I'd waited for Asher to balk at our questions, and that one did it. Standing from his chair, he straightened his tie and curtly said, "I don't think I have anything more to say about this because you don't have any right to be questioning me. Please see yourselves out."

Before Alex could explain his version of the truth, I jumped up to try to make Daniel Asher understand how important it was to find this person. "One of the people your firm worked with at *The Sunset Ridge Eagle* news-paper was murdered Sunday night. Bethany Lewis? We're here about a man named Michael who knew her because we have these letters which show how much in love he was with her. We need to find him to tell him and give him something she'd kept for him, hoping they would get back together. She was my best friend and I'd hate to not be able to do this one thing for her."

Daniel Asher's sharp intake of breath told me the news of Bethany's death stunned him. Knitting his brows, he frowned and said, "I'm sorry to hear that.

Bethany was a delight to work with. She'll be missed."

My pleading tone hung in the air as I waited to see some softening in Asher's stance. Finally, he nodded and called his receptionist. "Get Michael Thompson's address for Officer Montero."

He looked over at me and frowned. "I'm very sorry about your friend, but I can't guarantee Michael will still be at the address we have for him. We let him go three months ago."

The receptionist returned with Michael's address and handed it to Alex. We thanked Daniel Asher and quickly left his office, even though my version of the truth had done the trick. By the time we reached the elevator, I could feel Alex's stare practically burning a hole in the side of my head.

I turned to look at him and saw him smiling at me. "Nice save back there."

"Well, you know how it is, me and my small town thing I have going on. Sometimes it works."

"You should know I'm impressed every day by you. This case might just be me waiting for Derek to haul me off in handcuffs if it wasn't for you, Poppy."

I secretly loved it when he said things like that, but I didn't want him to know how much I adored hearing his compliments about my work as his partner. Shrugging, I waved him off. "It's nothing. Grasshopper has learned her lessons. So where are we off to now, teacher?"

Turning away, I faced forward and saw in the shiny metal doors in front of me that he was still smiling as he looked at me and said, "We get to head out to Ellicott City."

WE PULLED UP to the white Cape Cod house on High Ridge Road in Ellicott City just after sunset and parked the car in front of a quintessentially suburban home. Once we got closer to it, however, it became clear that it was anything but an average house. We peeked through the windows on the front porch since none of them had any curtains or draperies and saw every room was empty. Not one piece of furniture sat in any of them.

"Did he move? This looks like the kind of house a family would live in, so do you think when he lost his job he simply packed up his wife and kids and left town?" I asked.

Alex looked around the neighborhood at the expensive homes nearby. "He might not have been able to pay the mortgage on a house in a place like this if he lost his job and didn't have enough savings. Let's check around back."

"It's getting dark. I'm not sure skulking around this guy's house at night is a good thing."

He chuckled and nudged me toward the front porch steps. "You'd know about that whole skulking around a man's house in the dark thing. Just pretend it's my house, and anyway, I'm here, so it's not like anyone's going to jump out of the bushes and attack you."

"Funny. If someone does, I'm going to run behind you. Just letting you know."

"I know my place here. I'm the muscle," he joked as we walked down the side of the house.

The house next door had no lights on in it either, so at least we wouldn't have to deal with a nosy neighbor wondering what we were up to. We climbed the five steps of the wood back porch and looked in through the windows of the back door that led into the kitchen since it didn't have any curtains hanging on it either.

Inside, I saw only a stove and a refrigerator. Not even a table had been left in the kitchen. Alex gently elbowed me in the side and pointed at the window. I looked in and saw what had caught his attention.

"Is that a knife with something dried on it?" I asked as I strained to see what it could be.

"Yeah. How likely is it that it's blood?" he asked me as he jiggled the door handle to find it locked.

"We need to get into this house, Alex. Let's go try the front door and see if we have any luck with that."

The two of us turned around to see a man with crazy eyes staring wildly at us with a shovel in his hands raised to beat our heads in. We froze without taking even a step, and he lowered it to point at us.

"I don't think you want to do that. I've lost too much already and killing you two won't make things much worse for me."

Chapter Eighteen

THE MAN'S EYES flashed a wildness I'd never before seen anywhere but in horror movies. Looking away for just a second, I saw his thin hands gripped that shovel so tightly his knuckles had turned white and appeared as if at any moment they would erupt from under his skin. His feet firmly planted in a wide stance, he appeared ready to lunge with the slightest provocation. Nothing about the man said either Alex or I was going to get off that porch safely.

I looked to my left and saw Alex staring just as intently at our would-be attacker as he was at us, but in my partner's eyes I saw not a wild look but a calculating one. Unlike me, standing in pure terror at the possibility that Michael Thompson would at any second swing that shovel and slam it into the side of my head to crush my skull like it was a rotten cantaloupe, Alex stood calmly assessing the situation and devising plans for our escape.

At least I hoped he was and I wasn't just letting my soon-to-be smashed in head fill with overly romantic notions of his cleverness and invincibility.

"What are you doing here? Did she send you? I told her there was nothing left to pick off my bones!" he yelled in a frantic voice that trembled when he said the word *her*.

Alex slowly pulled me behind him and held me there, but his worry that I'd move or try to run was unnecessary. I had no intention of attempting anything stupid like that. I liked my skull just as it was in one piece, and if he could stop this madman from trying to kill me, I was all for standing behind him and letting him take lead.

"We just came here looking to talk to you, Michael," Alex said in a soft voice barely above a whisper. "You are Michael Thompson, right?"

"I don't know who I am anymore. Who are you? Why are you trying to break into my house?" he shrieked.

Raising his hands in surrender, Alex continued to gently try to make him understand why we were there on his back porch, even though we looked like common criminals trying to break into his house, just as he thought.

"Michael, we mean no harm. My name is Alex and this is Poppy. We just want to talk to you."

He narrowed his eyes to slits, like he didn't believe what Alex had said, and then looked back and forth between us. "Poppy isn't a real name. It's a flower. You're just trying to trick me."

I'd gotten that every day of grade school from every teacher who refused to accept that I felt more comfortable with my nickname than I did my given name. I couldn't react as petulantly now as I had at school, though, or we were sure to feel the sharp edge of that shovel against our heads.

Giving him my sweetest smile, I said, "Hi, Michael. Everyone calls me Poppy ever since I was a little girl, but you can call me by my given name, if you want. It's Elizabeth."

His expression softened, and he repeated my name like he couldn't believe it. "Elizabeth?"

"Yes. It was my grandmother's name, and I've always loved it," I lied in the most sincere way I knew how. I had been named after my father's mother, but I'd never liked the name as much as my nickname. My paternal grandmother never found anything nice to say about a single person in all the time I spent around her. At her death when I was six, I had no tears, as much as I wished I could have cried at her passing for my father.

"She took my two kids and one day when I was at work, she cleaned out the house. I came home to nothing. I know I made mistakes, but she took everything I had."

Alex and I looked at each other as Michael Thompson began to unravel right there in front of us. Whatever fear I'd had of him and his shovel faded away, replaced by sympathy for the obvious pain he was in.

I mouthed the words, "Let me talk to him a little more," and slowly crept out from behind Alex to see if I could at least make Thompson see we didn't want to hurt him. He stood at the edge of the porch with his head hung, and when I looked more closely, I saw tears rolling down his cheeks.

Reaching out my hand toward him, I smiled and said, "I know how bad things can seem, but you're going to be okay, Michael. Do you want to talk? I'd love to talk to you."

He looked up and began sobbing loudly as he nodded. "I would. I don't have anyone to talk to anymore. I don't have anything anymore. It's all gone."

I took his hand in mine and led him to a wooden bench at the far end of the porch. Behind me, Alex moved to where Michael had stood on the edge of the porch near the stairs. I didn't know what I would say, but I let my heart lead the way instead of my head. He didn't need to be interrogated now. He needed a shoulder to cry on and someone to lend their ear for a while so he didn't think he was all alone in the world.

Still holding the shovel, he sat down and cried like a baby as I held his hand. I didn't know him and he didn't know me, and it was quite likely he had murdered my friend, but at that moment I felt so much sympathy for him that I had to help.

"It's going to be okay. I know it doesn't seem like it will, but I promise no matter how bad you feel, once you let it all out, then you can start to feel better. Just let everything you're feeling come out."

I hoped what he was feeling was simply distraught and not full of rage that would turn on me at any second. He stopped crying and lifted his free hand to wipe his eyes, but the shovel got in the way.

Quickly, I said, "Here, let me take that so you don't hurt yourself with that."

He didn't fight me, and once he released it into my hold, I held it out for Alex to take. Without a weapon, I saw Michael Thompson not as the terrifying madman who I was afraid would crush my skull but as the broken person he truly was.

"I never wanted anyone to get hurt. I didn't mean to do all those things to my wife," he said quietly as he wiped the tears from his cheeks.

I wasn't sure what he meant by that. Had he hurt his wife at some point other than cheating on her? Part of me didn't know if I should ask what he'd done, but I knew if I didn't Alex would and I had a feeling Michael would be far more receptive to my questions.

Gently stroking the top of his hand, I tentatively asked, "What happened that they got hurt, Michael? Maybe we can help them get better."

He shook his head and began sobbing again. "No, no. She says nothing will ever make things better. She says I made my bed, so now I have to lie in it. She doesn't understand that I'd do anything to fix my mistake."

I looked over at Alex, who didn't look nearly as affected by Michael's breakdown as I was. That didn't surprise me, though. He was a cop down to his marrow, hardened over after years of the job and everything he'd gone through in his own life. I'd seen my fair share of heartbreak, but it hadn't made me retreat into my shell like him, so I empathized with what my father liked to call "the hard luck stories that tug at the heartstrings."

"Would you like to go inside and talk where I'm sure it's warmer?" I asked Michael, instantly knowing I'd made a mistake asking that when he ripped his hand from my hold.

"No!" he screamed at me. "We can't go in there!"

Alex rushed over to my side to stop him from grabbing me, but I had the sense he just didn't want to talk about the house, so I wouldn't ask again. Holding my hand up so Alex wouldn't move close to him, I lightly touched his sleeve and smiled.

"Okay, we can stay here if you want. Is that okay?"

Strangely calm after lashing out just a few seconds ago, he nodded and repeated my words. "We can stay here. That's what I want."

"Okay. I like it here too, so we'll stay. Do you need anything, Michael? Food? Medicine? Because if you do, we can get it for you. We're happy to help."

He shook his head so fast his dark hair fell down onto his forehead and began rambling, "I want to stay here. This is my house. That's what I want. All I need is my house and my family. I need them back here." Turning to face me, he stared into my eyes and asked, "Can you bring them here? I need them here."

"They're not hurt, are they, Michael?"

His body sagged, and he hung his head. "She says I hurt them, but I would never do that. I love them. I just didn't think when I did it."

I looked up at Alex and saw his mouth open to ask the obvious question of what it referred to, but I stopped him and asked myself. "What did you do, Michael? Will you tell me?"

"She says I broke my vows. I guess I did," he said in a faraway voice as he buried his head in his hands. "I couldn't help myself. She was just too beautiful and she said she cared about me."

"Who was she? Can we call her so she can come over and be with you?"

Michael began sobbing and shaking his head violently back and forth. "She won't! She doesn't love me anymore. She said she'd love me forever, but she lied. She lied to me!"

His words echoed in my ears, and I leaned back against Alex in fear that Michael was about to lash out at me this time. The she he was talking about was Bethany by the way he'd talked to her in those letters.

"Why aren't you at work?" Alex asked.

Looking up at him, Michael's lip quivered as he

answered. "When she left me, I didn't know what to do. This whole house seemed like it was against me. My alarm didn't work, and I began missing days. Then an account I'd been working on was taken away from me because one of my co-workers complained about me always missing work."

"You lost your job," I said sadly as he nodded in tears.

"I lost everything because of that bitch! She told me she would love me forever, but that was a lie. It was all a lie!"

I didn't have to hear any more. The story was all together clear and too familiar. Michael had cheated on his wife with Bethany, and when his wife found out, she left him and took the kids. Now he was all alone and in the middle of an emotional breakdown.

The question was why was he breaking down now? Was it because two nights ago he killed the woman who he thought had ruined his life and now guilt tortured his madness addled mind?

Alex tapped me on the shoulder while Michael sobbed into his hands again. Leaning down, he whispered into my ear, "We need to get into that house."

"I know, but he freaked out when I asked him the last time."

"I can ask this time. Maybe he won't freak out. I'm a guy, so it might not upset him as much."

Mouthing okay, I turned back toward Michael and rubbed his back as he cried. Behind me, Alex cleared his throat and then in his softest voice asked, "Michael, why don't we go inside so we can get you warmed up?"

"I can make you tea," I offered enthusiastically

before remembering his wife likely had turned off the electricity which had made his alarm stop working.

He dropped his hands, and for the first time, he smiled at me. "I love tea. I want you to make me some tea. That would make me happy again."

I didn't have the heart to remind him that without a working stove or microwave he wouldn't be able to have tea. Necessity was the mother of invention, so if I had to run next door to his neighbor's house and beg for hot water and a tea bag, I'd do that. Anything to give him something to be happy about because the man looked like he didn't have a shred of goodness left in his life.

"Then I'll make you tea, Michael. We can go inside and make tea and talk about things, okay?"

Smiling broadly, he nodded. "Okay. I'd like that."

He and I stood to go into the house, but when he saw Alex standing next to me, he gritted his teeth and his eyes flashed the anger I'd seen in them a short time earlier. I tried to remind him of the tea I'd make him, but he didn't want to hear about it.

"You're just like her! You're with him, aren't you?" he shrieked, taking a step back toward the kitchen door and pointing at me. "You never cared, just like her!"

"I do, Michael. We can make tea and talk, right?" I said, but whatever calm he'd felt only seconds before had disappeared. Now he was just that crazed man who had wanted to beat us with a shovel.

"No! I won't let you trick me. All you women do is trick me and I won't let you," he answered before launching into a barely intelligible tirade about how all women lie and cheat.

With each flail of his hands, he descended further and further into whatever madness afflicted him. Alex wrapped his arms around me to protect me, but I wasn't sure Michael could even comprehend hurting anyone. All he wanted was the hurt inside him to stop.

"He's not going to give us anything more," I admitted sadly and stepped toward the stairs to leave. "We better go."

"Not yet. I want to ask him something first," Alex said as I moved away from him. "Michael, that knife on the counter in your kitchen there. What did you use it for?"

Startled by the question, Michael stopped his ranting and grabbed hold of the screen door. "You need to go now. I can't talk to you anymore."

Alex took a step toward him to stop him from running inside the house, but he slipped away and slammed the kitchen door closed in his face. Peering out through one of the windows, he stared at him and screamed, "Go away! I don't want to talk to you anymore."

I rushed to Alex's side to look in through the window and saw Michael grab the knife. He ran away into the living room and waved it around in front of him before taking off up the stairs with it. Stunned, I looked at my partner, not quite sure what we'd just seen.

"What happened there?"

"He's crazy. Something inside him snapped. What we need to know is did it make him kill Bethany?"

I took one last look inside Michael Thompson's empty house and sighed. "Did you notice he never said her name not even once?"

"He never said his wife's either, Poppy. I wouldn't be surprised if he can't remember they had names. He just sees them as the reasons he's so unhappy."

Alex tugged me by the arm away from the back door, and even though I didn't feel right leaving Michael there all alone with the demons in his head and that knife as his only company, I left and followed him to the car.

"Should we tell someone he needs help, Alex? I'm worried he might do something to himself."

"I'll call county services, but I doubt they're going to be much help. They can't force him to go with them. They can't even force him to answer the door. I think we'll have better luck getting back to Sunset Ridge and telling Derek so he can get a warrant for him. That way he has no choice but to let people in."

I closed the passenger side door and leaned back against the seat exhausted. Michael Thompson's madness had taken everything out of me. Looking over at Alex as he started the car, I wondered if he'd ever unraveled like that after losing his wife.

"I feel bad for him. He's lost everything. That must be devastating, don't you think?"

Alex frowned even as he nodded his agreement. "It is devastating. I feel for the guy too, Poppy, but as messed up as he is, I think he's our murderer. He's got motive. He thinks Bethany ruined his life and made him lose everything. He's got means. That knife on the counter looked like a hunting knife and had some kind of dried liquid on it."

I finished his rundown of Michael Thompson's possible guilt, hating what I had to say. "And he had opportunity. He's got no one in his life and he lives alone, so he could get to Sunset Ridge to kill Bethany without even being missed by a soul."

Just saying that made me feel bad for him. That he

could drive to Bethany's, kill her in cold blood, and then come back to his empty house without anyone missing him was possibly the saddest thing after Bethany's death.

Alex weaved his fingers through mine and brought my hand to his lips in a kiss. "Cheer up. We might have just solved this case."

I forced a smile, knowing it was a good thing that we could now show Derek someone else could have killed Bethany. "I know. I just wish there wasn't so much misery at every turn in this case."

He smiled at my naiveté and kissed my cold knuckles. "It's a murder case, Poppy. We rarely get anything but misery with them."

As we drove down Michael's suburban street on our way back to Sunset Ridge, I knew he was right. Murder was always miserable. Thankfully, we had each other to chase away the ugliness that came from our cases. I wasn't sure what I'd do if we didn't.

Chapter Nineteen

THE SUNSET RIDGE police station looked like the place had been abandoned. Nobody sat at their desks in the outer office area, and every office we passed was empty, even Derek's office. As Alex and I walked to the back of the building hoping to find anyone at all, I wondered if something terrible had happened.

Again.

"I know you guys don't just sit around during your shifts, but shouldn't someone be here? This feels like the beginning of some zombie movie or something where aliens have taken everyone but the two of us," I said as we looked around the empty station.

"Zombies don't exist, Poppy. I'm sure someone's here," Alex said in that way that told me he thought little of my theories.

We turned the corner and began walking down the hallway to the interrogation and break room. I elbowed him for discounting my zombie idea. "I noticed you didn't say anything against the alien theory. Does this mean you're a believer?"

He stopped walking and turned to face me. Raising his eyebrows as high as they could go onto his forehead, he stared at me like I was an alien. "What's wrong with you? Did that fifteen minute nap in the car do something to you?"

"No. I was just trying to lighten up a dark situation. This whole case has been nothing but sadness and misery, like you said, so I was just trying to add a little happiness to it. I also believe in aliens, so it's not like I'd have to lose my mind to mention them. That's all."

I didn't mean to sound as defensive as I did, and I saw by the way Alex's expression softened that he thought my feelings were hurt. "It's okay, Poppy. Some cases are harder than others. This one's been tough, and I don't think I realized how much you've been affected by it."

He lifted his hands to cradle my face, but I shook my head to stop him. I wasn't embarrassed by our relationship and had no problem with the rest of the world knowing we were together, but something about one of his fellow officers seeing us get all romantic in the back hallway felt wrong.

"It's okay. Let's see if we can find somebody in the break room. Maybe they're all gathered in there to share some crappy police station coffee and old vending machine candy."

I turned away from him and began walking away when I heard him say very quietly, "Sometime soon you and I are going to have a conversation about how you hide your true feelings behind jokes, Poppy McGuire."

That he knew me well enough to see right through the goofing around I used to hide how I really felt unnerved me more than I wanted to admit at that moment. I wasn't sure I was ready for him to understand me that well yet.

So I said nothing to that promise of us talking about

my defense mechanisms and kept walking toward the break room as he silently walked behind me.

He caught up just as we got to the room and saw Derek sitting there with none other than Mariah Lewis. Practically her sister's twin in everything but a few extra pounds she carried around her waist, she sat with her head in her hands sobbing.

Alex and I stopped at the door, unsure if we should interrupt Derek's questioning, but as soon as he saw us, he waved us in. "Join us, please. Alex and Poppy, this is Bethany's sister Mariah."

As Bethany's friend, I felt bad standing there in that interrogation room not knowing much more than her name. I guess I always thought since they were repairing their relationship that I'd get another chance to know her better when she visited again in the future.

Except now that future was gone, cut down by some maniac I had a feeling I'd just spent a few uneasy minutes with in Ellicott City.

Mariah looked up at each of us and smiled meekly before drying her eyes. "Your police chief just told me what happened. Who could have done this?"

We pulled up chairs and sat down away from the table so as not to intrude on what was Derek's case and questioning as he explained how Mariah had come to be sitting in the interrogation room of the police station.

"The Pennsylvania State Police found Mariah broken down on the Pennsylvania Turnpike near Pittsburgh this morning and brought her here after seeing the APB on her. I've been telling her what we know so far about her sister's case."

The mention of Bethany's murder started her sister crying again, and in between sobs, she asked, "Do either of you know what happened? Who did this?"

Derek answered her question with one of his own, startling me with how he cut to the heart of the case as he saw it. "Do you recognize this man, Mariah?"

She looked over at Alex intently, as if she was studying him. My heart slammed into my chest as I waited for her answer, which would go a long way to showing Derek he was wrong about Alex being his best suspect. Narrowing her eyes, she looked him up and down and then again but said nothing.

Finally, she nodded. "Yes, but I only saw him once on the street. My sister pointed him out. He was wearing a policeman's uniform that day, though. She said they used to date, but he broke up with her."

I didn't know how Alex kept his face so passive as he listened to the way that final statement came out of Mariah's mouth so full of anger and disgust. I knew my expression showed how guilty I felt about being the one she likely thought he'd left her for.

Derek continued with his questions. "Mariah, did you hear your sister and Alex fighting the night of her murder?"

"Yes. They fought outside the apartment."

"Did it sound like the fight was violent or that Bethany was in any danger?"

I had no idea why Derek was working so hard to put ideas into a suspect's head that Alex had been the killer, but with a gentle touch of his hand on my leg, I got the hint that he didn't want me challenging Derek on this. Alex smiled at me like he couldn't have been more sure whatever Derek was doing would help him, so I took a deep breath and kept my mouth shut, as hard as that was.

Mariah shook her head and screwed her face into an expression that said she thought his description of the fight was way off-base. "Yes, but it wasn't anything he'd murder her over. They were just fighting because she thought he was playing games with her after he sent the flowers and then acted like he didn't really want to see her when he came over after she called."

"So nothing other than that fight happened that night? He didn't come back in the time you were still there at your sister's apartment?"

"No. When I left right around eleven, he hadn't come back. Bethany had pretty much told him never to come back again, so I wouldn't be surprised if he never did."

I felt my body ease with every word she said. She didn't believe it was Alex either. Now if only Derek would open his eyes and see it too.

"Why did you end your visit to your sister's early?" he asked.

I listened with interest to hear her answer. It felt entirely too coincidental that she left just in time to not be around when her sister was murdered mere feet from the apartment where she'd been staying for weeks.

"My boyfriend Kenny back in Ohio asked me to come home because he missed me, and since Bethany was in such a bad mood for the past few days, I figured it wouldn't be a big deal. I told her I had to go back and she understood."

Interrupting Derek just as he opened his mouth to ask another question, I asked the one that I had to know the answer to. "Why would you leave so late at night? Why not wait until Monday morning?"

Mariah didn't seem to be sure if she should answer

my question or not. Looking across the table at Derek, she waited for him to tell her to either answer my question or ignore me. After he shot me a nasty look I knew was meant as a warning to not get in the way of his questioning, he nodded his head and smiled.

"Go ahead. Answer Ms. McGuire's question. It's one I'm interested in hearing myself."

"Okay. Well, I try to drive only at night. I'm terrified of driving, really, but at night there aren't as many drivers on the road so it isn't as bad. That's why I'd only gotten as far as I did when my car broke down. I stop during the day and rest and then I drive again at night. It takes longer, but I feel safer that way."

Looking over at Alex, I saw nothing to say he believed her or not. For me, the answer seemed entirely plausible, if not somewhat bizarre. But then again, I didn't fear driving so being on the road when other cars were there didn't bother me. It did make sense that she would have only gotten to western Pennsylvania driving only at night for a couple days, though.

Derek seemed to believe her too, if the way he was nodding his head was any indication. When he hadn't resumed his questioning after over a minute, I took the opportunity to ask another question I worried he probably wouldn't.

"Why was Bethany in such a bad mood, Mariah? It was the holidays and you two were mending your relationship after all this time. What did she have to be upset about?"

As soon as the words left my mouth, I regretted asking them. Not because it upset Derek because he seemed just as curious as I was to know what was bothering Bethany. No, as soon as I finished speaking, I felt Alex's stare nearly boring a hole in the side of my face. I'd asked a question that could possibly lead to Mariah pointing the finger at Alex for being the reason why her sister was so unhappy, and that wasn't a good thing.

Suddenly, it felt like the whole world had frozen in time, and I turned to see him staring at me not with a look of anger but with a look that said he was hurt by my question. I silently mouthed that I was sorry, but it didn't change the fact that the question had been asked and now we'd all have to listen to her explain just what was making Bethany so unhappy in the days leading up to her death.

I just hoped it wasn't what Alex feared it would be.

And then Mariah answered, and thankfully, what had been upsetting Bethany had nothing to do with him. "My sister was having a hard time at work with someone. She was worried she was going to be fired. Bethany hated the fact that she'd taken a few well-earned weeks off from work, the first real vacation she'd taken in years, and the newspaper was thinking about hiring some woman behind her back. She thought they waited until she went on vacation to do it and worried it was because they wanted to replace her."

Excited to hear it wasn't the breakup with Alex or anything to do with him, I said, "I met this person Bethany disliked at *The Eagle* this morning when I was there at Bethany's office. Her friend Erika told me about the trouble she'd had with her before she left in November. Now she's back and she's a real piece of work. Her name is Samantha Cooper."

Derek pushed his chair out and stood from the table. "Mariah, give me a few minutes. I'll be right back in. Do you need anything? Please feel free to help yourself to coffee. I won't be long."

Without a word to Alex or me, he waved his hand for us to follow him out into the hallway. I had a feeling I was going to get a scolding to rival the one I'd gotten from Mrs. Chester, my third grade teacher, when I took it upon myself to liberate the class ferret because I'd seen a show about how all animals should be free the night before and wanted to help Squidly the Third Grade Ferret to freedom. She barked at me for nearly twenty minutes that day after having to run up and down four floors of the school to catch poor Squidly.

I closed the door behind me and found myself facing not only Derek's stern look but Alex's too. Figuring my only way out of trouble was to turn on the sweetness, I smiled my cutest smile and said, "I know what you're going to say, but I just figured I could help in there since I knew Bethany better than you did."

"I have a feeling your partner would have given anything for a muzzle to keep you quiet."

I saw Alex look away in disgust, but I didn't know if it was because of what Derek had said about me needing to be forced quiet or what I'd done in that room. Clearly, cute and sweet wasn't going to do the job.

So I'd have to go with Plan B, a frontal attack. I just hoped Alex would forgive me after I was done sparring with Derek.

"Well, you weren't exactly getting to the heart of the matter, so I figured I'd do it for you. It all turned out for the good anyway because she said she didn't think their fight was anything he'd want to murder Bethany over, and anyway, she wasn't even upset about him. It was all Samantha Cooper, who by the way is the world's biggest bitch and someone you should definitely be looking into. At the very least she needs to be brought down about ten pegs off her high horse. I mean, for God's sake, she practically threw me out of Bethany's office this morning as if I was trespassing or something. Definitely look into her, Derek. She hated Bethany with a passion, I can tell you that."

When I finished, I saw both men staring at me like I was one of those aliens I believed in come down to earth. I couldn't tell if they were interested in what I had to say or something far less complimentary.

"Are you done?" Derek asked.

Looking to Alex and seeing he had no intention of helping me out of the scolding I was set to receive, I nodded. "Yeah."

"You know, Poppy, if you'd come up for air once in a while, you might find out what I have to say. I'll look into this Samantha Cooper and find out how badly she wanted that job. If Bethany was in the way of her getting it, that might be a motive for murder."

"They had problems before she left in November too," I reminded him, hoping to be helpful.

"Got it. Now as for Alex here…"

I opened my mouth to blast Derek for still believing Alex was a real suspect, but before I could say a word, Alex spoke up for the first time. "You still think I did this? Christ, Derek! I'm not your killer."

Derek didn't frown like he usually did when anyone pointed out his faults but smiled. Patting Alex on the shoulder, he said the words we'd waited so long to hear. "I've known you didn't do it for about an hour. The coroner said your DNA wasn't found on Bethany at all—no blood, no skin, no semen. Plus, the state police found the car. Something about a clerical mix up."

Stunned, Alex turned to look at me with a broad smile and then back at Derek. "So I can work this case officially?"

"You'll find your badge sitting on your desk waiting for you."

Barely able to contain my excitement, I forgot where we were and threw my arms around him. "See? I told you he'd come around. This is so great! Now we can move on Michael."

Alex released me from the hug as Derek asked, "Who's Michael?"

"Nobody yet, but we're going to look into a lead we have from some letters Poppy found in Bethany's office this morning. Once we find out anything, I'll let you know what we know."

Derek leveled his gaze on me once more in that way that told me he disapproved of something I'd done. "That Samantha Cooper might be a bitch, but it sounds like you were trespassing. When did you plan on telling me about these letters?"

I flashed him my sweetest smile again. "When you figured out Alex was innocent."

He wanted to read me the riot act about my behavior, but Alex spirited me away with the excuse that we needed to get something to eat and get back to work. We hurried to his office to grab his badge, and as he put it back in its usual place on his belt, I felt happier than I'd felt in days.

"I knew you didn't do it. I never doubted you."

He looked up at me and I saw disbelief in his dark eyes. "Never? Not even once for a second?"

I had doubted him, but that had been my jealousy

coloring the truth more than anything else. He didn't need to know I'd been weak for a few minutes that first day.

"Nope. I've been Team Alex all the way since the beginning of this case. But hey, why didn't you want to tell Derek about Michael? I thought we were going with him being the killer."

Not noticing how I'd changed the subject, he motioned for me to close his office door. When we were alone and no one could hear what we were talking about, he said, "I think it's better for the two of us to investigate Michael and let Derek investigate Samantha. Kill two birds with one stone."

"Is that the only reason?"

He shook his head and twisted his face into a grimace. "The truth is I'm worried Derek won't do well if he has to deal with the county police, which he would in Ellicott City. They won't take him seriously because he's a small town police chief."

I felt a little bad hearing him say that. Derek had never been a great cop, but I had a feeling he did the best he could. "It doesn't sound like you have a lot of faith in him anymore. Is that because he hung on to you being guilty for so long?"

Alex shrugged, but it was clear he did hold that against Derek. "He's a great guy when it comes to cats in trees and making the neighbor stop parking in your spot, but he's not very good when it comes to detective work."

"Ouch. You're going to make me want to defend our chief with that kind of talk."

"Maybe you're right. Maybe I'm still angry about how easily he thought I could kill Bethany like that. Whatever it is, I think you and I have better resources to get to the truth of this case and Michael Thompson, so better to leave Derek in the dark for a little while longer. On that note, I think it's time I call in one of those better resources."

Taking his phone out, he dialed a number as I wondered who this resource could be. "Have you been holding out on your partner?" I joked, hoping that's all it was. I didn't want to think he'd truly been hiding things from me. Not knowing he'd gone to see Bethany after leaving my house on Sunday was more than enough secrets for me.

He dodged my question and began talking to his friend from his days on the force in Baltimore. "St. Clair, it's Alex. How've you been?"

John St. Clair's answer made him chuckle. "Nope, still just partners in crime. That's what I'm calling about. I need your help with a case we're working. I need to find out if a man named Michael Thompson has a record, but I need to see the reports on any arrests too. He's from Ellicott City, though."

Alex stood silently listening to St. Clair for a few moments more before he said, "Okay, anything you can find out I appreciate it. Nine o'clock sounds good. If it's good for Poppy, I'll bring her along too."

My curiosity piqued, I waited until he ended the call and asked, "Where are we going at nine o'clock? Are we meeting St. Clair somewhere?"

"Yeah. He's going to get all he can on Michael Thompson and meet us at Schultz's at nine."

"Schultz's? Is that an old haunt of yours?" I joked, happy to think I'd get to see more of his life before he came to Sunset Ridge.

"One of the oldest. It's not much, but hopefully, you

won't hate it."

Looking across the desk at him, I smiled and reminded him who he was talking to. "I've spent many a night at the corner bar, Alex. You're looking at the poster child for old haunts. I'm sure I'll love it."

I liked the idea of seeing St. Clair again since I'd enjoyed the time we'd spent with him a few months before. He was funny and brought out a lightness in Alex I rarely saw. But why did we need his help?

"What can John do that you can't? Don't you two have the same ability to check if Michael Thompson has a record?"

Sitting behind his desk, he explained, "I can find that out, but I can't get a look at the reports since Ellicott City is under the county control. St. Clair has a connection with the county, though, so I'm hoping he'll be able to get the details."

"Is there some reason they wouldn't just give them to you, a Sunset Ridge police officer?" I asked as I threw my coat over the back of a chair and took a seat.

"It seems our illustrious police chief got into it with someone in the sheriff's office a while back, so we haven't had an easy time getting much of anything you'd call support from them since. Now you see why I didn't want him handling this part of the case."

"Ah, so there is method to your madness."

He smiled that sexy grin that never failed to make my stomach flip and arched a single, dark eyebrow. "Always."

Chapter Twenty

S CHULTZ'S REMINDED ME of my father's bar in some ways. Although it was certainly dingier than McGuire's and had a far grittier feel to it, the place had a warm, friendly vibe that made me feel right at home. We walked in through the front door to find the bar empty, except for the bartender and a few patrons who sat in front of him watching an old television above his head. John St. Clair sat on a barstool near a red and blue neon sign advertising some beer I'd never heard of. Smiling when he saw us, he opened his arms wide and came to greet us.

"Alex Montero, good to see you again!" he said as they shook hands. "How the hell are you?"

"Too long away from this place, I think. How've you been, St. Clair?"

"Same old, same old. You know it is."

St. Clair looked past Alex and pushed him out of the way to say hello to me. "Poppy McGuire, the investigative journalist turned detective and the best looking partner this guy has ever had. How are you, darlin'?"

He encircled his arms around me to give me a bear hug that nearly took my breath away and made answering how I was doing impossible. When he finally released me, I inhaled deeply for a few seconds and answered his question, happy to see him again.

"I've been okay. It's good to see you again, John."

My use of his first name made him laugh, and he clapped Alex on the back as he led us to a table near the back of the bar. "I think she's the only person other than my mother who calls me John. So what's going on up there in that tiny town of yours? It sounds like you two are neck-deep in something."

We all sat down at a round table with uneven legs that made his beer splash over the sides of his glass. Realizing we hadn't gotten drinks when we walked in, he raised his hand and waved to the bartender at the front of the room.

Alex stopped him, though. "I can get our drinks. You two talk while I grab a scotch for me and…" He looked down at me for an answer to what I wanted. "Light beer?"

This case had been too hard for a light beer. Shaking my head, I pointed at him. "I'll have what you're having."

For a moment, Alex looked surprised that I'd want a scotch too, but he simply smiled and headed off toward the bar to get the drinks, leaving me alone with St. Clair.

"He's a good guy, you know?" he said as he raised his glass to his lips.

I did know that. In the months that I'd worked with Alex, he'd shown me time and time again how good a man he was, and this case, even though it had made me question him for a few hours, had ended up only strengthening my belief in that goodness I'd found in him.

Turning my head to watch him as he made small talk with one of the men sitting at the bar, I nodded my agreement with St. Clair's assessment of him. "He is."

"So what about you, Poppy McGuire? What should I know about you?"

I looked over at him, unsure where the conversation was going. "There's not much to know about me, to be honest. Small town girl living a small town life. Pretty boring stuff compared to you here in the big city."

St. Clair shook his head. "I don't think so. My friend wouldn't spend so much time with you if all you were was some ordinary, run-of-the-mill, small town girl. If Alex finds you interesting, there's a whole lot more going on with you than meets the eye."

I had to smile at his assumptions. I liked to think there was more to me than what the gossips in Sunset Ridge liked to tell everyone, but most days I simply felt like ordinary Poppy McGuire.

"What makes you think he finds me interesting?" I asked, knowing that he probably thought I was fishing for compliments. What I really wanted was some clue to understand why the man I loved still hadn't let me into his heart like I believed he could. While the reason for my joking around to hide my true feelings was something he knew all about, Alex's way of keeping himself closed off from even me made me unsure we'd ever move from where we were to something more.

St. Clair looked up toward the bar and then back at me. His dark brown eyes filling with admiration, he smiled and said, "I've only seen him look like this with one other person. Since I know how he felt about her, I have to assume he finds you far more than merely interesting."

Her. St. Clair wouldn't even use her name, like some word he didn't want to say in front of me for fear I'd know the importance it held. But I knew what she was to Alex—what she continued to be to him.

I couldn't go on with her specter haunting my time with him, though, so I swallowed hard and said her name. "Helena. His wife."

"The only other person I've ever seen Alex truly care for. He cares about his friends. We all know that, but it's not the same. I see it whenever he looks at you, and I hear it when he talks about you."

The right words suddenly seemed impossible to find, so I sat silently smiling at the compliment I understood in St. Clair's words. Nothing would make me happier than to know I came anywhere close to the place he held her.

"And you care about him too. I don't know you nearly as well as I do him, but I see it written all over your face. Have you told him? Not that he wouldn't know, but we men can be stupid sometimes."

My cheeks flushed the warmth that came from my usual blushing when I was embarrassed, and St. Clair chuckled. "Maybe you are that simple small town girl you claim to be, Poppy McGuire. What do I know about anything, right? I'm just a single guy, but I remember when Alex and Helena were dating. I knew it was real then too."

"Did you tell him you knew?" I asked, curious how Alex and his friends acted around each other when they weren't talking about work or drinking beers together.

"I mentioned it once or twice, but everyone knew and we were happy for him. Well, most of us. Ken didn't think she wasn't right for Alex. I never told him what he said and I know Ken never told him. It was probably just him being jealous. Guys are like that. We all want to be happy and to have our friends be happy, but sometimes we can't find the right way to say it."

Curious, I started to ask more about Ken Bryer but Alex returned to the table with our drinks and I didn't have to chance. St. Clair and Alex immediately launched into a discussion about how Schultz's hadn't changed in all the years they'd been coming there, so I quietly listened as I sipped my very strong scotch and soda and liked that his friend had the ability to bring out a side to Alex I hadn't seen much of since this case began.

"Do you remember the time I got so drunk after fighting those guys from the tenth and you had to carry me home up the three flights of stairs to my apartment?" St. Clair asked with a big belly laugh.

Alex smiled and turning toward me, explained, "You see how big he is? Try carrying all that up all those stairs. This guy was like dead weight. I wasn't sure I'd see him at work the next day, but lo and behold, he showed up right on time for his shift. He looked like a bus had hit him, but he was there."

I chuckled at the thought of St. Clair that drunk. Much larger than Alex, I imagined it would take nearly a bottle of whisky to get him that loaded. "I bet you were hurting that day."

He closed his eyes and grinned. "You have no idea. I swore off the hard stuff since that night and haven't gone back to it." Raising his glass, he said, "Now it's just beer for me, but it's still good enough for a toast. To my good friend and his good friend."

Alex and I clinked glasses and then tapped ours on

St. Clair's while he toasted his friend in return. "To the kind of friendships that last forever."

I took another sip of my drink and curious about their third friend asked, "Why didn't you ask Ken to join us tonight?"

St. Clair quickly answered, "Ken doesn't drink. Hasn't for years. So asking him to hang out at a bar would be a waste of time."

"You guys do make an odd group, you know that? You're gregarious, St. Clair. Alex is quiet but when he comes out of his shell, he's got that life of the party thing simmering in there. But Ken is nothing like you two."

They looked at each other and nodded. "I guess you're right," Alex said. "Ken's a unique kind of guy, but that's probably because he spends so much time with the dead."

St. Clair joked about how he could never do a coroner's job, and Alex and I agreed. For me, the whole dead thing definitely creeped me out. I considered telling them how odd even his office felt when I visited just a few days earlier, but I assumed they knew since they'd been friends with him for all those years. So I kept my comment to myself as they gradually finished talking about the old days and turned to the case at hand.

"So, what's going on with this Michael Thompson guy? You sounded like you were dealing with something big when I talked to you on the phone," St. Clair said before taking a swallow of his beer.

Alex took a deep breath and let it out slowly. "Bethany was murdered Sunday night. I've been the prime suspect since about two minutes after she was found."

It felt like the entire bar fell silent. I saw the pain in

his eyes when he said those words and wondered if it would ever leave him. Or me.

"Who'd want to kill Bethany?"

St. Clair's question was the same one everyone had asked and we still didn't know the answer.

"We think it was Michael Thompson," I said. "They had been dating a while back and he didn't seem to be able to let go when they broke up. I found threatening letters he wrote her."

Alex took a sip of his drink and slowly lowered his glass to the table. "They slit her throat."

"Like Helena?" St. Clair asked in horror. Shaking his head, he added, "No way is this a coincidence. Nobody has two people in their life murdered the same way. Would this Michael Thompson know how Helena died?"

"I don't know. All we know about him is he was seeing Bethany before I started dating her and he's lost his mind now because his wife took the kids and left him when she found out he was cheating on her."

His shoulders sagged as he explained what we knew about Thompson, and I knew the stress of this case was finally getting to him. I gently touched his hand resting on his thigh to let him know he wasn't alone and I believed in him.

"Did you find out anything about him, John?" I asked. If he could give us something that would show Michael was the kind of man who would be violent, we could take that to Derek and have him brought in.

St. Clair reached into his coat and took out a sheet of paper he began to read from. "He's been through the ringer lately, it seems. The police have had to go out to his house eight times in the past six months. Most of the calls have been about him doing strange things like blasting music out his window in the middle of the night and sitting in his car for hours on end. He doesn't sound balanced. Once, though, back in September, was because the neighbors reported hearing screaming between a man and a woman."

"That was probably when his wife left him," Alex suggested. "Anything else?"

"The report said that the woman involved in the incident was named Mariah Lewis," St. Clair said. "Maiden name? The officers noted that Thompson was clearly upset when they arrived and spoke to them, but the female, Ms. Lewis, appeared calm."

Alex and I looked at each other in stunned confusion. What would Mariah Lewis have been doing with Michael Thompson at his house in Ellicott City?

I asked, "Did they describe the woman? Was she injured? Had he hurt her?"

St. Clair scanned his notes and then lifted his head. "No injuries. It seems that they were just making too much noise with their fighting and the neighbors called because they were afraid it was getting out of hand. All it says about the woman was she was in her early thirties."

What was going on? Why had Mariah been anywhere near Thompson when she lived in Ohio? Had she been a part of some conspiracy with him to kill her sister? And if so, why?

Clearly shaken by the information, Alex thanked St. Clair for his help and stood to leave. "We better get going. I'll be in touch."

Before I could get my coat on, he walked away toward the door. I gave St. Clair a meek smile, not knowing what to say, and finally just said, "He's taking this case hard. Thanks for your help, though, St. Clair."

He stood to hug me goodbye and joked, "You finally got my name right, Poppy. Take care of our guy there. He says you have the best instincts he's ever seen. Use them and figure out who the hell is trying to make it look like he's a killer again."

I promised I would and ran to catch up with Alex, who stood waiting for me on the sidewalk outside, his coat wide open in the cold night as he stared straight ahead with a look of stunned sadness.

Cradling his face, I kissed his lips. "It's going to be okay. Let's get home. It's getting late."

He just stood there staring down into my eyes. He looked lost, like he didn't know where to turn now. My heart broke for him seeing him like that, and as I buttoned up his coat so he wouldn't freeze to death, I wished I knew a way to bring him the peace I knew he so desperately wanted.

Peace about what happened to Bethany, but even more now, peace about the death of Helena.

He stopped my fingers as I moved to the top button. "We need to talk to Mariah Lewis tonight. I don't want her leaving town without explaining why she was with Michael Thompson."

"Are you sure? You look pretty shaken up."

"Michael Thompson is the best lead we have to solve Bethany's murder, and now we know Mariah was with him recently. That's too much of a coincidence. We need to find out what happened to make him kill her and if her sister was part of it."

I brought his ice cold hands up to my lips and kissed them. "Then let's go and talk to Mariah."

Chapter Twenty-One

DEREK HAD PUT Mariah Lewis up at the Hotel Piermont, and she was awake when we knocked on her door at nearly eleven o'clock. I knew Alex wanted to force answers out of her, but I hoped he wouldn't be too hard on her, just in case she had nothing to do with anything Thompson had done and was truly just a grieving sister.

We sat down at the round table too large for the hotel room, and as I stared at her, struck by how similar she looked to her sister, he didn't waste any time getting to the heart of the matter. "How long have you known Michael Thompson?" he demanded to know.

Mariah narrowed her eyes in confusion and shook her head. "I don't know anyone by that name. Who is he?"

"The man whose house you were at in Ellicott City in September when the police were called because you and he were fighting so loudly his neighbors worried someone might get hurt. Your name is on the police record. So what's your relationship with him?"

"I don't have one! You're confused. I've never met this Michael Thompson person. Why are you asking me this?"

Alex continued to press her to admit she knew him. "Police reports don't lie, Mariah, so you can drop the act. You were at his house with him, so you obviously know him. I want answers, and I want them now."

She jumped from her seat and began to cry. "I don't have any answers for you! Why are you doing this? I just lost my sister. Are you being this way because everyone in this town thinks you're the one who killed her?"

I saw Alex wince like what she said pained him. Even hearing her say that made me sick to my stomach, but in the state she was in, she wanted to lash out.

"Yeah, I've heard all about it since they dragged me back to this godforsaken town. They think you did it, and now you come to me looking to blame my sister's death on me in some way."

Before things got out of hand and there was no turning back, I stood from the table and walked over to talk to her and hopefully help her see that's not what we wanted to do to her. I approached her as she began to sob harder and said, "We aren't blaming you, Mariah. That's not what this is about. Alex cared about Bethany. He would never hurt her just like you wouldn't. We just want to understand why you would be at that man's house, a man who wrote Bethany letters threatening her after she broke up with him."

Mariah stopped crying, and looking away, she quietly said, "The only thing I can think of is this thing we used to do when we were younger. Whenever one of us got into trouble, we'd claim to be the other. We even have fake IDs with our pictures but the other's name on them. We looked so much alike that it was easy to fool people. Maybe she gave the police my name when it was her."

Behind us, Alex said angrily, "I'm assuming you can prove you weren't in Ellicott City when this incident occurred?"

She nodded and dried her eyes. "The first time I've left Ohio in years was to visit Bethany in December. If it was September, it was her, not me with him."

While I tried to get my brain around all she'd said and all we'd found out about Michael Thompson, Alex stood and brusquely thanked her as he walked out without another word. I apologized for upsetting her and ran after him. When I finally caught up with him in the art-deco style lobby of the hotel, he looked more lost than earlier when I'd found him outside Schultz's.

"Hey, what's going on? This is good news, Alex. If it was Bethany there with Thompson, then we know they fought and he was upset with her. I don't know why he waited all these months to finally lash out, but he's our guy."

Almost as if he didn't hear me, he nodded and said, "Yeah, I guess that's it."

A group of people coming back from a night of drinking stumbled past us, so I pulled him by the arm toward the door and out of their way. "Let's go talk to Derek and tell him what we have. He'll be able to bring Michael Thompson in and then this will all be over."

I saw a look of recognition came over Alex's face, and he smiled. "Let's go talk to him then."

Ten minutes later, we sat in Derek's living room decorated in typical bachelor fashion with a ridiculously large TV and little else but two chairs and a couch for visitors to sit on. Wearing a pair of sweatpants and a Ravens t-shirt, he propped his feet up on the coffee table to listen to us unravel our tale of Michael Thompson and his need to hurt Bethany because she'd left him.

When we finished laying out our case, he put his hands behind his head and made a clucking sound.

"Sounds pretty good to me. I never knew Bethany the way you described her, though. She sure changed from that sweet girl I knew when she first arrived in town."

His comment made me realize in some ways she really had changed. But in other ways that I hoped people would remember her for, she was the same great girl who had come to Sunset Ridge after college at the University of Maryland and fell in love with the small town she said reminded her of the one she grew up in.

"I'll have him brought in for questioning in the morning. You two can feel free to sit in."

Alex said nothing and turned to leave, but I figured I should warn Derek about Michael Thompson's tenuous hold on reality. "He's got problems, so keep that in mind when you talk to him."

Derek looked over at Alex as he walked out his front door and then back at me. "It looks like he's not the only one."

I found Alex waiting for me once again, this time looking up at the night stars as he stood in the cold. Wanting to help but not knowing what had made him so unhappy, I said, "How about we go to McGuire's for a drink? It probably won't be too busy, and we can talk."

He closed his eyes and took a deep breath in before opening them again and lowering his head to look at me. Blowing the air out of his mouth so it billowed like frosty white smoke next to my head, he nodded and in a resigned voice said, "Okay."

It felt like it took everything he had inside him to say that one word.

WE FOUND THE table furthest away from the bar where my father and a few diehard McGuire's regulars sat talking about the upcoming Super Bowl and the Patriots' dynasty. I poured us two glasses of scotch and promised I'd tell my father about the case later before returning to join Alex.

I placed his drink in front of him and sat down. He still wore that lost look on his face that bothered me. I wanted to rid him of that, to remind him that he was exactly where he belonged with the one person he never had to doubt.

He took a few gulps of his drink and finally said more than a single word. "I wasn't looking for forever with her, but I thought we were at least truthful. It seems like I was wrong in that too."

"I'm sorry, Alex. I'm sure she just went there to talk to him. She was crazy about you."

He sighed and a frown replaced the lost look he'd worn for the past hour. "You know when Helena was murdered, they thought it was me at first, and then when that didn't work out, they told me it was probably someone she'd been seeing on the side because the way they killed her was so personal. It didn't matter how many times I told them she wouldn't do that to me. They still kept saying it was a jilted lover who did it, not that they ever really stopped believing it was me. They never thought for a minute that neither one of those theories were right."

I wanted to say Bethany was never right for him, no matter how much she liked him. I wanted to tell him that she hadn't lied to him so much as just acted the way she always did with men. I couldn't do that to him, though. He deserved to think of their time together as more special than that.

"A lot of times the police don't see the people involved in a case, Alex. All they see are victims and suspects and evidence."

He took a drink and smiled at me. "Not you, though. Maybe that's why you have such good instincts for this. You see the people."

I wanted to change the subject, if only to get his mind off what he'd just found out about Bethany, so I said, "I can't figure out what you three guys—you, Ken, and St. Clair—had in common to make you all get together to be such good friends, you know that? You're three totally different people."

Just the mention of his friends appeared to ease his mind. With a grin, he explained, "We all began working in law enforcement around the same time. Ken was a little older than John and me and wasn't a detective, but he was an interesting guy. He knew Helena before I did because Manger was his favorite restaurant. That's why he was so thrilled when we got together. He liked to say that he'd always have a great table there from that point on because I was with one of the chefs."

As he sat there enjoying memories from long ago, I wondered what to make of the contradictory statements about the trio's friendship I'd heard from all three men. Then again, it all had been so long ago, and from what I'd seen, men simply didn't seem to read people well, no matter if it was professionally or personally.

Well, most men. I was willing to give my partner a pass on that, and whatever his memories of that time were, they were clouded by a loss he still hadn't gotten over.

Chapter Twenty-Two

DEREK WAITED FOR us outside the interrogation room, his happiness at nearing the solution to this case evident by the huge grin on his face. I wasn't sure I'd ever seen him look so happy when he didn't have a drink in his hand or a woman on his arm.

Not that I blamed him. I, too, couldn't wait for this case to be over and done, but more than that, I worried the longer it dragged on, the longer Alex would suffer not only because of this case but also because of the one he never was able to solve.

Rubbing his hands together, Derek said, "Good morning! You ready for this?"

I looked at the closed door of the room and wondered how crazy Michael Thompson was this early in the day. He definitely seemed like the kind of guy who could go around the bend with just a tiny bit of caffeine in him.

"How is he?" I asked, bracing myself for some madness to come.

"Yeah, he was a mess when we saw him," Alex added.

Derek shrugged. "He doesn't seem too bad to me, but I only saw him as they were bringing him in. I had them keep the cuffs on him just in case, though. I don't need some crazy bastard tearing up the spot where I get my coffee every day."

A chuckle escaped my lips, and as Derek walked into the room, I turned and whispered to Alex, "Glad to see he has his priorities straight."

The smile he'd worn since we met at The Grounds that morning grew until it nearly stretched from ear to ear. "That's our chief. Let's hope he can handle this guy."

"If not, I'm ready. He liked me last time."

My first look at Michael Thompson told me something had drastically changed in him. The wild-eyed look he'd worn the entire time we spent with him on that back porch had softened so he looked like any ordinary person handcuffed and waiting to be questioned by the police. Even his posture had relaxed, making him look almost comfortable on the metal folding chair he sat on.

Alex saw the change too, and his face showed his mix of concern and confusion as he sat down across from Thompson. Studying him, he looked at me and shook his head as if to ask what had happened to the man we'd seen.

"Mr. Thompson, I think you know Officer Montero and Miss McGuire. They're going to be sitting in on our meeting," Derek announced as he opened up the case file and began to flip through the stack of pages the investigation into Bethany's murder had become.

"Elizabeth, right?" Michael Thompson asked timidly. "You were named after your grandmother, you said."

Impressed he remembered, I nodded to let him

know he was correct. "I'm happy to see you doing better today, Michael."

He smiled and it went all the way up to his eyes. "Thank you, and thank you for trying to help me the other night. I wasn't doing well."

"Okay, we need you to answer a few questions, Mr. Thompson," Derek said, ending the brief moment of kindness I'd shared with Michael. "First, how did you know Bethany Lewis?"

"I loved her. She loved me. We were going to be together forever."

An uncomfortable silence hung in the air, and I looked to my right to see Alex silently waiting for Michael to continue. I knew what he was doing as he stared at the man. He was adding up the months to figure out if Bethany had been telling Michael she loved him while she was dating him.

"When did you and Bethany begin dating?" Derek asked, and I couldn't help but marvel at the fact that I sat surrounded by three very different men who'd been with her.

"We started seeing each other last spring. At first I couldn't offer her anything, so it was just once or twice and then we stopped. But then we realized we still cared for each other and started seeing each other all the time by the Fourth of July."

I listened to Michael talk about his relationship with Bethany and tried to remember if she ever mentioned him even in passing in any of our conversations, but she never said anything about anyone named Michael. She hadn't talked about anyone in her life during the spring and summer. She'd appeared to be interested in Alex that whole time.

"What do you mean you started seeing each other all the time by the Fourth?" Alex asked, his characteristic coolness absent from his voice.

"Whenever she would come to where I worked because her paper used us, we got together."

"Asher and Mitchell?" I asked.

Michael nodded. "Yes. I worked there until they let me go a couple months ago."

"Okay, now about the incident in September when the police had to come to your house because you and Bethany were fighting. What happened?"

Knitting his brows, he frowned as he answered, "She told me that she'd fallen in love with someone else. She said she met someone here in Sunset Ridge and she couldn't see me anymore. I told I couldn't let her go, so we got into a fight. I never hit her or did anything but yell. I was upset. I loved her, and I thought she loved me. I lost everything just to be with her, and then she wanted to leave me for someone else. I couldn't let her do that."

Derek stopped writing in his notes and looked up. "So all those months passed by and you couldn't handle that she left you and you killed her."

"What?" he shrieked, his expression pure horror at what he'd just heard. "I would never hurt Bethany. Someone killed her?"

He buried his face in his hands and began sobbing like a baby as the three of us looked at each other. Was he just acting like he didn't know she'd been murdered, or was this truly the first he'd heard of the crime?

Never one for having much respect for emotions, Derek asked, "Are you saying you didn't know Bethany Lewis had been murdered, Mr. Thompson?"

Michael dropped his hands from his face and the realness of his tears was evident all over his drenched cheeks. "Of course I didn't know. How could you ask that? I loved her. If I knew she died, I would have been beside myself with grief."

Derek seemed confused as to what to ask next, so I jumped in and said, "Because the letters you wrote her sounded pretty threatening. You didn't sound like you'd be beside yourself with grief in them."

Wiping his face, he stopped crying and looked toward me with horror in his eyes. "You think I'd kill her? I loved her. I would never hurt her for anything in the world. I couldn't hurt her like that."

"Like what?" Derek asked, jumping on his comment as an admission that he knew more than he was pretending to.

"Like murder," Michael answered, much to Derek's disappointment. "I would never do that. Why would anyone kill her? She was beautiful and sweet. I loved her."

"You didn't sound like this in those letters you wrote her. You sounded like a man who wasn't going to let anyone else have her if you couldn't, even if that meant killing her," I said even as my gut began to tell me Michael could no more kill Bethany than I could.

Confused, he shook his head and asked, "What letters?"

I looked over at Derek as he lifted them out of the file. "The letters you wrote telling her you couldn't go on without her and you couldn't let her continue living if she left you."

Michael raised his still handcuffed wrists to move the letters in front of him and began to read. He scanned the words he'd written, and I saw the sadness settle into his face as they came back to haunt him.

He looked up, his eyes full of sorrow, and fighting back tears said, "I know what these look like, but I would never kill anyone, especially not Bethany. I wanted her back. I never gave up on the idea that we'd be together again."

"They look bad, Mr. Thompson," Derek warned. "You pretty much say you're going to kill her."

"No!" he cried out. "I was just out of my mind when my wife left me and took the kids. I got help, though, and once they put me on my meds, I was okay. I didn't mean to make it seem like I would ever hurt her."

"But you weren't that way when we were at your house yesterday," Alex quietly said next to me. "You didn't look okay then."

"I didn't take my meds for a few days and I went off the rails by going back to the house. But as you can see, I'm okay now. As long as I take the pills my doctor gave me, I'm okay."

He didn't seem to be lying about that. Compared to the wild man I'd tried to connect with the last time we were together, now he seemed downright relaxed, even calm, except for protesting his innocence and mourning the news of Bethany's death. His eyes didn't flash the madness I had seen in him, and his voice remained level, for the most part. Whatever he was taking, it was working this morning.

Alex leaned back in his chair and folded his arms across his chest. "What about the bloody knife on the counter we saw? How do you explain that?"

Hanging his head, Michael pushed up his left sleeve to show us a fresh wound a few inches above his wrist on his forearm. "I wanted to kill myself, but I couldn't when I thought of my kids hearing their dad killed himself, so I didn't do it right. Not even deep enough for stitches."

My heart went out to him. He looked so disappointed that he couldn't even kill himself to put an end to his pain. Next to me, Alex sat crestfallen after hearing Michael's explanation. Like me, he no doubt understood that Michael Thompson probably wasn't Bethany's killer, which meant we were back at square one again with no suspects.

Except him.

Only Derek's mood remained the same after Michael's confession. Pressing on, he asked, still obviously believing he had the killer sitting right in front of him, "Where were you Sunday night between midnight and five in the morning?"

Barely whispering, Michael answered, "My mother's."

All three of us looked at each other in disbelief at his answer. Unable to even keep the sneer from his face, Derek said, "So your answer is that you were at your mom's? Seems pretty convenient, and I'm not sure we're going to be able to take your mother's word for where you were that night. Moms tend to not be very reliable witnesses, Mr. Thompson."

He looked up at Derek and nodded. "I know what it sounds like. I'm a grown man who has to stay at his mother's. You think I'm pathetic. Well, I guess I am. It's just too painful to stay in my own house at night anymore. There's no furniture on the first floor and there's only beds and empty dressers in his kids' rooms and the master bedroom, and all they do is remind me that I have nothing. So I began staying at my mother's every night a few weeks ago around the holidays."

"Wow, that's sad," Derek said quietly as he turned away, unable to even look at Michael after that pathetic explanation.

"Do you have anyone other than your mother who can back up your alibi?" Alex asked.

Michael's eyes opened wide and suddenly he looked like the man we'd met on his back porch. Excited, he nodded his head up and down. "My mother's next door neighbor, Jeanette Childers, called the house at right around one in the morning about her furnace turning off and on and wondering if my mother could send me over to see what was wrong. She woke me up out of a sound sleep. I ended up in her basement for nearly three hours trying to figure out that damn furnace. All you have to do is ask her. She can tell you I was there all night before I got it fixed."

"Your mother's next-door-neighbor?" Derek asked in disbelief.

"Please, just ask her. Mrs. Childers will tell you I was in her basement for hours on Sunday night," Michael begged.

Derek pushed a piece of paper and a pen toward him. "Write down the name and number."

His handcuffs clanking against the metal table, he did as he was ordered and pushed the information back toward Derek. "You'll see. She'll tell you I was there all night."

Alex and I stood to follow Derek out of the room so he could call Michael's mother's neighbor. It seemed like a flimsy alibi to me, but my gut still said this guy wasn't Bethany's killer.

Closing the door, Alex grimaced. "That was not the

man we met at his house. Those pills must be wonder drugs to make him seem normal because he was anything but last night."

Derek shook his head. "I believe you. What I can't believe is that I have to call a suspect's mother and her neighbor to see if his story holds up about the old lady next door with the faulty furnace. It sounds like some kind of awful mystery novel title. The Old Lady and the Faulty Furnace available now in hardcover. Find out what's hiding in that basement."

I stifled a giggle at Derek's joking as Alex's expression told me Michael Thompson's questioning had been an even bigger disappointment to him. I could only imagine how he felt now that our best suspect seemed to be yet another example of a false lead.

"What about Samantha Cooper?" he asked, his voice full of hope.

Shrugging, Derek said, "Nope, she had an alibi. She was at the Hotel Piermont that night with some guy who likes to be smacked around. I had no idea Sunset Ridge was this exciting. Who knew all these people in town had such freaky secrets?"

"So nothing with her?" I asked, hating that she was slipping from our grasp too.

Turning serious, Derek patted Alex on the shoulder. "I'm sorry, but none of the suspects so far have panned out, and if this guy's mother and next-door-neighbor say he was there and there's nothing else to point to him, I'm going to have to let him go."

Quietly, in a voice full of disappointment, Alex said, "I understand."

"That doesn't mean I think you did it, Alex. It just means we're going to have to take a better look at this case and find the clue we've been missing so far."

Derek left us standing there in the hallway to call Michael Thompson's mother, and I hated what I had to say. Taking Alex's hand in mine, I gave it a squeeze of support and said what I knew he had already admitted to himself.

"He's not our murderer, Alex. I wish it wasn't this way, but Derek's right. He's not the killer."

Struggling not to frown, he nodded and said in a low voice, "I know, but that leaves us back at square one. Mariah didn't do it. Samantha didn't do it. Michael didn't do it. Then who murdered Bethany and why? We've looked into her life and only found those three people who seem to have any motive. But none had opportunity. Did she have other enemies we don't know about?"

I hated seeing the pain in his eyes when he said that. I knew what he was thinking, but I couldn't let him get discouraged about this case.

"We'll find the answer, Alex. Don't get down about this. We will. I'm not giving up, and I won't let you give up."

He tried to put on a good face, but he couldn't pretend enough to smile. "I know. I can see why I was the prime suspect, though. I'm the only one who doesn't have an alibi other than being alone, which you know as well I do is no alibi at all."

I kissed him on the cheek and wished we were alone in my house so I could take him into my arms and kiss him long and deep to take his mind off all the terrible things surrounding us. It broke my heart to see the man I loved so disheartened.

"Don't worry. We'll figure this out."

Lowering his eyes, he looked away and said, "I'm sorry, Poppy. If I never answered her call or never went over there when she asked me to, you wouldn't have to be standing here with the only person the police should be looking at."

I cradled his face and looked into those brown eyes so full of sadness. "Don't think that way. Please listen to me. You went to a friend when they asked you to. You have nothing to apologize for with that. Come back to my house with me and we'll curl up on the couch and watch a movie. We won't think about this case for a few hours. We'll just let our minds go blank and enjoy time together."

He gave me a tiny smile but shook his head. "I think I'll just go home for a little while since I'm not scheduled until tonight. I'll give you a call later, okay?"

"Okay. My invitation will be open all day, so if you change your mind, my couch and I will be waiting."

He nodded, and as he walked away down the hall toward the door of the police station, he said, "Thanks, Poppy. I'll talk to you in a little bit."

I wanted to run after him and tell him how much I loved him and that we wouldn't stop until we solved this case, but he needed time to be alone, even if it was only going to end up making things worse. I understood, though. Sometimes a person just had to be with themselves when everything in life looked bad.

As I walked toward my house, I promised myself and him no matter what it took, I'd figure out some way to get a break in this case. Alex deserved at least that from someone he loved.

Chapter Twenty-Three

CURLED UP UNDER my throw, I sat on my couch and prepared to binge-watch TV until I heard from Alex. The Weather Channel had a marathon of some monster storm show I hadn't seen many episodes of yet, so I settled in with a large glass of root beer, my favorite drink of choice for long term television viewing, and a bowl of buttery popcorn and began watching about some supercell tornado that ravaged the Midwest in November 2001.

I wanted to get lost in the program, but try as I may, I couldn't stop thinking about the case. The Weather Channel usually helped me forget my troubles through some strange way of replacing concern for whatever bothered me with concern for those terrorized by the storms, but this afternoon even the devastation wreaked by Mother Nature couldn't push my own worries about Alex out of my mind.

He looked so sad when he left the police station. When Derek thought he was the killer, he'd been hurt by the betrayal of the people he worked with, but this was different. Now he wasn't the main suspect anymore, but the question of who killed Bethany still hung over his head. It didn't matter that Derek and the rest of the force didn't think he was guilty. As long as her killer remained free, there would always be that niggling doubt if Alex had anything to do with her death, just like with Helena's murder.

I thought about calling him to see if he needed anything, but I knew what he needed, even if I didn't want to give him that. I worried that if he spent too much time alone, he'd crawl inside his own head and get lost in the misery that always remained somewhere hidden but always threatening to take him over. Just as he'd never really gotten over Helena's death, Bethany's now pressed on him, and I wasn't sure he could handle wondering if people blamed him for both.

Reaching for my phone, I let my finger hover over his name in my contacts for a moment. No, I had to give him what he needed now, but a need of my own simmered inside me, so instead of calling Alex I called my father.

"Poppy, I was hoping you'd call me today. When you called yesterday and had to get off the phone so quickly, I worried something terrible had happened."

"Nothing more terrible than what's already happened, Dad," I admitted sadly. "I would have told you if anything else came up in the case."

My father's voice eased my mind, just as I knew it would. "I saw Derek last night and he told me Alex was probably going to be in the clear today. So why do you sound like you lost your best friend?"

I knew that was just my father's way of saying I sounded sad, but that description was more accurate than he could know. I was afraid I was losing my best friend. This case had been torture for Alex, and now it felt like he was slipping away into something I wasn't sure I could save him from.

"It's nothing. This case. We've run into another dead end, and I don't know what to do."

"What you always do. Look for the question you haven't asked yet. Then you'll find the answer, and hopefully it will be the answer to this mystery of who killed poor Bethany."

Poor Bethany.

In all the investigating leads and worrying about Alex, I hadn't thought much about her, except for feeling guilty about how bad a friend I'd been. I hadn't told a soul about it for fear of what they'd think of me and my petty jealousy, but I needed to get it off my chest. Only my father knew how wracked with envy I'd been when she and Alex got together, so I took the opportunity to unburden my conscience to him and hoped even he didn't think I was an awful person for what I'd felt.

"Dad, can I tell you something?" I asked, knowing the answer but dragging my feet about finally telling someone about who I really was.

"Of course, Poppy. You can tell me anything, honey," he answered in his usual sympathetic voice, giving me the green light to confess my darkest sin.

I took a deep breath and let it out in a rush. "I wasn't a very good friend to Bethany, Dad. Her death has forced me to see that, and I can't seem to get past it."

The phone fell silent for a long pause until he asked, "Why would you say that?"

"You know how I felt about her and Alex dating. I was a horrible person the whole time, even after I convinced myself that I accepted they were together. I never stopped wishing they'd break up. That's not a good friend, and she never knew how terrible I was."

"Oh, Poppy, I know it's hard to fight making her a saint, but like everyone else, she was human. You're no different. You liked Alex and were jealous that she was with him. That doesn't make you a terrible person. It makes you human."

Tears welled in my eyes, ready to roll down my face. "I wasn't a good friend, Dad. Not one minute the whole time they were together did I really want them to be happy. I was so consumed by jealousy that their happiness never even occurred to me. What kind of person does that with people they care about?"

As I began to cry at the truth of what I'd been, my father said, "You're being too hard on yourself, Poppy. You didn't do anything to break them up, did you? I can't imagine you did."

"No, I never did anything like that. I just secretly hoped she would get tired of him and move on, like she always did. But even that shows I wasn't as good a friend to her as she was to me."

"Again, you're making her a saint when she was a mere mortal like the rest of us. Bethany was a girl who liked to have a good time. There was nothing wrong with that, so don't think I'm saying there was. But even someone on the outside like me knew she and Alex wouldn't last very long. She was a woman who needed attention and a lot of it. She'd gotten used to having that in her life, and I don't think Alex could ever give her enough of what she needed."

She couldn't get what she needed from him. He needed things from me I wasn't sure I could give him. I didn't give her the support she needed from a friend. He might never be able to give me what I needed because he was still in love with a ghost.

Was love in all its incarnations just need none of us seemed to be able to fulfill?

"I wish she was still here so I could apologize for being a petty, jealous fool."

"Poppy, Derek told me she was seeing some married man when she was supposed to be dating Alex. I think it's possible you're not seeing the real person because your view is clouded by guilt, but you have nothing to be guilty about. Caring about someone doesn't make you a bad person."

"I think it breaks one of the commandments to covet thy neighbor's boyfriend, Dad."

My father had strayed from the church after my mother's death, so any quoting of scripture fell on deaf ears. "Yeah, well, I don't think that's how the commandment was written and you weren't coveting Alex as much as secreting pining away for him. Does that make you feel better?"

I couldn't help but smile at the way he phrased things sometimes. "Not really, but now I'm just a little creeped out by you saying I was pining away for him."

"All I'm saying is Bethany was a flesh and bone human being with all the flaws that come with having feet of clay. Don't beat yourself up for how you felt about her being with Alex. Something tells me she may have felt very much the same way when she found out you were with him. That didn't change how she cared for you just like it didn't change how you cared about her. Give yourself a break. You never did anything to sabotage their time together. Your conscience can rest easy, Poppy."

Sighing, I tried to believe what he said, but I couldn't. My conscience wasn't convinced. "Maybe someday. Now I guess I just need to accept what happened and hope she is somewhere knowing that I wish I hadn't been so jealous that I couldn't be happy for her."

"Jealousy is like a cancer, but you didn't let it overtake you. Give yourself some credit. Others have done far worse when that green demon has taken them over. Just like you hope she can forgive you, you have to forgive yourself. When you do, you'll see you aren't that person you're making yourself out to be."

I dried my eyes and took a deep breath to let what my father was saying settle into my head. He was right. I hadn't done anything so awful it couldn't be forgiven. This was just my sadness at her death and regret I'd never get to see her again to tell her how much I admired her love of life. The truth was, like me, she had been human in all her choices. I needed to remember that.

"Thanks, Dad. I'll try. Maybe when we solve this case I'll be able to finally see things like you say."

"About that, have you and Alex had any success after finding that man in Ellicott City? Derek seemed to think he'd be able to wrap this case up today. He was buying drinks for the whole bar to celebrate last night."

The disappointment from Michael Thompson's alibi turning out to be good made my shoulders sag. Lead after lead had seemed so promising, and yet every single one had turned into a dead end. Alex may not have become the prime suspect again, but we had nothing to go on after Thompson's mother and her next-door-neighbor happily gave Derek chapter and verse about how Michael had spent all those hours working on that broken furnace.

"No. It appears Derek's celebrating was a little premature. The guy turned out to have an ironclad alibi during the hours when the murder took place, so it can't be him," I admitted, not able to hide my disappointment at how this case had turned out so far.

"Well, I'm sure you two will be onto the next suspect in no time," my father said trying to be supportive, even though he had no idea what he was talking about.

Normally, I didn't mind my father's empty platitudes since I knew they were meant to make me feel better, no matter how little they succeeded in doing that. Today, though, it wasn't enough.

"I don't see how, Dad. We have nowhere else to look. Bethany had a few enemies and none of them seem to be our killer. I'm not sure what theory we can turn to now."

"It seems to me that if Bethany wasn't the reason for this, then you need to find another reason and there you'll find your murderer. Just be careful, Poppy. I know Alex will be by your side, but be careful all the same. I'd feel better if it was Derek and Alex handling this one, to be honest."

Chuckling, I thought about what Alex had said about Derek's detective skills and tried to imagine the two men working together on a case. Nothing good could come of that.

"I think Alex would rather work alone if that was the case. Derek isn't exactly great when it comes to this kind of thing."

My father made a clucking voice with his tongue meant to show his disapproval of my attack on our police chief. "You underestimate Derek, Poppy. He's far more clever than you or Alex give him credit for."

On this point, I wouldn't bother arguing with him. He'd always had a special place in his heart for Derek Hampton. I wasn't sure if it was because he admired him for the football star he'd been in high school or simply because the Sunset Ridge chief of police had always been good to me, but my father wouldn't hear anything truly negative about Derek.

"Ok, Dad. Thanks for listening. I'm sure you didn't call to hear today's episode of true confessions, but thanks."

"Nonsense. I call my daughter to hear whatever she has to say, good or bad. I just hope you'll listen to me, which you so rarely do," he said with a teasing lilt to his voice that told me no matter what I thought of myself, he still saw me as the best daughter in the world.

"I'm going to go watch about some monster storm in Florida on the Weather Channel and just let my mind relax for a while until Alex calls me. I'll talk to you later, okay?"

"Okay, honey. Call me if you need anything. I'm here with both ears open if you want to talk."

"Thanks, Dad. Love you."

I ended the call after he told me like always that he loved me too. Once again, my finger twitched to press Alex's name in my contact list, but I didn't and tossed my phone on the couch next to me. He'd call when he was ready. Until then, I'd watch more disasters from Mother Nature and hope the Weather Channel's obsession with death and destruction would take my mind off my real life problems.

Chapter Twenty-Four

T HE CURRENT EPISODE featured a breakdown of the storms Florida had suffered through in the spring of 2011 to show how what was going on now in January five years later was so similar. Torrential rains, high winds, and even tornado outbreaks had ravaged the entire state back then, and the way it was looking with the forecast for the rest of this month, Florida would be going through much of the same horrific weather patterns it had that spring of 2011.

Halfway through the program, the hosts began talking about highs and lows and other weather features I wasn't really interested in, so my mind turned on again and I began to think about what that clue my father had mentioned could be. Then I remembered that book with the bloody fingerprint I'd found in Bethany's that night Derek and I had gone there. Now that Alex was cleared by the DNA tests, the fingerprint could be the solution to this whole case.

Throwing off the blanket, I tore up to my bedroom to get the book from between my mattress and box spring, excited about what I believed would be the clue Alex and I would need to find Bethany's killer. I found it right where I left it in that space below my head where I slept each night and took it back downstairs examine it once again. I knew it had one fingerprint the police would be able to use, but maybe it held other clues too.

As I sat on my couch literally on the edge of my seat, I slowly flipped through the pages, looking for anything that might shine even the tiniest bit of light on who had hidden in that car and slit Bethany's throat that night. In the margins, I saw scribbles she had made on some of the self-help ideas the author suggested, but none of them seemed to have anything to do with much more than her work at *The Eagle*. I reached the end of the book to find a few more insignificant words jotted down on the inside back cover, but there were no more fingerprints left and no other clues I could see.

I needed to get it to the police, but instead of taking it to Alex, I decided to ask John St. Clair for help. My gut told me to keep this from my partner and anyone in the Sunset Ridge police department for now. Derek would likely read me the riot act about touching his crime scene when he found out, so it was a better choice to ask St. Clair for help and give Derek the answer to who the killer was when I found out. Even he wouldn't be able to reprimand me when he had that in his hands, so better to go with the fait accompli instead.

I called St. Clair hoping he would be willing to help me, even though I wasn't following procedure. "I'm sorry to bother you, John, but I was wondering if you could help me with something. Alex doesn't know about this, and I'd like it if he didn't know."

St. Clair chuckled in that deep way only a big man like him could. "I knew there was more to you than the small town girl. What can I help you with?"

Looking down at the dried bloody fingerprint on

Bethany's book, I said, "I need you to help me figure out whose fingerprint is on a book I have. It has to do with the case."

"And you don't want Alex to know? I'm not sure I like where this is going."

I knew what St. Clair was thinking and quickly explained about what Donny and his guys had found. "No, no, it's not that I think it's Alex's. We got the DNA results back from the coroner. Alex is in the clear."

Relieved, St. Clair returned to his usual jovial self. "Good to hear. Well, if you want, you can come into the city and we can see if we can do it tonight. I'm working for a few more hours, so come on down."

"Okay! I'll be there as soon as I can. See you soon!"

Excited, I jumped off the couch to put my shoes and coat on. If luck was on my side, I'd have the killer's identity by the time Alex came on duty.

ST. CLAIR WAVED me toward him as the uniformed officer escorting me into the station pointed in his direction to let me know where to go. Clutching the book tightly in my right hand, I hurried over to his desk and sat down in the chair next to it.

"Thanks so much for helping me. It really means the world to me."

He smiled and squeezed my left hand. "I just hope you aren't too disappointed by the reality compared to what you've seen on TV. Fingerprints don't exactly work like they would have you believe in Hollywood."

I chuckled at the way he pronounced that as Hollaywood. "Well, I'm just hoping it leads us to something that could give us a break in this case. That

Michael Thompson lead turned out to be a dead end."

St. Clair shook his head and frowned. "I had a feeling it didn't turn out well when I called Alex to see what happened and he didn't answer."

"He's pretty down about this whole case, so I'm hoping this fingerprint will give us something to go on." I lifted the book for him to see. "It's on the first page of this book."

He took it out of my hand and opened the cover to see the dried, red fingerprint. "Let's see. It's a good one. Whoever it was, they gave us pretty much a full print. Let me take it to the lab and see what they can find. I'll be back in a couple and we can talk about how we're going to get my good friend out of the funk he's in."

St. Clair returned less than ten minutes later with the promise that the lab guys would put a rush on the identification. "Just so you know, it can take a couple hours. As I said, it's not like on TV and in the movies."

"That's okay," I said as I shifted to get comfortable in the chair beside his desk. "It's not like I was going to be able to do much tonight anyway. My mind is too full of this case."

Nodding, he leaned back in his chair and folded his arms behind his head. Everything about the man exuded confidence and strength. As I sat there studying him, I understood why Alex and he had been drawn to each other to become friends.

"I think Alex has the same thing, but he has the added problem of not being able to forget the past. It's a hard thing to be saddled with that."

St. Clair probably knew better than I how much of the past weighed on Alex every day. For me, it always felt like he couldn't escape what had happened to his life that night when someone took Helena from him. He had opened himself up to me as much as he could, but there was still that part of him that remained hidden away with that past he never let go.

"It's his nature, I guess."

"No, that's where you're wrong," St. Clair said, correcting me. "Alex isn't sullen and quiet by nature. You've never seen the lighter side of him?"

I tried to think of one time when I could describe Alex as light. I couldn't. No matter how much he smiled at the funny things I said or did, never had he ever seemed truly lighthearted.

"No, I guess I haven't. I just naturally assumed he was serious by nature and the death of Helena had made that part of him the only part he showed."

John shook his head and leaned forward to take his wallet out of his pocket. He opened it up and pulled out a picture of Alex and himself from years ago and handed it to me. Instantly, my eye was drawn to how happy Alex looked, his face full of happiness as he and St. Clair posed for a picture in front of an Inner Harbor bar.

They both looked so young and so carefree that I couldn't help but be envious of St. Clair for knowing that man back then. In all the months I'd known Alex, I'd never seen him like that.

"That was Alex before he got shot. We used to joke around all the time that life was good, and we believed it. Then in one night it all changed for him. Gone was the carefree guy who loved life, and in his place came the guy you know. I wish you could have known him back then, though. You would have loved him."

Smiling, I thought about how much I loved him just the way he was, but to know that he wasn't quiet and withdrawn because of his wife's death somehow made me feel better about us. I didn't need him to be the life of the party like he'd been when he was younger. I just wished he wasn't so burdened by that past.

"I love hearing he was happy was like that once."

"I miss that guy," St. Clair said wistfully. "I haven't seen him in a long time. I can say this, though. He's happier when you're around than he's been since he lost her. You bring out that smile I only saw when he was with her."

"That's good to hear, but I'm not sure he's ever going to be able to move on from that time in his life, and this case has brought it all back, I think. I'm worried that finding Bethany's killer won't be enough because even though he hasn't said anything, I think the fact that Helena's killer is still out there is something he can't deal with."

St. Clair's furrowed brow told me he worried about that too, even as he tried to ease my mind. "It's true he never did find who took her away, but I think he could be happy again with the right person. Don't let yourself get trapped in the idea that Helena was some perfect woman. She was great, but you are too, Poppy."

I thought back to how Ken Bryer had described Helena to me just a few days before and was struck by the difference between the way he spoke about her and how St. Clair did. A lot of time had passed, though, and he had been closer to Alex than Helena, so it wasn't entirely surprising that he would see her more realistically. Ken had been friends with her before Alex met her.

And I couldn't forget what I knew to be true—men rarely read people well.

"I was sorry to hear they were having problems before Helena was killed. I'm sure that weighs on Alex's mind still to this day."

A look of confusion settled into St. Clair's features, and he shook his head before I even finished my sentence. "They weren't having any problems. Who told you that?"

"Ken. He told me they'd been having problems ever since he got shot because Alex didn't want to have any children and Helena did."

St. Clair waved away everything Ken said. "Don't listen to a word that guy has to say about Alex and Helena. He had no idea what was going on. Alex wanted children as much or more than she did. He loved her and wanted to have a family with her. They were trying to start one when she was murdered."

"Really?" I asked, baffled how these two men who called themselves Alex's friends could be so different in their opinions about Alex and Helena's marriage. Maybe Ken had been privy to more intimate knowledge of their relationship because he was closer to Helena than St. Clair. Whatever it was that made the two men think so contrarily, I had a feeling it didn't really matter which one was right.

All that mattered was Alex had been in love with her and someone brutally took her life and altered his forever.

I changed the subject to lighten our conversation since nothing he or anyone could say would change what happened. We talked for over an hour more, mostly about life in Sunset Ridge and how I was sure even a guy who loved the city life like he did could find some good in a small town like the one I'd grown up in.

Whatever he wanted to believe, I still was that small town girl, maybe just with a different outlook on the world than most of my fellow citizens possessed.

His entire body shook from a deep belly laugh at the thought of him living in what he called "some Podunk town", but we were interrupted by an older man with grey hair who appeared in an office doorway behind St. Clair and barked, "St. Clair, I need you in my office now!"

Turning around, he quickly stood from his desk and answered, "Yes, Captain." Turning to face me, he said, "Looks like my fan club wants to hear from me. I shouldn't be long, and I told the tech to put a rush on those results, so it shouldn't be too much longer you'll have to wait. I'll be back in a few."

I felt like I wanted to wish him good luck since his captain looked like a rabid dog thirsty for blood. He trotted into the man's office, leaving me there to think about how much I hoped closing this case would ease Alex's mind. No matter how serious we ended up being or if we ended up just as work partners, I wished for nothing more than for him to get some piece of mind. Solving this case wouldn't change the fact that Helena's murder remained unsolved, but at least it would mean this one wouldn't end up plaguing him like hers had.

As I sat there lost in thought, a man appeared in front of me dressed in street clothes like St. Clair and holding a file folder in his hand. "I'm looking for Detective St. Clair."

I pointed toward the captain's office. "He's in there getting chewed out, I think."

The man looked toward the office and then back at me. Hesitating for a moment, he lay the folder on St.

Clair's desk and said, "Tell him we rushed as fast as we could."

He left me sitting there with the file that contained the answer to my case, and even though I knew it was wrong to open it before St. Clair returned, I lifted the corner to take a peek and began to scan what the report said. What I saw made my chest feel like someone had slammed a sledgehammer into me. There, among a handful of other names, was one I knew like my own.

Stunned, I sat in that chair in the middle of St. Clair's precinct as my brain conjured up a million reasons why the report could be wrong and then it all dawned on me. The eagerness to see Alex in the worst light possible. The willingness to believe he had something to do with Helena's murder. The ability to influence this case so we wouldn't find Bethany's killer.

I needed to get to Alex and find out how this could be. Grabbing the folder from St. Clair's desk, I yanked my coat off the back of the chair and ran out of the building as my mind swirled with fear that nothing had been as I'd thought.

Every step of this case had been in error, but now that I had the proof I needed, finally it would come to an end.

Chapter Twenty-Five

MY FOOT JAMMED the gas pedal to the floor, sending my car tearing down the streets of Baltimore as my brain scrambled to remember the directions back to Sunset Ridge and my fingers fumbled with my cell phone to call Alex. Three, four, and then five times I called, but each one ended with his deep voice telling me to leave a message and he'd get back to me soon.

"Alex! If you hear this message, I need you to call me now! Where are you? Call me!"

Blowing through red light after red light, I drove as fast as I could out of the city, unsure if I would stop if I saw the red and blue lights of a police car behind me things were so desperate. I needed to get back home to see Alex before everything in my life blew up in my face. All I had to do was drive fast enough to reach him so he could see what I'd seen in that report.

My palms dripped with sweat and made holding on to the steering wheel and my phone next to impossible. Shaky fingers pressed TWO on my speed dial to call Alex again, and as I raced down the highway toward home, I heard his voice once again intone that silky smooth command to leave him a message.

I didn't have any more to leave. Anything else needed to be said in person as he stood in front of me so I could see the look in his eyes when my words sunk in to his brain and he saw the results of the fingerprint analysis.

With every exit, the numbers grew smaller and I made my way back to the person this whole nightmare had started with—the man I loved still more than I ever thought I could love someone. My mind filled with what I'd say when I saw him in front of me. What he'd say when he heard me tell him I now understood how every clue and every lead had been wrong in this case.

I looked to the side of the road through bleary eyes full of tears and finally saw the green highway sign for my exit back to Sunset Ridge. I'd try the police station first and prayed to God I'd find him there.

JAMMING THE CAR into park, I turned the engine off and leapt out from behind the wheel. My legs felt like every muscle in them had been tensed since I first read that fingerprint analysis report back at St. Clair's desk, so now as I ran toward the police station, they cramped painfully making me slow down even as my brain screamed for them to push harder to let me run faster than I'd ever done before.

I tore down the hallway to Alex's office and found it dark and empty, like much of the police station was each night. Hoping beyond reason Derek might have decided to stay late for once since he'd become chief, I ran to his office, each step feeling like my thigh muscles would explode out of my skin. I found his dark just like Alex's, and real panic settled into my brain.

"Isn't anyone in this damn police station after dinnertime?" I screamed as I ran toward the front door.

"Hello?" a voice called out in response to my frantic yelling. "I'm in here."

I followed the sound to the dispatcher's office and found Andie, the young woman recently hired to work at night. She looked at me with terror in her eyes as I struggled to catch my breath in her doorway, her big blue eyes opened wide with fear.

"What's wrong?" she asked as she looked around me for anyone to help her.

"Where's Alex? Alex Montero. He's one of the officers who's supposed to be on tonight. Where is he?"

She shook her head so fast her long poker-straight hair fluttered around her head like fringes. "He's not on. He didn't check in when he came on his shift."

"So he's not working?" I asked, panicking even more.

Andie shuffled through a stack of papers on the desk in front of her and read through them, shaking her head again. "No. I don't have him out tonight."

I stumbled into her office like a drunk fresh off a bender and grabbed the papers from her hand. My eyes didn't focus, though, so I couldn't understand a thing written on them. Throwing them back onto her desk, I tried to keep calm even as my worst fears were coming true.

"Where is Derek? The chief, where is he?"

"He doesn't work nights unless it's a serious emergency. I don't know where he is. Home, maybe?"

"Call him and tell him I need to speak to him now. Tell him to call Poppy on her cell phone. If he asks, it's an emergency!"

I didn't give Andie time to ask me any questions and tore out of the building to get to my car. Alex hadn't shown up for work, which meant he was still at his house, so I'd get him there.

At least I hoped I would.

THE LIGHT IN Alex's living room glowed a soft yellow through the closed blinds. I stood on his front porch as my heart pounded and my brain spun from fear at what would happen next. I knocked hard on his front door, my adrenalin pumping through me, and I waited to see his face appear in front of me.

"Alex, open the door. I need to talk to you!" I yelled.

But he didn't answer. I thought about walking around to the back door, but his car parked in his driveway and the light on inside told me he was in there, so once again, I knocked hard enough so wherever he was in the house he'd hear me.

The hair on the back of my neck stood at attention with every second I waited for the door to open, and I looked behind me as I stood in the darkness, feeling like some kind of danger lurked nearby. I'd always hated how secluded his house was out here in the middle of nowhere. During the day, it was a beautiful place, but at night it frightened me.

Finally, as my imagination began to spin out of control with thoughts of deranged killers and wild animals attacking me as I stood defenseless on that porch, the door slowly opened but Alex wasn't there. Was he injured and only able to open the door before he collapsed behind it?

Quickly, I entered the house but saw no sign of him

as I scanned the living room. How had the door opened then?

Before I could look behind it to answer my question, I felt a wet hand cover my mouth. I fought against the person's hold on me, but it was no use. They were much stronger and determined to force me into the kitchen.

They threw me on the floor, and I saw why Alex hadn't reported for work or answered the door. There, next to me, he lay in a pool of his own blood from a knife wound to his stomach, his eyes closed. Horrified, I cradled his face and prayed he was still alive.

"Alex, open your eyes. Open your eyes and look at me. It's Poppy. I'm here. Oh, open your eyes, Alex. Please!"

"I know how to use a knife, dear Poppy. It's one of the few things I'm skilled at. His wounds won't kill him. He's just in incredible pain for the moment. But when I want him to die, I'll use this knife one more time and he'll die."

That voice so familiar and now so evil echoed behind me, and when I turned to look at the man's face, I saw what I had feared as I sped all the way there from St. Clair's office. Those eyes that had made me so uneasy when they looked at me that day as I sat with him hoping for help to find who had killed Bethany now flashed hatred like I'd never seen before.

"Alex told you when we first met that I was a knife expert. Didn't you listen?"

"Why did you do this to him?" I sobbed as I turned back to look at the peaceful expression on Alex's face as he lay there next to me.

Ken Bryer didn't answer, but I didn't need him to. Why he'd done it didn't matter at that moment. That he said Alex's wounds weren't fatal did.

"Alex, open your eyes for me. It's Poppy. I'm here. I just need you to open your eyes for me."

"See, that's the problem with you women. It's always you need. You need him to give you a baby. You need him to be more serious about the relationship. You need him to live. Need, need, need."

Ken's voice verged on manic, his words expelled from his mouth with such venom I knew it was just a matter of time before he took that knife to me. His hatred for the women in Alex's life meant he wouldn't spare me like he had his friend, so if I could just get him to confess to what he'd done, maybe Alex would live and see him behind bars even if I couldn't.

Lowering my mouth to Alex's ear, I whispered what I hoped wouldn't be the last words I'd say to him. "I don't know if you can hear me, but I'm going to try to get him to admit he killed Bethany. He's going to kill me. I know it as sure as I know my name, so listen to what he says so if you live you can put him away for what he's done."

ALEX'S EYES FLUTTERED open for just a moment, and I saw he'd heard me, so I whispered, "I love you. If I don't get to tell you that again, I want you to know that at least."

Groaning, he said in a faint voice, "Keep him talking. Get him to confess. Trust me."

"No more of you two lovebirds sharing secrets. Time for you to go the way the others went, dear little Poppy," Ken said low and ominously in my ear as he tugged me by my hair across the kitchen floor and slammed me into a cabinet.

My head throbbed where it hit the wood, but I had to try to do as Alex asked, so I said, "At least explain why you killed Bethany before you kill me. Why kill her? What did she do to you?"

"Because Alex introduced her to me."

"That was it?" I asked in shock at his answer.

His pale blue eyes flashed rage at my question, but he held back from striking me, clenching his fists tightly at his side. "He brought her to lunch—the lunch he was supposed to have just with me. She was all over him, just like Helena used to be every time she intruded on our time together. I could tell this one loved him too, but I knew he didn't care for her because he kept pushing her away instead of fawning all over her."

"You killed her because she loved him?" I asked, barely able to form those horrible words.

Ken answered my question as calmly as if he was telling me the time. "I killed both the women who loved him."

Out of the corner of my eye, I saw Alex's face as Ken's confession sunk in. He'd killed Helena that night behind the restaurant and all these years he'd pretended to be Alex's friend knowing he was responsible for taking away the woman he loved.

"Oh my God! You killed them both?" I cried out as Alex closed his eyes and turned away in agony.

"Of course. I couldn't let them live. They had to go."

"Why? He cared for them. You were his friend. Why would you want to see him so miserable?" I asked, not even sure I wanted to hear this madman's answer. Whatever twisted logic he'd employed to justify killing two people wouldn't make sense to me anyway.

"He cared for me, not them," he answered. "Not them."

All of a sudden it all made sense. Amazed at the clarity his answer had given me, I said, "You love him. That's what this is about. You love him and couldn't stand to see him with anyone else."

I look over at Alex lying still and wished he didn't have to hear what I was about to goad Ken into telling me. I didn't have a choice, though.

"How long have you been in love with him?"

Smiling like he was thinking back on a fond memory, he looked down at Alex and said, "Since the first moment he came into my morgue."

"But he's not gay. He wouldn't be with you. You had to know that."

Ken snapped his head around to face me and barked, "This isn't about sex, you provincial little bitch! True love has very little to do with sex. It has to do with one soul meeting another and seeing what they've been looking for all their lives."

As much as I wished I could honestly disagree with him about that, I couldn't. Somewhere in that mind filled with homicidal craziness was a tiny spot of romantic idealism that made him love Alex.

I needed to get him to tell me the details of how he killed Helena and Bethany, so I silently asked Alex for his forgiveness for what I was about to do and said, "I bet you planned out both their murders to the tiniest detail. You're that kind of person. You wouldn't leave any stone unturned when it came to doing it right."

Picking up the bloody knife he'd left on the counter after cutting Alex, he waved it in front of his face like some kind of murderous version of a metronome, all the while staring down at me with a look that told me I didn't have long before he used his deadly weapon on me.

"You think you're so clever, don't you, Poppy McGuire? Is it because Alex said you have good instincts? I nearly vomited when he told me that. Like some small town nobody like you could have better instincts than he has. You want me to tell you the whole story because you think you're going to be able to pin the murders on me, but you forget one thing. You two will be dead, so who will know?"

I sat up straight and pressed my back to the wood cabinet behind me, my head throbbing less now so I had my wits about me again. With a smile, I taunted him to reveal everything about his crimes, sensing he was the type of murderer who wanted to brag about what he'd done.

"Humor me then. If I'm going to die, at least give me one last request. Tell me how you did it."

Ken stepped toward me and nodded before looking over at Alex still lying motionless on the floor on the other side of the kitchen. "He's going to hear it too. Are you sure you want to put him through that?"

"In a few minutes, it won't matter what either one of us heard. We'll be dead and that's it. So at least let me hear how it all went down with them."

"I'm surprised not to hear you say you and he will be meeting in some fictitious afterlife in heaven where all your dead friends and relatives hang out waiting for you," he said, raising his eyebrows in surprise.

"I'm small town, but that doesn't mean I believe in heaven," I lied even as I prayed to God I hoped would save me and Alex from going to that very place shortly.

Ken seemed impressed by my lack of belief in an afterlife and leaned against the counter a few feet away from me. Nodding his head, he smiled. "Very well. I'll give you this last request. I only hope you appreciate my handiwork, especially with your friend Bethany."

He stopped to take a breath and knelt down next to Alex. Pushing his dark hair off his face, he said something I couldn't hear before standing again to begin his story.

"Helena knew me as a friend, so when I showed up behind Manger that night, of course she opened the door for me. She thought we were the closest of friends, even though I'd fantasized about the way I'd kill her for weeks before that night. It took nothing to slit her throat, and then I threw her on the ground to watch her bleed to death. It all happened so fast. I'd never killed anyone before, but I'd seen victims on my table every day for years. I never realized how fast life left the body until that night."

He stopped for a moment before continuing. "The homeless guy who hung out in that alley nearly shit himself when he saw, and I worried that he would tell someone until he showed up on my table three months later. Without Helena to feed him every night, he had to return to stealing and he was found dead from a gunshot to the chest. Problem solved."

Slowly, as he told me how he murdered her, I inched myself toward Alex until we were only a few feet away from each other. So enthralled with his own story, Ken didn't seem to notice or care.

"Weren't you afraid Alex would be charged with her murder since the husband is always the first one they look to when a wife is murdered like that?"

I asked the question like nothing about where I sat had changed, and for a moment, Ken looked down at me like he knew there was something different but couldn't put his finger on it. Then he appeared to forget anything about it and answered, "He didn't do it, so how would they charge him for her murder?"

"You never know. It was a bold move. You risked everything, but in the end, you got what you wanted."

He smiled that evil grin for a second and then it faded away as he remembered he didn't get what he'd hoped for. "For a little while. He was all mine, but then he said he had to move away from the city because there was too much haunting him there."

"You saw him grieve every day and knew you'd done that. It takes a strong mind to be able to handle that."

I hated complimenting him, but I had a feeling he wanted someone to say he'd done well, no matter how twisted his actions had been. I also suspected he wanted Alex to see what he'd done had been all for him.

"But you did it because you loved him, right?"

Ken nodded, and with a tilt of his head, stared down at Alex with what I imagined was love for him. "I was willing to be patient. I knew he needed to put the past out of his mind, and what better way to do it than move to the middle of nowhere and start over? I knew him as well as I knew myself, so I wasn't afraid he'd find new people to go with his new life. That wasn't who he was anymore."

Alex stirred next to me, but I needed him to remain silent, and for all intents and purposes, not there, so I touched his arm and quietly said, "Shhhh."

"But then another one of them popped up. This one was even worse than the first one. I blamed myself, though. I'd given him too much time alone out here."

"So once you realized another woman cared for Alex, you had to kill her too?"

"Helena's had been more spur of the moment, but this one was planned out to the second. I heard from Alex that they weren't together anymore, but I knew that would only be temporary. She'd find some way to insinuate herself back into his life, so I had to do it."

I gently stroked Alex's arm to let him know I was there with him and prodded Ken to continue his terrible tale. "It was you who went to Carson's florist and sent the flowers to Bethany, wasn't it?"

Waving the knife around again, he smiled. "Of course it was. I knew she'd think Alex sent them and would call him, thinking he wanted to get back together. When she went to her car to go to see him, I'd kill her. But then he showed up there and fought with her. She was already upset, but Alex's usual way of not showing much emotion really sent her over the edge. It's what they always say. No matter how well you plan these things out, something always comes up. She really wasn't a terribly stable person, as it turns out. So I had to wait a few hours longer, but I knew she'd eventually go running after him. They always do."

Bethany had been going to see Alex when Ken killed her.

My stomach roiled at how easily he dismissed Bethany's feelings for Alex. I could only imagine how confused she must have been to get those flowers and think he wanted to get back together with her after all those weeks of only being able to tell her diary of her love for him and then to have him act like he was there to see her only because she'd asked him to come and not because of the desire the card had promised.

I wanted to lash out and hurt Ken for all that he'd done, but I had no way to do that. Alex lay injured next to me, and without a weapon, I'd be dead before I even got to my feet. He'd slit my throat just like he planned to but before he'd told his whole story, and even though I didn't understand how Alex intended for anyone to know about what he'd done when we were both dead, I had to keep going and get Ken to tell me everything.

"She must have been beside herself with confusion about how he felt," I said, hating how true that was.

Puffing out his chest, he no longer merely told the story of how he was Bethany's killer but bragged of his prowess at murder, even in the fact of unseen obstacles. "Then her sister left her alone, and the stage was set. The sister had been a tiny snag in my plan, I admit. I would have just killed her too, though. Kill one. Kill two. Whatever. She left her apartment and I planned to get her, but then she had to run back in for something, leaving the car unlocked, so I took my opportunity and jumped into the back seat to wait. I mean, she left the car wide open. It was like providence was smiling down on me. She came out with a book in her hand, and as soon as she settled in and put her seat belt on, I leaned forward and slit her throat before she could say a word. I picked up the book from the passenger seat and grabbed the keys out of the ignition to put the book back inside before coming back out to put the keys in the ignition again. And then I left."

Morbid curiosity filled my mind at why he bothered to do anything with the book at all, so I asked, "Why put the book in the house? Why not leave it on the seat?"

He nodded his head quickly and crouched down beside me. Pointing the knife toward my face, he explained, "It didn't belong there, so it had to be put back where it belonged."

I had no idea what that meant, if it meant anything at all except to him, so I tried to make it look like I understood. Remembering the old adage, I said, "A place for everything and everything in its place."

"Yes! You do get it!" he said excitedly. "I bet your house is neat like mine, isn't it? Everything and everyone has a place in this world. Mine is with Alex, but I'm sorry to say you don't have a place here."

And in a flash, we'd gone from two people who understood one another to murderer and his next victim. Pulling me by the hair, he thrust my face near Alex's so close I heard him breathe and behind me Ken said, "I'm going to finally let you watch a woman you care for die. You don't love her, but I can see you care for her. This is my gift to you."

Tugging me backwards, he sat me down on the floor in front of Alex and placed the knife to my neck just below my ear. "Open your eyes, Alex. I'll let you say your goodbyes before I slit her throat."

Alex lifted his head to look at me, and I saw in his brown eyes pain like I'd never seen before in my life. His voice gravelly, he said, "I'm sorry, Poppy. I'm so sorry."

I felt the tip of the blade pierce my skin and forced my eyes to remain open so the last sight I saw was him. If I had to die at the hands of a madman, then I was going to do it gazing at the man I loved as he looked at me.

In that moment, just as I accepted no matter what I

did I was going to die, I silently told my father I loved him and then said, "I love you, Alex."

Ken moved to slit my throat and behind me I heard a noise like a gunshot. The knife fell from his hand as he collapsed on top of me, pressing me to the floor. Stunned I'd been saved, I pushed him off me and turned to check on Alex as I saw Derek coming toward us saying something about making this a habit.

He smiled down at me, but I didn't care to think about what he meant or didn't mean by that. All I cared about was Alex. Cradling his face, I kissed him on the lips and whispered against them, "Everything's going to be okay. You're okay. I'm here and I'm not going anywhere."

Just before he closed his eyes, he lifted his hand to touch my face and smiled. "Thank you."

Chapter Twenty-Six

I STOOD HOLDING Alex's hand as the chilly February air whipping across Ridgewood Cemetery stung my cheeks even as it made me appreciate life in that place where he'd buried his wife all those years ago. Then he hadn't known who had taken her from him. All he'd known was she was gone and he'd never have the chance to tell her all the things he thought he'd have the rest of his life to say.

When he asked me if I'd come with him to see her, I didn't hesitate in saying yes. From the very beginning, she'd been a part of first our friendship and then what had blossomed into love afterward, a third soul never seen but always there. Sometimes I'd hated how much she affected him, but now as I stood in front of her grave with him, I didn't feel that way anymore.

Alex took a deep breath and let it out, sending a stream of smoke into the cold air as he stared down the hill. "Right after we met and were still getting to know each other, I found out she fed that homeless man behind the restaurant. I walked past homeless people every day, preferring not to think of them as I went about my life. I asked her why she did that. To me, it was only enabling him to never seek a better life."

Turning to face me, he asked, "Do you know what she told me?"

I shook my head and smiled. "No."

"She told me it wasn't her job in life to do anything but help if she could. She was kind and good, and I wanted to believe I deserved that in my life after what I'd seen in my job."

My heart ached for what he'd lost. I understood the loss of a parent, but that was different than losing someone you'd promised to love and cherish for the rest of your life.

He looked away and in a sad voice admitted what I'd known since that first time I met him. "I've never really let her go. I know that. I know it's been unfair of me to not move on, but it was like as long as I didn't know who had taken her away, I couldn't let her go. Bethany wanted more from me, but I couldn't give it to her, and she paid the price for being with me just like Helena did."

Squeezing his hand, I leaned my head on his shoulder. "Don't say that. You were honest with Bethany just like you've been honest with me."

"Was I? Maybe I shouldn't have even started seeing her since I knew I hadn't let go of Helena, even after all those years. If I hadn't, she'd still be here today."

He looked at me and I saw how much he blamed himself for both her death and Helena's. "This wasn't your fault. Neither of them deserved what Ken did, but you aren't to blame for his actions, Alex. Don't do this to yourself."

"What about you? Can you really say I've been honest with you about how much I still keep of the past?"

I thought about that and couldn't blame him. It didn't matter that he'd never actually said to me that he still loved his wife. I didn't need to be told that.

Standing on my toes, I kissed his cheek and smiled up at him. "You have always said I have such great instincts, yet you think I didn't know you were still in love with ghost? Trust me. I knew from the moment I met you. Anyone willing to really look can see it in your eyes."

"I still wake up in the middle of the night and reach over to the other side of the bed expecting to find her there."

"So that's why we've never…?"

Alex nodded. "It's not that I didn't want to stay with you all those times I pretended to be tired or sick. I just didn't think I could do that to you. I did it to Bethany, and it wasn't right. I didn't want to admit I'd never moved on, even though I wanted to with you. I need to tell her goodbye and move on, but until recently I haven't been able to. Now I know it's time."

I slipped my hand from his and looked down at Helena's grave. "I'll leave you so you can have some privacy."

As I turned to go, he grabbed my arm, and I looked back to see his eyes pleading with me to stay. "Don't go. I want you to hear this too."

Weaving our fingers together again, he kissed my cheek and sighed. "Helena, I'm so sorry you had to pay for Ken's madness, but he's finally paid the price for what he did to you. After all this time, I never stopped loving you. I couldn't as long as your killer was still out there. But now you can rest in peace and I can begin living life again."

He stopped talking as the last words got caught in his throat and hung his head. I wanted to make his pain go away, but I knew I couldn't. What I could do was show him I loved him and be there for him now.

I leaned against him and whispered, "You're a good man, Alex. Don't ever forget that."

Turning to look at me, he smiled. "She used to say that to me too."

"Then you should believe it."

He looked down toward the headstone that read Helena Montero, loving wife and beautiful soul, and said, "I know what you'd tell me, Helena. You'd say it's time, Alex. It's time to be happy again. I think you've tried to tell me that a number of times over the years, but I wasn't ready to listen. I'm finally ready, so I wanted you to be the first to know."

His words sounded like they were torn straight from his heart, and as he finished, I couldn't keep my tears from falling any longer. Tears for her and Bethany and what they'd suffered. Tears for Alex and all he'd endured since that night Ken killed Helena. Tears for all the love he had held onto all those years because he'd been unable to let go.

He looked over at me and smiled as he wiped my tearstained cheeks. "She'd like you, Poppy. She'd like how you make me want to live again."

Just then, a bird landed on her headstone and made a noise like it wanted to sing. Struck by this singular bird in the middle of winter appearing at that moment, I pointed to it and said, "It's like a sign, don't you think?"

He tilted his head and studied the bird for a moment. "That's so strange. Helena had fed two birds on our balcony and when she died, I didn't continue it and they stopped coming around. This one reminds me of the one bird that used to always be there. It had a tiny yellow spot on its chest just like this one."

We watched it and it stared up at us, like it was taking one last look before leaving. After a few moments sitting there, it flew away, and I couldn't help but think it was a sign that she too thought it was time for him to move on.

**Poppy and Alex return in Happy Hour:
A Poppy McGuire Mystery (Poppy McGuire
Mysteries Book #5)**

About The Author

Anina Collins has always loved a good mystery. From Agatha Christie's Hercule Poirot to Sir Arthur Conan Doyle's famous detective Sherlock Holmes to Dan Brown's intrepid Professor Robert Langdon, she's spent some of her favorite reading times with mystery novels. When she's not writing her favorite mystery couple, she can be found watching entirely too much Supernatural and dreaming about the beach.

Visit Anina's Facebook page at facebook.com/Anina-Collins-429334270597293 for news about her books, along with giveaways and other fun stuff!

And sign up for her newsletter today for exclusive news first! Visit her website at aninacollins.com for more details.

Books by Anina Collins:
The Eleventh Hour (Poppy McGuire Mysteries #1)
After Hours (Poppy McGuire Mysteries #2)
Top of the Hour (Poppy McGuire Mysteries #3)
The Darkest Hour (Poppy McGuire Mysteries #4)

And look for the next book in the series, **Happy Hour (Poppy McGuire Mysteries #5)**, coming soon!